MURDERER'S CHOICE

by Anna Mary Wells

"One of America's top-notch mystery novelists...Miss Wells puts all excitement into her stated plot from start to finish.... Miss Wells not only holds her own in the mystery field, but also contributes to raising the literary standard of this popular but too often shabby writing endeavor."

—Dallas News

"Miss Wells has employed her sound comprehensions of character in building a story which demonstrates more than the mere attempt to place responsibility for alleged murder."

—Detroit Free Press

"Ingenious plotting."

—Detroit News

Titles by Anna Mary Wells available in Perennial Library

MURDERER'S CHOICE
A TALENT FOR MURDER

MURDERER'S
Choice

BY

ANNA MARY WELLS

PERENNIAL LIBRARY
Harper & Row, Publishers
New York, Cambridge, Hagerstown, Philadelphia, San Francisco
London, Mexico City, São Paulo, Sydney

A hardcover edition of this book was originally published by Alfred A. Knopf, Inc. It is here reprinted by arrangement.

First PERENNIAL LIBRARY edition published 1981.

ISBN: 0-06-080534-X

81 82 83 84 85 10 9 8 7 6 5 4 3 2 1

FOR

JEAN MARIE

who likes Sherlock Holmes better

MURDERER'S CHOICE

Chapter 1

FRANK OSGOOD leaned back in his chair and puffed nervously at his cigarette. He was conscious that the gesture was fidgety, and the consciousness annoyed him and thus increased his nervousness. He took a deep breath and tried hard to relax. The meal had been good; an ounce of excellent brandy in a balloon glass invited his attention; there was every reason for him to enjoy to the full the sense of physical well-being. More than that, he wanted to be at ease. His cousin's cool, supercilious observation was missing none of his discomfiture, and that enraged him. Charles always affected him this way, had ever since they were boys. He should not have accepted this invitation to dinner; he'd known that even as he accepted it. It did seem, somehow, as if a time ought to arrive in his adult life when he might be free of this absurd domination. He could see through Charles now; the legend of the older man's infallibility had been destroyed years ago. And yet whenever they were together Frank reverted to the awkward schoolboy overwhelmed in the presence of superior sophistication.

"Drink your brandy," Charles said with his lazy grin. "It's not poisoned."

"I didn't think it was." Frank deliberately avoided touching the glass. It was a slight and futile gesture of opposition to his host's will; Charles drove him into corners that forced such childish absurdities. It made no difference, of course, whether or not he drank the brandy, but he resolved stubbornly that he wouldn't touch it and that he wouldn't lose his temper about it either. He was a man now, and a reasonably successful one. With everyone else in the world but this cousin he felt himself a man, fully competent to deal with any exigencies that might arise. With Charles alone he was still an awkward schoolboy. He came to the end of the cigarette and pressed it out in the ash tray on his right. That left him with nothing to do with his hands unless he drank the brandy. He fiddled with the stem of the glass and then, conscious of the other man's amused stare, set it down abruptly.

"It's been nice seeing you," he said on a sudden impulse, "but I think I'd better be shoving off. Mother gets lonely in the evenings."

"Aunt Martha can do without you for one night," Charles said authoritatively. "Besides, I haven't told you what I brought you here to tell yet."

"Oh, you really did have some business in mind?" Frank was relieved and more nearly master of himself than he had been at any time during the evening. He picked up the brandy glass and took a swallow abruptly. "To tell you the truth, I'd been wondering," he said. "It struck me as a bit odd that you asked me to come here. We don't really have enough in common to make us want to dine together without some special reason, do we?"

"No, we don't." Charles shook his head negatively. For some reason his inner amusement appeared to be increasing rapidly; the smile that crossed his lips as he spoke suggested a spontaneous and irrepressible amusement. "I wanted to tell you," he said, "that I've just taken out a hundred thousand dollars' insurance in your favor."

"In my favor?" The younger man made no attempt to disguise his astonishment. A wave of angry red mounted from just above his collar up toward his forehead.

Charles laughed out loud.

"You don't seem much pleased or flattered, I must say," he commented.

"I'll wait and find out what's your game," Frank said drily. "Then if any thanks are due I'll offer them. I don't want your money. I can earn a living. I do earn a very satisfactory one."

"More than that," Charles said, "I've made my will and named you as residuary legatee after a few little bequests to charity, and of course the taxes, are paid off. You get everything else, my boy."

"Am I supposed to laugh now, or is the point yet to come?"

"You'd better laugh now." There was something wolfish about Charles Osgood's good-humored smile. "You may not think the point's so very funny."

"I'll wait," Frank said grimly.

"For reasons that need not concern us now," Charles said lightly, "I intend to kill myself within the next six months."

"Then the insurance policy would not be valid." Frank

was rather proud of that reply. It was in the conversational key that Charles had set, and he flattered himself that it startled Charles a little. Undoubtedly he had expected protestations either of horror or of disbelief.

"Ah, yes," Charles said, "but I don't intend the insurance company to know that I've killed myself. What they don't know won't invalidate the policy."

"That's nonsense, Charles. No insurance company is going to pay a hundred-thousand-dollar claim within six months after the policy's taken out until they've made a very careful and thorough investigation."

"Possibly, possibly!" Charles waved his cigarette in an airy gesture. "After all, that's really your problem and not mine, isn't it? I shall be dead, you know."

"I really do believe you'd be capable of that," Frank said thoughtfully. "There's no other man in the world of whom I could believe it, but I honestly think you would kill yourself just to play a rotten joke on me. Well, let me beg you not to bother. I shan't take the money, and I shan't let the insurance company wrest it away from me; I'll simply go to them and tell them that you killed yourself, and that will be the end of that."

Charles laughed out loud as he quenched his cigarette. "This is delightful," he said. "You know I'm really enjoying this a great deal more even than I expected to, and I expected to enjoy it considerably. I haven't come to the point yet. You may tell people I killed myself all you like, my dear cousin, but they won't listen to you. They won't pay you the least mind. Your motive in saying that will be so pitifully obvious. Here's the point, Frank, and I think you will have to admit that it is ingeniously contrived. You are going to the electric chair for murdering me."

Charles leaned back in his chair to his full length, teetering ominously on the two back legs of the frail contrivance, and grinned amiably at his cousin.

Frank felt a roaring and a pounding in his ears. There was no longer any question of keeping the conversation in the key Charles had set. For a horrible moment he was afraid that he might cry. It was the childhood drama all over again; the big boy had twisted his own words against him; he was helpless and furious in the grip of a senseless and powerful malevolence. It was typical of the relations between the two men that the younger one did not for a moment doubt his cousin's absurd intention. He drew a deep breath and fought hard for composure.

"That won't be so easy," he said at last. The words were light, but his tone wasn't; Charles could judge exactly how much the threat had perturbed him.

"It won't be too hard," Charles answered. "You see I have the advantage of being able to choose my time and place; it doesn't matter to me particularly how I die, or exactly when. I have no business to occupy my time; I'm entirely free to watch my opportunity to die in the manner that will be most certain to incriminate you."

Frank glanced quickly around at the adjoining tables, and Charles laughed aloud again.

"Oh, no," he said. "No one's overhearing us. I've guarded against that. The waiter's done with us, and we are well out of earshot from the closest table. I thought of that well in advance—not that it would matter, really, if anyone did overhear us. They'd only assume I was drunk and pay us no mind. Perhaps I am drunk, you know, have you thought of that?"

Frank shook his head. "I believe you," he said dully. "I know you, you see. I know how much you hate me. You couldn't tell me why, could you?"

"I don't think there is a why to such things," Charles said meditatively. "It's like love in a way. Hatred like ours is a remarkable thing—almost classical in its simplicity. I couldn't give you a reason, no. I've always hated you. If I believed in reincarnation it would be because there doesn't seem time enough in an ordinary life to build up the sort of feeling I have for you. Rather amusing thought that— that we've gone through lifetime after lifetime feeling this way about one another—except it's rather beastly to think I'd go to all the trouble of killing myself and you just to start it over again. 'When I was a king in Babylon and you were a Christian slave—' you're just the type for a Christian slave, Frank; the line might have been written for us. Next time we may crop up as members of the OGPU and the Gestapo respectively—no, no, no, no, bad casting. I could be either of the two, but you belong in one of the downtrodden classes. It's your metier. Jew or Pole or disinherited bourgeois, it wouldn't much matter; you're the type for any of them. There, that's it, if you must have a reason. It's because you're so meek. You're a goody-goody, Frank, and I never could stand a goody-goody. From the moment it first occurred to me how funny it would be to see you in the electric chair—and for a crime you hadn't committed—it was too good to pass up. You mustn't feel sorry for me, you know; it's quite worth killing myself for."

"I think it is," Frank said, and he spoke now with entire self possession, calmly and coldly. "I am quite able to believe that you would die happy if you thought your death would cause mine, and in disgrace. And I'm glad to know that there isn't any reason for your hating me except what's inherent in our genes or chromosomes or whatever. It's always bothered me a little to know why. I never did anything to you, Charles."

"Oh, Lord, you're not going pathetic! Pull yourself together, man, have you no sense of humor?"

"No, I don't think I have," Frank admitted. "Not your sort anyway. Your idea doesn't seem in the least funny to me. I believe you all right; no one else would of course, but I know you well enough to realize that you're telling the truth. But it's not a very practical idea. Evidence isn't so easy to manufacture. And forewarned is forearmed, you know."

Charles laughed again. "Yes, I know," he said. "Why don't you step over to the next table and tell that man with the high forehead that I am threatening to kill myself so that you will be punished for it? He looks intelligent; he might be a lawyer or a detective. Don't you think he could advise you what to do to circumvent me? Or go to the police tomorrow—now there's an idea. Tell the police the whole story. Do you think I hadn't thought of that, cousin? Tell the police this story tomorrow, and they will laugh at you; yes, certainly, but when within six months I die under highly suspicious circumstances, will they laugh? If I know the police mentality they will bestir themselves to find the odd chap who came in with some crazy story that Osgood was planning to kill himself. Too good, altogether too good. The police would judge that you had overreached yourself, my dear Frank. Your attempts to explain would be exquisitely amusing. I must admit I was a good deal tempted by the idea of staging some sort of disappearance so that I could see you squirm. But it's awfully hard to fake a death; the authorities are most insistent on a *corpus delicti*. It looks as if I shall simply have to resign myself to passing on before your troubles begin —except that I do derive a certain amount of anticipatory pleasure from imagining it all. You shouldn't grudge me this evening, my dear cousin, it is one of the few exquisite pleasures left me in a very short life. All such pleasures have a peculiar savor when you know that your days are numbered. You ought to begin to realize it too. That brandy, for instance, ought not to be gulped by a man in your position. You can actually count—not, perhaps, on the fingers of both your hands, but still without being a very good mathematician you can certainly count the number of such glasses you will consume before your untimely demise."

"You're not interested, I suppose, in giving me a sporting chance?" Frank inquired. "This isn't a game in that sense?"

"Oh, not at all. The only reason I'm telling you now is that it gives you longer to worry. My original plan was to arrange the incriminating details in advance, kill myself, and allow your arrest to take you entirely by surprise. There's a lot to be said for that plan; I still regret having had to abandon it. The notion of your astonishment, your bewilderment, your struggle, your growing horror as you become aware of the weight of the evidence against you, your disbelief, your alternating moods of terror and in-credulity, your final despair—that's a fascinating drama, my dear Frank, and very tempting. If I had been sure enough of your intelligence I'd have followed it. But I should have wanted to be sure that at the very end, as they shaved your head and fastened the plates to your ankles and read the service for the dead over your breathing body you'd know—not just suspect, but know for certain—that I had done it. And I regret to admit it, Frank, but I couldn't count on you unaided for that. And of course I can't leave you any sort of written communication, for that would be evidence, so I am forced to tell you now. But not in order to give you a sporting chance, oh dear no. I haven't the slightest desire or intention of giving you a sporting chance. A very childish and goody-goody idea. I fully intend to have you convicted. And there is really absolutely nothing you can do about it."

"I could enlist," Frank said reasonably.

"If they'd overlook your ulcers, yes, that would hurry me a little. I'd have to attend to it before you could be sent overseas. But in a way it would help too. In the army your movements would be pretty circumscribed; it would be simply a question of being on hand when you had leave in order to stage the crime. Of course that possibility does give you your choice of electrocution or shooting. Courts martial are more prompt than civilian criminal courts too, I understand. If you're anxious to get it all over quickly, enlisting might be your best bet."

"Do you want to die, Charles, or are you planning this altogether on my account?"

"Your solicitude is touching. You're about to suggest

that if I want to die I can enlist, and die nobly. But why should I trade my life for that of a German or a Jap I've never seen and certainly have no grudge against when I can equally well trade it for yours? Besides, the army doesn't want potential suicides. It seems the will to live is an important constituent of a good fighting man."

"Then I'd make a good fighting man," Frank said. "I want to live. I'm not going to let you do this to me, Charles."

Charles laughed again. "The beauty of the idea will grow on you as you think it over," he said. "How are you going to circumvent me? Study up on various methods of inflicting violent death in order to try to guess how I'll do it? Be sure to use a false name at the book stores where you buy the books or the libraries where you borrow them. And cover the whole field—poison, guns, stilettos, blunt weapons. I haven't decided myself just how I'm going to do it, so you can see the field is wide open. If I were to throw myself under your car, and it could later be proved that you had been reading up on rare South American arrow poisons, some bright young newspaper reporter might be struck by the odd coincidence. Your one chance, Frank, is to persuade me not to do this. Why don't you start begging? It's about the time you usually do."

"It's really Kay, isn't it?" Frank spoke with apparent irrelevance. "You say there isn't any reason for your hating me as you do, and in a way that's true. You've hated me since we were children. But you've always come out on top; you've always been able to terrify and humiliate me whenever you chose. Hate hasn't very much to feed on there; you'd have outgrown it by now if it hadn't been for Kay. You know that the reason she wouldn't marry you is that she loves me. None of us has ever admitted it before, but you know it, don't you?"

"Well then, my dear cousin, if you can only manage to beat the murder rap that will be facing you in a few months, you'll be in a financial position to marry the girl. Now that's what I call a sporting chance; all my money, and if you can prove you didn't kill me it will be yours to marry on."

"I shan't marry Kay on your money. Perhaps you will be interested to hear that we have already decided we can afford to be married this year."

"What about Aunt Martha?"

"I'll be able to let mother keep the house, and Kay and I will have an apartment. I never thought it would be fair to Kay for us to marry if it would have meant all living together. I suppose that to you that's just part of what you call being a goody-goody. I'm cautious, I'm prudent, I've put off marriage until I'm thirty-five rather than incur undue risks for the girl I love. Nevertheless, you will observe that Kay has been willing to wait for me, although she might certainly have married more advantageously— that is if your money could be called an advantage when one considers that you go along with it."

"Bravo, bravo, my dear cousin. Your style in insults is improving. I've always heard that the fear of death brings out the best in a man; I shall follow your development during the next few months with the greatest of interest."

"And now, if you've had your fun," Frank said, "I think I'll be running along. I don't believe I need thank you for the dinner; I've paid for it with a very realistic performance

of alarm; you say you've enjoyed yourself, and I believe
you have. As a matter of fact, to be perfectly frank with
you, you frightened me for a few minutes; I know you well
enough to believe fully in the malevolence of your intentions. But I also remember your little jokes when we were
boys, and I realize that the price you set on my life must
look very high to you, disregarding how it might appear to
anyone else. I'm not a schoolboy to be frightened with
ghosts any longer, though apparently you believe that I
am."

"Good night," Charles answered with perfect good
humor. "Do think it over, Frank. I assure you the idea will
grow on you."

Frank walked out onto a dimmed 47th Street fairly
well pleased, on the whole, with his departure. The idea
was, of course, absurd, fantastic and unthinkable. It was
like Charles's perverted sense of humor to try to frighten
him so, and in a way it was a good thing that he had been
so obviously frightened. Charles had had his money's
worth out of the idea, and perhaps now he would be ready
to drop it without squeezing it for any further juice. Frank
drew a deep breath and stepped out briskly toward the
Times Square subway station. He could make the 9.57
from Hoboken if he hurried, without having to spend a
quarter for a taxi. He breathed more freely away from his
cousin, and began to plan what he would tell his mother
about the dinner. She had always liked Charles, perversely,
like all women—all women except Kay, of course. What
luck for him to have found just the right girl, and what
incredible luck that she should have preferred him. Plenty
of women would suit Charles, but for a man both shy and

finicky, as Frank recognized himself to be, the chances were all for going through life without ever finding a woman who would both suit his taste and be attracted to him. And he had found Kay, and she'd waited eight years for him, though she could have had Charles or any number of others. Good old Kay! What would Charles want with a schoolteacher anyway? He'd probably been interested in her only because he knew Frank wanted her.

Kay was one he could tell about this fantastic threat, but not his mother, no, definitely not. She wouldn't take it seriously, of course, but she would be worried and upset; she didn't see why the boys couldn't get along together.

Frank stopped and looked both ways meticulously before stepping off the curb. It was the sort of thing in him that irritated Charles. A cruising taxi idled by, and he shook his head impatiently and waved the man on. It picked up speed abruptly and went in pursuit of another fare. Frank had a sudden, vivid mental image of a dark figure stumbling and sprawling in front of it. If Charles were to do something like that, how could he ever prove that he hadn't pushed him? He looked quickly behind him down the dark street, and hurried on across, suddenly heedless of traffic, eager only to put as much space as possible between himself and his cousin. That was all that was necessary; even if Charles meant what he said he had only to keep an adequate amount of space between them to protect himself. Kay would laugh at the story. Suppose, though, that he told Kay, and a few months later Charles did die under mysterious circumstances. Would Kay doubt him? Frank Osgood shrugged his shoulders impatiently and ran down the steps inside the kiosk.

Chapter 2

"It's all set, Pomeroy," Dr. Hillis Owen said, sprawling his ungainly length in his desk chair tilted back at a precarious angle. "We'll have to start referring the serious cases and winding up the hypochondriacs for the duration." He held out the commission in his left hand for her to read.

"Why don't you apply for one too?" he demanded. "Best damned nurse in the United States. Not that I suppose we could get the army to let us work together—"

"No thank you, doctor," Miss Pomeroy said politely but firmly. "You'll have enlisted men to do your record work. Army nurses are needed for more—" she hesitated for a word.

"For messier work," he supplied for her. "Yes, you're right, Pomeroy, and you've done your share of that. You've saved your money too, haven't you? All set to retire and take it easy for life, or can I persuade you to help me get started again when I come back?"

"The army isn't accepting women my age for nursing duty now," she said. "When it does I'll go, of course. After all, the messier the work the more it's needed."

She spoke matter-of-factly; the pink, placid, unlined face beneath her snowy cap and equally snowy hair was professionally expressionless, but Dr. Owen saw it suddenly through an unprecedented mist as it would look to a shattered boy ten thousand miles from home, calm, cheerful, competent and motherly.

"That's right, Florence Nightingale," he said. "They

can count on you in the pinches."

"For the present," she said, "I've been offered a job outside my own field. It's rather unusual, but it's attractive. I think I'll accept it."

"A job outside nursing?" Dr. Owen's astonishment was frank. "Good heavens, Pomeroy, what else can you do? Haven't you been nursing ever since you were born?"

"I went into training when I was twenty-one, just after I finished college. It's all I've ever done, yes. I wouldn't have thought of looking for anything else, but since there is someone who thinks I'm capable of another job, I thought I might try it."

She didn't elaborate the statement, and after a moment the doctor inquired curiously: "Well, aren't you going to tell me what it is?"

For almost the first time in his memory of her, Miss Pomeroy looked embarrassed.

"Don't if you don't want to, of course," he added hastily, some of her confusion communicating itself to him. "I don't want to know your secrets. Just leave me a forwarding address, and drop me a line occasionally."

"Of course I want you to know," she said, but there was still a little constraint in her tone. "I'm to be a special investigator for the Keene Detective Agency."

Dr. Owen whistled. Her embarrassment was, of course, accounted for; she disliked to mention anything that might suggest to him the events connected with the murder investigation which had brought him his wife. He respected the delicacy of her feeling even while he smiled at its inappropriateness. Doris had daily to suffer reminders more painful than the name of the detective agency. He made no reference, however, to the cause of her embarrassment.

"You a sleuth, Pomeroy?" he said jovially. "Don't tell me you're going to wear false whiskers."

"They want me for special cases," she explained. "I've hesitated to mention it to you, but I really should like your advice, doctor. Mr. Keene says that from time to time things come in that are entirely out of the line of their routine investigators. He keeps several special people for that sort of thing, and he thinks I might be good as one of them. You don't think I'd be taking his clients' money under false pretences, do you?"

"No, I don't," the doctor said decidedly. "Whatever you might do, Pomeroy, you'd give full value received for your money. I think you'll be a first class special investigator, and I'm glad you're going to have a fling at it. When do you start?"

"Why, as a matter of fact," she said, "there's a case right now they want me to work on. I said of course I'd have to wind things up here first."

"Nonsense," he said stoutly, though with a sinking heart. "I can get somebody in for that. You go ahead if you want to."

She shook her head with gentle obstinacy. "No one else can do your work as well as I can, Dr. Owen," she said. "Besides, there's no hurry on this case. It's rather odd, but not at all urgent."

The doctor did not ask for her confidence, but she proceeded without hesitation, and without any apparent qualms as to the ethics of discussing the matter with him. They had shared so many professional secrets that each trusted the other's discretion completely.

"It's a matter in which my nurse's training will be of value," she said. "A man came in to them recently, the heir of rather a large estate from a recently deceased cousin. The cousin had died what had all the appearances of being a natural death; it was properly certified and he was buried in due course. But the heir says the man had intended to commit suicide. He wants it investigated."

"In heaven's name, why? If I ever heard of a case where sleeping dogs had better be left to lie, that's it."

"I don't really know why. I haven't talked with the client yet. Mr. Keene outlined the case to me—in confidence, of course," she added as an afterthought, and blushed when the doctor laughed.

"I'll keep your secrets as well as you keep mine," he told her.

"Mr. Keene says the man doesn't want the insurance money if he isn't entitled to it."

"Then why didn't he go to the insurance company with his suspicions?"

"He didn't want to make them suspicious in case there was nothing in it. After all, once the idea of suicide's suggested, it would be in their interest to prove it was correct, of course. The man said he preferred to have detectives without prejudice working on it."

"It's funny all right," the doctor said. "I don't believe I've ever encountered a conscience quite that tender. By all means take it on, Pomeroy, and if you're allowed to tell me the answer when you get to it, please do. It'll be something for me to think about while I'm supervising mental tests."

"I shall be very grateful if you'll let me ask your advice from time to time," she said.

He laughed. "You've kissed the Blarney Stone for sure, Pomeroy," he said. "You know more than I do about every case that goes through this office. You'll be good at your new job, all right. After all, psychiatry's just a form of detecting—matter of putting two and two together and trying to figure out why the heck the answer isn't four. More power to you, my girl."

"Oh, doctor!" Miss Pomeroy said, blushing like one, "and you talk about my blarney!"

She was wishing for the comfortable support of the doctor's presence two weeks later as she sat in a small cubicle shut off from the rest of the office of the Keene Detective Agency by frosted glass partitions, looking across a cramped and scarred desk at Mr. Frank Osgood. She felt uncomfortable without her uniform; for years ordinary dress had been to her a symbol of the fact that she was off duty and could relax; it was strange and awkward to be at work in a tweed suit, and to be interviewing a patient—client, she corrected herself mentally—on her own responsibility. She missed the reassurance of the forms with their ready-made questions, and she missed the dignity of Dr. Owen's Park Avenue office with its thick rug and the big polished desk over which she had presided. However, as she reminded herself grimly, there was work to be done and no sense in repining. Dr. Owen was busily weeding out the psychologically unfit from the ranks of men newly recruited for the army, and the Park Avenue office was closed for the duration. This was her job, and since she'd accepted it, it was up to her to do it as well as she possibly could. Mr. Osgood was a nervous, rabbity little man. She sternly repressed in herself an impulse to describe him in more technical psychiatric terms. Awkwardly, haltingly, fumblingly he told her the story which she had already heard and passed on to Dr. Owen.

"You haven't questioned his doctor?" she asked.

"I haven't spoken of the matter to anyone outside of this firm except the woman to whom I'm engaged. I respect her judgment."

"Are there any other relatives who might be consulted?"

"Charles and I are—were—the last flowering of the Osgood family. It was one of those big families that runs to seed all of a sudden. My grandfather Osgood had five sons, the youngest not much older than Charles. He was killed in the other war. Two never married, and Charles and I were both only children, he of the oldest son and I of the third. Charles wouldn't have left his money to me if there'd been anyone else to leave it to."

Miss Pomeroy did not miss the note of bitterness, and she was more than a little curious about it. It was not the tone in which a man usually spoke of a cousin who had just left him a very sizable legacy. Frank Osgood looked as if he could use the money, too; he was not actually seedy, but he had none of the appearance of well tailored success which marks the man who has arrived in New York.

As if he had divined her thought he said: "Of course, whatever you find out I'll have money enough to pay you. Charles took care of that. If it weren't for his money I shouldn't have been able to come to you at all." He laughed mirthlessly.

"You want us to find out whether or not your cousin

committed suicide?" Miss Pomeroy inquired. "And when we find out, you want the report to be given to you in confidence, so that you may do what you like with it?"

Privately she thought that he was inviting blackmail.

"I know he committed suicide," the little man said violently and suddenly. "I can't stand sitting around any longer waiting for things to start to happen. He framed me. He fixed it to look as if I'd killed him. He told me he was going to. And he's been dead six weeks now, and nothing's happened. I can't stand waiting any longer. There's no statute of limitations on murder; when his clues start turning up they'll get me. I can't stand waiting any longer."

Miss Pomeroy looked as calm and untroubled as if they were discussing the state of the weather.

"You think I'm crazy, don't you?" he challenged.

She smiled a polite denial.

"I didn't mean to tell you all this," he went on. "I just wanted you to find out whether it wasn't really suicide. But there's something about you that makes a person feel like confiding everything."

Miss Pomeroy knew this already. On the verge of nodding complacently she checked herself, wondering uncomfortably for the first time how it was going to be to use that power of gaining people's confidence to wring guilty secrets from men who trusted her. At least she needn't worry about that in this case, she thought, bringing her attention back to the problem in hand.

"All I ask is that you won't laugh," Frank Osgood was saying. "I know just exactly how foolish this sounds, and what sort of an ass it makes me out, but now I'm started

I may as well tell you. Charles has always hated me. When we were youngsters he used to pretend he was trying to toughen me up for my own good, but since we're grown he's been satisfied to let it stand as the simple, unadorned hatred it was. We used to spend the summers together on Grandfather Osgood's farm in Michigan. He was good at all sorts of outdoor sports and I wasn't, and he devoted himself to making my life miserable. Grandfather Osgood liked him the better of us two, and so did his father, naturally enough, and even mine. We grew up finally and of course I kept out of his way as much as I could. But then we had the infernally bad luck to fall in love with the same woman. At least I don't know whether it was bad luck or whether Charles set out to win her because he saw I wanted her. She was a Michigan girl. She's here now, and we're going to be married in a few weeks—not just because I'm the survivor, either; she'd turned Charles down while he was alive and had all the money. Well, anyway, a few months ago he asked me out to dinner and told me he was going to kill himself and fix things so the blame would fall on me. Absurd, of course. Ridiculous. No sensible man would pay the least attention. But I knew Charles. He was perfectly capable of doing it."

Miss Pomeroy was having no trouble now in keeping her attention fixed on the matter in hand. She stared at Mr. Osgood speechlessly.

"Well," he said, "go ahead and laugh. I expect it. You won't hurt my feelings."

"It's no laughing matter," she answered, shaking her head soberly. "It was a dreadful idea, but he must have

changed his mind. He's been dead how many weeks, and
all properly certified and buried. What is there to worry
about now?"

"I tell you he fixed it so the clues would turn up bit by
bit," the little man said violently. "It doesn't matter when;
if it's twenty-five years they can still electrocute me.
Charles said something that night about wanting to keep
me in suspense and enjoy my torture. He planned it that
way on purpose, and I can't just sit around and wait any
longer."

"But that would be awfully difficult even if anyone were
diabolical enough to want to do it," Miss Pomeroy objected, frowning.

"Not for Charles. He wrote mystery novels for a living.
He must have had twenty rejected or half hatched plots
jingling around in the back of his brain. He knew all about
poisons and post-mortems and anatomy—vulnerable
points and things, you know, the knife wound that the
detective can point out *had* to be the work of someone
who had studied medicine—and *rigor mortis*. He'd have
taken a considerable scientific pleasure in working out one
of his schemes."

Miss Pomeroy regretted, not for the last time, that she
had left her original profession. When you were at a loss
with a patient you could always stick a thermometer in
his mouth while you collected yourself or appealed to the
doctor, but now it was up to her to keep the ball rolling.

"And you want me to find out what the clues are and
try to destroy them?"

"Not necessarily. Forewarned is forearmed, you know.
If you can just find out what the line is likely to be so

that I'll have some chance of a defense. I don't know whether I'm supposed to have hit him over the head and left him to die of concussion or sent him poisoned chocolates through the mail. I don't know whether proving I haven't been near him since that night at dinner will be the best thing or the worst that I could do."

"How is he officially supposed to have died?"

"Heart attack."

"That rules out shooting or stabbing, doesn't it? If he died that way it couldn't be your fault unless it could be proved that you'd frightened him to death."

"How do I know that was what he died of? It's what the certificate says, is all. But he wasn't cremated. He's lying there in his coffin waiting to be dug up and analyzed, with goodness knows what contusions and abrasions on him, or what sort of poison he may be full of."

"It couldn't have been a caustic poison or an opiate," Miss Pomeroy said thoughtfully. "Not if he expected to get a certificate for heart failure. No doctor could miss those."

"But, hang it, we don't know that he expected to get a certificate for heart failure. Maybe his plan went wrong right there."

"Or maybe he really had heart failure before he had a chance to carry out his plan," Miss Pomeroy suggested. "After all, planning suicide is a very depressing business, and has its effect on the whole organism. Do you know why he wanted to kill himself in the first place?"

"No, I have no idea. I've thought about it a good deal, too. I kept thinking it would give me a lead on what to do. It seemed as if he had everything to live for. Those fool stories of his had made him rich; women were crazy over him. I've thought—I don't know whether I should mention this, and I hope you'll understand that if I do it's in strict confidence, Miss Pomeroy—I've thought possibly it might have been Kay. Not that he ever took on much over her turning him down, but pride might have prevented that. I can't really believe that he cared enough for any human being except himself to want to commit suicide over a rejected love, but it's the only explanation that occurs to me."

"I suppose there's no question that he *did* die," she offered tentatively. "He couldn't have had a doctor acting in collusion with him and planned some sort of disappearing act?"

"I saw him in his coffin," Osgood said grimly. "As his heir it was the least I could do. He's dead all right."

"The evil that men do lives after them; the good is oft interred with their bones," Miss Pomeroy quoted softly. "Well, let's hope that the Bard was wrong this once."

"You know I really didn't expect to find a private detective quoting Shakespeare in the line of duty," the little man said. "I hope you'll pardon me if I'm unduly personal, Miss Pomeroy, but I'd like to tell you that I think I'm very lucky to have found you."

"I hope you won't be disappointed," she said, pulling a pad toward her and beginning to make notes in her neat, precise hand. "Now I think I'd better have a few names and addresses, and then I can get to work. First the insurance company?"

"I don't know," he said. "I haven't heard anything from any company, and I haven't felt it was quite the thing to make inquiries in view of all the rest of the money I'm coming into. None of the lawyers has mentioned a policy to me as yet."

"That's curious, isn't it? How much was it supposed to be?"

"A hundred thousand dollars. About as much more as the estate I'm inheriting after taxes and fees are paid."

"And he didn't mention the company, and you haven't heard any more? That's very odd." Miss Pomeroy tapped the pad with the pencil.

"Yes, I think so too. You understand that I'll be in a financial position to pay your fees whatever they may be and whatever you discover. If you can prove it was suicide and I don't get the insurance I still have the rest of the estate."

"Yes," she said. "Now who was the attending physician?"

"Dr. James Laurence. I don't know anything about him."

Neither did Miss Pomeroy, which pleased her. It wasn't agreeable to suspect a man you knew of carelessness with a death certificate, and in spite of Mr. Osgood's certainty she intended to hang on to her notion that perhaps a disappearance had been arranged until it was definitely and finally disproved.

"Family?"

"No surviving relatives closer than myself and my mother. There were a couple of servants. He had one of those farmhouses in Connecticut that literary men favor. Going to barricade the doors and live off the land come the revolution. Of course he didn't know a carrot from a ragweed, but that doesn't deter his sort of farmer from boasting that he's invented the simple life."

"Where are the servants?"

"The man's in the army; the woman has a place in New York now. I believe the man attended Charles in his last moments. He died before the doctor reached him."

"And what are their names?"

"Nora and Richard Johnson." He gave her the woman's address.

"I'll talk with them and see what I can find out," Miss Pomeroy said. "Try not to worry too much."

Frank Osgood stood up and inhaled deeply. "You know," he said, "I think that's the first free breath I've drawn since Charles died. You are a woman to inspire great confidence, Miss Pomeroy."

Chapter 3

DR. JAMES LAURENCE (Internal Medicine) was one of the tanned and breezy practitioners whose faces are more familiar at their golf clubs than at their hospitals. The accoutrements of his office were conventionally luxurious. Miss Pomeroy, whose ideal of a perfect doctor had been formed around the figure of the first one she had known at the age of six—F. D. Darrow, Physician and Surgeon, with a slick horsehair sofa in the waiting room of his office above the drug store—didn't like Dr. Laurence. She had served a good many doctors she didn't like in the course of her professional career, and she flattered herself that her manners had always masked her emotions as successfully as now. Dr. Laurence didn't know, of course, that she was a nurse, although it seemed to her that the air which had become second nature to her, respectful but not subservient, must surely give her away. Office hours were over for the afternoon, and Dr. Laurence was devoting a brief period to interviewing salesmen for pharmaceutical houses and other unremunerative callers. He plainly regarded Miss Pomeroy as one of the least attractive of this unattractive class. She stated her errand directly and without preamble. His expression when she announced that she was a private detective indicated a degree of surprise which she found somewhat embarrassing, and when she added the subject of her present investigation he was definitely astounded.

"I understand that there are ethics in your profession, Dr. Laurence," she said hastily, "and of course I don't want you to violate the confidence that exists between physician and patient. But a close relative has positive first-hand information that Mr. Osgood intended to commit suicide, and for sufficient and entirely creditable reasons he is eager to establish the facts in the case. I'm not even asking you to express an opinion as to whether he did so or not; I'm only asking whether the circumstances of his death could admit of that interpretation."

"Good Lord, yes," the doctor said. "He could have committed suicide any day he chose during the last six months of his life and defied anybody to prove it. He had a heart condition that was going to kill him off within the year whatever he did, and all he'd have needed to do to hurry it up a bit was not take his medicine when he had an attack, or, say, run upstairs carrying a dictionary."

"But however did he get the insurance then?" Miss
Pomeroy asked, and immediately wished she had bitten
off her tongue instead. A private detective, Mr. Keene
had explained, acquires information without giving it. In
this case, however, her slip, if it was a slip, was effective.

"What insurance?" Dr. Laurence asked, and then continued positively: "He didn't get any insurance within the
past year unless the company employed a dumber doctor
than I've ever met. Anybody who'd ever been within a
mile of a stethoscope could diagnose that heart. Besides,
I've been his doctor for about five years and I haven't had
any inquiries about him from insurance companies—or
hadn't until you came along."

Miss Pomeroy smiled at the pleasantry, but her brain
was working furiously. Hundred thousand dollar life insurance policies weren't handed out like War Bonds. Had
Charles Osgood succeeded in fooling an insurance company doctor—(unlikely)—or had he been lying about the
insurance, or could this man be lying about the disease?
And if so why? What advantage could accrue to a doctor
from saying that a man had perished of heart disease if
he had really committed suicide? Offhand she couldn't
think of any. Of course it was entirely possible that a doctor who had diagnosed heart disease would stubbornly
refuse to retreat from that position even if faced by irref-
utable evidence that the death had been a suicide. She'd
tried to guard against that in her approach, but she had
realized it wouldn't be easy. And certainly if Charles Osgood had been suffering from an incurable heart disease
the physician attending him could very easily have been
misled into reporting suicide as the result of the disease.

No carelessness or inefficiency need be sought for there.

Her silence, she realized suddenly, was stretching to an awkward length, and Dr. Laurence was showing signs of impatience.

"You think he hadn't taken out any life insurance policies since you first attended him then?" she asked.

"If he did there was something underhanded about it, and damned clever too. You know it's routine to send an inquiry to the regular attending physician—and besides that, the physical examination for any substantial policy is very thorough. He certainly couldn't have passed it during the last year."

"He's been ill for that long?"

"His heart hasn't been bad for that long, but it was brought on by a nephritis of long standing. That is, his kidneys were damaged and eventually his heart was affected also. But the nephritis alone would have been enough to keep him from getting any insurance."

"And of course he knew all this?"

"Of course. He was a mature man, independent and quite solitary. No immediate family; there was no one to tell if I didn't tell him, so I told him. It was the only sensible thing to do. He needed to wind up his affairs, and he could take it."

Yes, he could take it, Miss Pomeroy thought. Apparently he had taken it standing up, sharing the knowledge with no one.

"Did he seem much upset?" she asked.

"He was a reserved man. I think he'd suspected for a good while before I admitted that he was right. He didn't show much visible reaction."

"Do you think he was the sort of man who might have killed himself because he couldn't stand waiting?"

"I don't know. I don't really think so, no, but I certainly couldn't be sure. After all, it was his life. If he wanted to cut it short and could so easily I'd hardly think it was my business to interfere."

"Yes, I can see that," she said slowly, and got to her feet, realizing that the interview was at an end. She wanted desperately to continue it, but she couldn't think of anything else to ask.

"Why should anyone care?" he inquired curiously. "The man's certainly dead; none of this can bring him back."

"There was the question of that insurance," she explained. "The heir feels hesitant about accepting the money since he knows that Mr. Osgood had intended to kill himself. But from what you say I judge there must be some mistake about that; the policy doesn't exist at all, so there really isn't any reason for further investigation, is there?"

"None that I can see," he assured her.

"Were you present when Mr. Osgood died?"

The doctor raised his eyebrows slightly as if he found this cross-questioning a trifle offensive, but he answered promptly.

"No, he was dead on arrival. That wasn't at all remarkable. His man phoned that he was having a bad attack, and I gave instructions by telephone. He had an adequate supply of digitalis with him at all times, and understood how to use it. However, he'd been dead for some time when I arrived."

"You went out to Connecticut to him?"

"Yes, I did."

"You didn't think it necessary to advise that they call in a local man from near at hand for the emergency?"

This time the doctor's eyebrows rose definitely. "I did not," he said quite sharply, rising to his feet as a sign that the interview was at an end. "I am glad to cooperate with you, Miss Pomeroy, but I can't feel that the medical treatment I recommended is a legitimate field for your investigation."

"No," she said. "No, no, of course not. I only wondered—he couldn't have taken an overdose of the digitalis?"

"He could have fallen downstairs or drunk himself to death, but he didn't. He died of a heart attack. I've certified that, and the case is closed."

"If the family were to want an exhumation would you be willing to cooperate?"

"No, I don't believe I should care to act for the family in that case. Good day, Miss Pomeroy."

"Good day, doctor, and thank you."

Miss Pomeroy rode down in the elevator and walked into the street engrossed in a brown study. The more she thought about Dr. James Laurence and his story the more curious she became. In the first place, a man of Charles Osgood's means was unlikely to have been satisfied with the diagnosis of a general practitioner when that diagnosis was such a gloomy one. There should have been a heart specialist somewhere in the picture, but Dr. Laurence had failed to mention any. In the second place, the hundred thousand dollar insurance policy didn't fit at all. There wasn't any conceivable reason why he should have told his cousin that such a policy existed if it didn't. Moreover, if Charles Osgood had been suffering from an incurable disease he had had no reason to conceal the fact from his family. That sort of heroism was understandable in a family man who feared to distress his loved ones, but here was no need. He could perfectly well have luxuriated in all the sympathy and attention his state could have commanded—if the story were true. On the other hand, if it weren't true an entirely extraneous element was introduced into the puzzle. If Dr. Laurence were lying he must be doing so for some private purpose of his own; it was inconceivable that this could fit into the pattern of Charles Osgood's plot against his cousin. That was the trouble with plots; they involved so many people and such complete synchronization in planning and action that only a genius could count on having one work out right.

On impulse Miss Pomeroy turned in to a strange and expensive beauty salon and ordered a shampoo. Her mind worked best when her hair was wet. The fact that she could get an appointment at all without having made advance arrangements was nothing short of phenomenal according to the young goddess in charge of the desk. Miss Pomeroy assented humbly, her mind still on her problem. In the privacy of her white-curtained cubicle she gave herself up to it and the grateful ministrations of a girl who had sense enough to recognize a customer who didn't want to talk when she saw one.

Suppose Charles Osgood, in perfectly good health, had planned and perfected the ridiculous scheme he had outlined to his cousin. Suppose he had carried it out, leaving all his carefully laid clues, and his manservant had sum-

moned a busy and not too bright doctor, and suppose the
doctor, anxious to get on to another patient or a game of
golf or a dinner date, had certified heart failure as the
easiest thing. After all, everyone died of heart failure although there were different contributing factors. It was
certainly a safe guess in a case where a doctor didn't know
what had happened. But suppose that afterward some of
the carefully laid clues had somehow been called to his
attention, or at least that he had gotten wind of the idea
that the death might not have been as simple and natural
as he thought. What would be his best defense against an
accusation of carelessness? Why, certainly to say that the
man had previously been suffering from a heart ailment
which made the diagnosis of the cause of death a matter
of routine.

And supposing that there was any truth anywhere in
this chain of supposition, where should she trip up the
doctor? Why should she trip up the doctor, as far as that
went? His evidence would certainly satisfy her client; the
death could never be certified as suicide or murder, whatever it might really have been. That thought, Miss Pomeroy told herself sternly, was unworthy of a private detective.
Moreover, she was suffering from a lively feminine curiosity as to what had really happened, and she hoped devoutly that her client wouldn't decide to drop the investigation before she should have a chance to find out.

All right then, if Dr. Laurence's story were true there
ought to be a heart specialist, and apparently there wasn't.
She considered telephoning the doctor again to ask him,
and decided against that. Perhaps the servants would
know. Obviously in any case the next job was to interview

the servants. They would be able to describe the circumstances of the death, and Miss Pomeroy felt that her knowledge was extensive enough to allow her to distinguish a genuine heart attack from a false one. They ought to know, too, whether or not the man had been ill, whether he'd been taking medicine. Miss Pomeroy jumped so that the attendant pulled her hair and apologized.

"My fault," she said, "quite all right," and returned to her meditations. If Charles Osgood had been taking digitalis for any length of time there would certainly exist records of the purchases. She ought even to be able to find out how much he should have on hand, and perhaps also how much he actually did have on hand at the time of death. The next thing was to interview the servants. What would have happened to the contents of a man's medicine chest by the time he had been dead for six weeks, though?

It was a peculiarly difficult problem, she thought, shivering pleasurably as the hot water was dashed over her scalp, because there were so many unknown quantities. In an ordinary murder investigation you had a dead person and a murderer; it was simply a question of eliminating suspects one by one until you arrived at the culprit. But here there were a whole series of questions. Had Charles Osgood ever intended to kill himself? If the answer to that one was yes, there remained the question whether it was because he knew he was fatally ill or for some other reason. His plans would be quite different under the two differing sets of circumstances. Then, supposing he had intended to kill himself, had he really intended to incriminate his cousin? And supposing he had, where had the plan gone wrong and why? Miss Pomeroy had no doubt in her own mind that it had somehow gone awry, but how could she hope to detect the errors without knowing the original plan? She couldn't expect to be able to believe what anyone said, even assuming no one was intentionally lying, for the essence of Charles Osgood's plan must have been to mislead observers. The key to the puzzle lay hopelessly beyond her reach in the dead brain of Charles Osgood.

And suddenly Miss Pomeroy realized that it did nothing of the kind. It wasn't easy, ordinarily, to get an insight into the mind of a dead man, but Charles Osgood had been a very special case.

"Do you ever read detective stories?" she inquired abruptly.

The suddenness of the question caused the operator to spill some of the cold rinse water on Miss Pomeroy's nose, and by the time apologies had been offered and accepted and the damage repaired, the question itself was forgotten and Miss Pomeroy was forced to repeat it, somewhat to the detriment of the casual effect she had hoped to achieve.

"Do you ever read detective stories?"

"Well, of course I really like good literature," the girl said defensively, "but naturally I don't get much time to read, and for when you just like to pick up something light I always say you can't beat a good murder mystery."

"That's what I always say too," Miss Pomeroy agreed. "Did you ever read any by Charles Osgood?"

"Charles Osgood? Is he the fat one?"

"I don't know. I don't think so. I never saw him."

"No, that's not the fat one's name. He might be the

one with the British accent or—no, it's not the Colonel. He's named after an animal or something. Do you mean the lawyer?"

"No, no, no," Miss Pomeroy said. "I'm talking about the author, not the detective. I don't know whether his detective is a herpatologist or a journalist; I never read any of his books. I just wondered whether you had."

"If he's the one that wrote about that Japanese, there aren't any more on account of the war," the girl said helpfully.

"I don't think he is; it doesn't matter; I'll go up to the library and look him up as soon as you're finished," Miss Pomeroy said, abruptly impatient for the shampoo to be over. The girl was maddeningly slow now, and when, an hour later, Miss Pomeroy presented herself at the central desk in the reference room of the Public Library she had another setback. The detective novels of Charles Osgood were not catalogued as reference works, and consequently were available, if at all, only in the fiction collection on the 42nd Street floor. Miss Pomeroy walked down three flights of stairs rather than wait for the elevator, and found that two Osgood novels were in and that she had no library card with her. The nearest Womrath shop was more productive, and in due course of time she was seated over her solitary dinner at Alice Foote MacDougall's with a pile of eight brightly paper-jacketed novels at her left elbow. The light was poor, and it hurt her eyes to try to read, but she was too impatient to wait any longer and sampled Murder by Magic with her tomato bisque.

She read rapidly, skimming lightly through essential scenes and skipping the recapitulations, but even so Murder by Magic carried her through vanilla ice cream and demitasse and left her seven more to finish at home during the course of the night. It was five o'clock in the morning when she closed Homicide at Hillsdale, switched off her bed light, and settled herself to sleep or to think.

Charles Osgood's detective was a rough and ready midwestern farmer named Silas Smith. In despite of a rustic appearance and manner of speech he was widely read in American literature and solved his cases either by analogy from the simple, homely experiences of the farm or by induction based on abstruse quotations from the works of Mark Twain or William Dean Howells. His surface simplicity threw people off, and he was able to ferret out plots because the guilty authors despised him.

The plots themselves were all of the hand-is-quicker-than-the-eye school; in the center of a brilliantly lighted ballroom hereditary jewels disappeared from around the neck of a young Polish countess rusticating in rural Michigan; a man sitting peacefully in a closed dining room in his club, with half a dozen cronies about him, dropped dead with a bullet through his heart; a young girl disappeared without leaving a trace in broad daylight on the street between her home and the corner grocery store. The solutions were ingenious and intricate, depending generally on the simultaneous evil designs of some half dozen characters acting independently.

Every novel had at least one scene of torture threatened or executed, generally at some length. Frequently the exigencies of the plot made it necessary for Silas Smith to be a witness of or even a participant in this scene, unwillingly if the victim were a sympathetic character, enthusi-

astically if it were a trapped villain. There had obviously
been a broad streak of sadism in Charles Osgood, and while
Miss Pomeroy recognized that he had found a harmless
and even wholesome outlet for it in his fiction, she found
her distaste for the author growing with every story.

She was glad Charles Osgood was dead. His profession
was one which furnished innocent amusement for thou-
sands of people; that she was willing to admit, and perhaps
they would miss him, but Miss Grace Pomeroy was glad
he was dead. The vicious degeneracy of the man's character, masked by the hollow and wholesome virtues of
Silas Smith, revolted her. She no longer had any doubt as
to whether or not he had intended to convict his cousin of
his own murder. The gesture was thoroughly in character
with the man. She found herself thinking of him not as
the victim but as the murderer he had intended to be. But
as to the nature of his plan she had not found a single clue.
The Osgood plots were deft and convincing enough for
fiction, but there was not one of the eight that could by
the remotest chance have stood the test of actuality. The
scheme Osgood had concocted must have depended on
himself alone; he certainly could not have expected anyone to share in his deviltry. It had to be elastic to cover
various contingencies concerning Frank's actions; it had
to be simple; it had to promise on the surface at least to
work out satisfactorily when his guiding intelligence was
removed. Miss Pomeroy had no idea what it could have
been nor where it could have snagged, and she devoutly
hoped that Frank Osgood would let her find out.

Chapter 4

THE next morning was Thursday, and it occurred to Miss Pomeroy that here should be an excellent opportunity to interview Nora Johnson. She was quite aware of the fact that in her new profession the direct approach was generally frowned upon. If she wanted to talk to Nora, the approved way to do it would be to secure a position as general maid in an adjoining apartment and cultivate the other woman on their days off. In the current state of the world it did not even seem to her that it would be likely to be particularly difficult to get such a job. But in her own person Miss Pomeroy preferred a less subtle method, and since Mr. Keene had given her a free hand to work on this case she decided simply to call up Mrs. Johnson, introduce herself, and ask for an interview. She was rather more than dimly aware of the fact that Mr. Keene had permitted a green hand such wide latitude only because the case struck him as screwy—mentally Miss Pomeroy enclosed the term in quotes—and unlikely to be very remunerative. She would have to work fast if she expected to find anything out before she was called off the investigation.

Mrs. Johnson on the telephone proved somewhat surprisingly cordial, and proposed that Miss Pomeroy should come over at once to the apartment on East 81st Street where she was installed as general factotum. She received her guest some forty-five minutes later in a spotless white tile kitchen, and offered her coffee and cake. Miss Pomeroy demurred at dipping into the coffee ration, but Nora silenced her firmly.

"They're hoarders," she said coldly, "and anyway the coffee's already made. If you don't drink it I'll have to throw it out. *She* wouldn't have it warmed over if she was starving."

Miss Pomeroy accepted a cup of coffee, hoping that this attitude presaged a generally critical viewpoint toward employers and not loyalty to a former one at the expense of the new. Nora did not wait to be questioned but opened the subject of Charles Osgood's death herself.

"Well, what do you want to know about Mr. Osgood?" she asked. "Anything that'll hurry up me getting my money I'm ready and willing to tell you."

"Did he owe you money?" Miss Pomeroy asked, forgetting again not to appear surprised.

"Of course not. I'm not dumb enough to work any place where I don't get my money every Saturday night on the dot. I mean the money he left me in the will."

Miss Pomeroy decided hastily that frankness was the best policy.

"I don't know anything about it," she admitted. "I have no connection with the lawyers probating the will. I supposed it had been done. But I don't think you need to worry; I understand those things always take time. There's no controversy over the will, and Mr. Osgood had plenty of money, so I'm sure you'll get yours in good time."

"I hope so," Nora said darkly. "One thousand dollars it said in the will for me, and another thousand for Richard. I hope he wasn't playing none of his tricks on us."

"I can't imagine a man playing a trick in his will."

"Then you didn't know Mr. Osgood. No time he'd rather play a trick than when he was dead and knew you couldn't get back at him."

"Didn't you like him?"

"I liked him all right, because he didn't have me buffaloed. He paid good wages and I knew my rights; nobody that couldn't stand up for themselves ever oughtta have worked for him."

"Oh," Miss Pomeroy said. "Well, I guess people always have to stand up for their own rights, don't they? But it was nice of him to leave you the money."

"I haven't got the money yet," Nora answered.

"Well," Miss Pomeroy said, "I'm sorry I don't know anything about it. I'll be glad to see the lawyers for you, but of course I can't promise anything because I don't know what the situation is. I wanted to ask you for some more information about Mr. Osgood's death. I understand the doctor didn't arrive until too late."

"Not until he'd passed away," Nora agreed with relish. "Richard and I was with him the whole time."

"Had you ever known him previously to have an attack similar to the one that killed him?"

"Never," she said positively. "He was a very healthy gentleman. He couldn't abide being sick or having anything to do with sick people. I never heard him complain once."

"He wasn't taking any medicine then?"

"I wouldn't know. He never talked about it if he did. There was things in the medicine chest, like anywhere else, and I suppose he took some of them sometimes. Do you think he was poisoned?"

"I haven't any idea. But some interested parties think he may have committed suicide, and I'm trying to find out."

"That's nonsense. He never killed himself, not him. I wouldn't put it past him to kill somebody else, but not himself."

"That's very helpful," Miss Pomeroy said. "Now could you tell me just about how he was taken ill?"

"He went into his study after lunch just like he always did. Sometimes he wrote and sometimes he laid down; he had a studio couch in there."

"Was he alone?"

"Just Richard and me in the house."

"Had there been guests recently? Was it usual for him to lunch alone?"

"If you'll let me tell you my own way and ask me one question at a time we'll get through a lot faster."

"I beg your pardon," Miss Pomeroy said humbly.

"He had his lunch and went in there. I heard the type-writer going some and I noticed it wasn't like he usually goes. Mostly he writes real fast for a while and then stops and then real fast again. This day it was uneven—slow and uneven."

"Has anyone looked at the pages he was typing?" Miss Pomeroy asked, her heart in her throat.

"Yes, the doctor looked them over and said they showed he was sick; they didn't make no sense. He threw 'em away."

"You're sure they've been destroyed?"

"Burned 'em myself."

"Well, then, go on," Miss Pomeroy said sadly.

"Pretty soon he came out in the kitchen for a drink of water; said he was awful thirsty."

"Did you watch him drink it?"

"I was doing my work; I saw him, but I didn't what you'd call watch him, no."

"Could he have taken anything when he drank the water?"

"Poison you mean? He didn't take no poison."

"What did he say?"

"Just kind of rambled on; I never paid him much mind. He always talked a lot of foolishness."

"But he didn't complain of feeling ill?"

"No, he certainly didn't."

"Then what happened next?"

"He went on back in the study and wrote a little while longer. Then he called me, and his voice was all funny; he called two or three times before I went because he wasn't making hardly any noise. He was standing there with his hand to his throat and his eyes all funny, kind of bowing. Like to scared me to death."

"Bowing?"

"Yes, sort of bowing to me. He could just barely talk; he said: 'Sick, get a doctor, water' or something like that. I got him some water first and then ran for Richard, and Richard stayed with him while I called the doctor."

"How did you know what doctor to call?"

"It was on a list of numbers in the front of the phone book."

"And what did the doctor say?"

"He told me some medicine was supposed to be in the medicine chest or maybe in Mr. Osgood's pocket—spelled the name for me and had me go look while he held the line, and it was there all right. He told me to give him a teaspoonful and keep him sitting up but quiet until he could get there, and to keep his hands and feet warm."

"Do you remember the name of the medicine?"

"It's on the tip of my tongue, but I can't say it."

"Was it digitalis?" Miss Pomeroy inquired, unblushingly leading her witness.

"Digitalis, that was it."

"And you gave him the dose the doctor prescribed?"

"Precisely. When the doctor got there he said we'd done exactly right; he couldn't have done more himself. It was his heart; took him like that and he was gone."

"What happened when you gave him the digitalis?"

"I couldn't see that it made any difference. Richard was having a terrible time to keep him sitting up; he kept slipping down and waving his hands around and trying to talk. Richard saw we couldn't hold him and sent me to get the Munroes to help. I ran all the way down there, but when we got back he was dead."

"The Munroes were the nearest neighbors?"

"They're the tenants on the place. Their house is maybe a quarter of a mile away."

"Half a mile round trip, and you ran. You were gone about ten minutes altogether then?"

"I guess so. Mrs. Munroe was in the house; he was out at the barn, and she sent the boy for him and came along with me. He followed about five minutes after us, but it wasn't any use; Mr. Osgood was dead."

"And the doctor?"

"It was an hour or more before he got there. The Munroes thought maybe we ought to call somebody out from the village, but Richard thought, with him already dead, there wasn't no sense in running up two doctor bills when neither one could do him any good. We kept rubbing his hands and feet like the doctor said, and we kept hot water bottles beside him, but I tried his breath with a mirror and I knew he was gone."

Miss Pomeroy looked at her helplessly. There wasn't anything else to ask. The report tallied in every way with what the doctor had said, and the symptoms were entirely consistent with the heart attack the doctor had diagnosed. It was a funny thing for a man with a heart as bad as that not to have let his servants know he was suffering, and yet it was not inconsistent with the known character of Charles Osgood. The presence of the digitalis in the medicine chest certainly tended to confirm what the doctor had said.

"That's all," Nora was saying belligerently, "except I'd still like to know when I get my money. If they're trying to prove Richard and I killed him so we won't get what he left us, they're barking up the wrong tree. We called the doctor the minute he took sick, and the doctor saw all we done and said it was all right. And he didn't have nothing funny to eat for lunch."

"Nobody thinks you poisoned him," Miss Pomeroy said. "You mustn't get such notions in your head. It's just— well, he was known to have mentioned suicide, and when a man dies suddenly after he's been talking about suicide it makes people wonder."

"Everybody talks about suicide one time or another," Nora said, "and very few does anything about it. I wouldn't put much stock in that."

Miss Pomeroy thanked her and set out for her office on West 45th Street, sorely troubled as to what to do next. The doctor and all the attendants at the death bed stated flatly that the death was natural and refused to be shaken in that belief. She remained skeptical herself, but her client ought to be satisfied; against such a phalanx any evidence that Charles had manufactured would inevitably crumble. It was a funny thing though; it seemed as if a man like Charles Osgood should have devised a scheme that would at least get past first base.

There was a note at the office that a Miss Kay Waterhouse had attempted to see her the previous afternoon and would try again this afternoon. Miss Waterhouse, however, could not come in much before five o'clock and she would be grateful if Miss Pomeroy would wait for her until that time. Miss Pomeroy passed the intervening hours in rereading more attentively some of the adventures of Silas Smith.

Miss Waterhouse telephoned at four to confirm the appointment and came in on schedule a little before five o'clock. She was a competent, pleasant looking young woman in her early thirties, wearing low-heeled oxfords, a tweed suit, and a knockabout felt hat. Her voice, her manner, her clothes all shouted "schoolteacher" and Miss Pomeroy thought that she would be a good one.

"I'm afraid I may be intruding in something that's not my affair," she said in her agreeable throaty voice after the introductions were completed. "I'm engaged to Frank Osgood and I understand he's retained you to make an investigation for him."

For once Miss Pomeroy reacted properly. "I'm very much afraid I can't give you any information," she said. "Perhaps if you and your fiancé could come in together if you have any questions—"

The girl made an impatient little gesture with her right hand.

"I know," she said. "I understand, of course; if he's consulted you it's in confidence and you can't tell me. But this is terribly important. A great deal more hinges on it than you have any idea. I'm not asking you to tell me anything; I know he came to you and I know pretty well what he asked you. All I'm asking you is to let it alone; don't do it whatever it was. Please don't. It's terribly important."

Miss Pomeroy looked at her curiously and coldly and did not say anything. This was largely because she had no idea what to say, but its effect on the girl was obviously unsettling.

"Don't you believe me?" she asked humbly.

"It's not a matter of believing," Miss Pomeroy said. "You're asking for information about the affairs of a client that we couldn't possibly give you—if he is a client."

"He is a client," the girl said, leaning forward and speaking with intense eagerness. "Please don't beat around the bush, Miss Pomeroy. Of course I know what I'm talking about; how else could I have known your name? Frank told me all about it. I don't want to be an interfering female; I'd have stayed away if I possibly could, but he's been so foolish; he's such a babe in the wood someone has to take care of him, and there's no one but me to do it."

Miss Pomeroy continued to stare at her without saying

anything; she was troubled and uncertain, but the girl did not realize it.

"Listen," she said. "Look at me. Look in my eyes. I've always been told I have honest eyes. It's so desperately important that you should believe me. My name is Kay Waterhouse. I'm thirty-three years old. I teach the fifth grade at the Theodore Roosevelt School in Brooklyn, and I'm going to marry Frank Osgood this year. I knew him out in Michigan when we were youngsters—him and his cousin. I've been engaged to Frank for eight years; he's had a lot of financial trouble, and we've never been able to marry. I came east in order to be near him and got the job in Brooklyn. For four of the eight years we've just been putting off marrying from year to year, thinking things would be better, and now at last we really can. Doesn't that agree with what he told you?"

"There's nothing in any of that to bring a man to a private detective agency," Miss Pomeroy said.

"He wants you to prove something about his cousin Charles's death," she said.

Miss Pomeroy stared back at her without the flicker of an eyelash.

"I know it," the girl said. "You don't need to admit it if you don't want to, but I know it. And he shouldn't have. He's such a silly fool, such a sweet silly—"

"Do you think Frank Osgood killed his cousin?" Miss Pomeroy asked suddenly.

The girl shrank back into her chair and put her hand across her mouth. Her eyes were wide with horror.

"Do you?" Miss Pomeroy insisted.

"Of course not." Kay's voice was breathless. "What a

perfectly ridiculous notion. What a horrible thing to say! What are you trying to do to me?"

"I'm trying to find the answer to a question that has baffled me for several days," Miss Pomeroy said. "I need to find someone who thinks Frank Osgood killed his cousin Charles. There has to be such a person somewhere. I've known that, but I haven't known who it was or where I'd find him. You're the one, aren't you? All right, then, if you want to help your fiancé I'll tell you how you can. Tell me the whole story, why you believe he did it—everything, every tiny detail that contributed to that belief. If you will I can answer my question, and I can help Mr. Osgood too."

Kay shook her head slowly, her eyes still frightened.

"He died of heart failure," she said.

"Somebody somewhere thinks there is awfully good evidence that his cousin killed him. Is it you?"

"I don't understand. I don't see what you can mean."

"You don't need to understand; if you'll tell me why you think Frank Osgood killed his cousin I'll promise to help you."

"I can't do that," Kay said.

"Then you're wasting your time and mine."

"I can't tell you why I think he killed him," she said, "because I know he killed him. I'll never repeat that to any living soul; I'd deny it under oath right now. I know he killed him, and you won't get any evidence out of me."

"My dear, I can assure you that you are mistaken," the older woman said kindly. "Moreover, if you'll trust me I think I can set your mind at rest."

The girl shook her head dumbly.

"Talk it over with him," Miss Pomeroy urged. "Talk it all out openly; don't go on letting such a horrible suspicion poison your life."

"Don't you think he might kill me if I told him I knew he was a murderer?"

"He may very well be tempted to if you insist on talking in riddles. It really would be better if you'd tell me. You'll upset and worry him, and I'm quite sure I can settle it for you."

"I shan't say any more," Kay Waterhouse answered. "I've said too much already. I wish you'd forget what I've said. I've been overwrought. I love Frank and I intend to marry him. I don't know why I've been talking this way."

"You really had better stop if you intend to marry him," Miss Pomeroy agreed. "I wish you could take my word for it that the one piece missing from my puzzle is your so-called evidence."

The girl smiled faintly. "I came here to persuade you that Charles Osgood's death was natural and that you'd better report it as such to your client and close the matter," she said.

"I was about ready to do that," Miss Pomeroy said, "before you came. Now I'm not so sure."

Chapter 5

RECONSTRUCTING the mental processes of a dead man was not, Miss Pomeroy concluded, quite such a simple matter as she had supposed when she first undertook it. It was reasonably safe to assume, she thought, that no one of the persons to whom she had talked was telling her lies dictated by Charles Osgood. Certainly he must have been too intelligent a man to rely for the success of his plot on the probability that anyone would stick to a false story under pressure when once its author was safely out of the way. He hadn't, therefore, primed Nora or Dr. Laurence or Kay Waterhouse. If there were nothing else against it, none of them seemed to like him well enough to have been chosen as an ally in his fiendish undertaking.

No, whatever anyone of them was testifying that was false Charles Osgood must have planted so successfully that the victim really believed it. He would have been quite capable of tricks of sleight of hand that could have deceived any of them. Miss Pomeroy wished with particular fervor that she might succeed in breaking down the distrust of Kay Waterhouse. A plot that had succeeded in making her believe that Frank was a murderer must have been a good one—unless, of course, she was a superlative actress.

Miss Pomeroy gave herself for a time to contemplation of the unpleasant possibility that Kay Waterhouse was trying to frame the man to whom she was engaged. There were several things to be said for it. She had sought the Keene Detective Agency on her own initiative and, for one as much in love as she pretended to be, she had arrived at a murder accusation in surprisingly short order. Miss Pomeroy was willing to believe that her own personality was one to invite confidence, as she had been told, but this was a more than ordinarily portentous confidence. If Miss Waterhouse wanted Frank Osgood accused of murder, how differently would she have acted? She might perhaps have gone straight to the police with a direct accusation—

or she might have thought an apparently reluctant suspicion expressed in the right quarter would be even more effective.

At this point in her meditation she turned to the Times for distraction, reading, in her usual methodical fashion, straight down one column to the end and then passing to the next, all the way across the page. She had progressed no further than page 12 when she was arrested by the name of Charles Osgood. It appeared below a small cut of a starry-eyed young woman somewhat inadequately clothed.

"Self Styled Widow Claims Osgood Estate" the cut line said, and the story continued:

"Miss Billie La Verne, night club dancer, today filed suit to have the will of Charles Osgood, novelist, who died last August 17, set aside on the ground that it ignored her dower right in the estate. Miss La Verne states that she and Mr. Osgood were married privately aboard his yacht, *Silas II*, in the summer of 1940. Thereafter they lived as husband and wife for the two weeks of the cruise, at the end of which they separated by mutual consent. However, according to Miss La Verne, there has been no subsequent legal separation nor any move toward divorce by either of the parties to the marriage. If the court supports her contention and declares the marriage legal Miss La Verne will inherit about sixty-five thousand dollars as the widow's share of the estate.

"Under the terms of Mr. Osgood's will, which was admitted to probate on September 25, most of his property passes into the possession of his first cousin, Frank Osgood, stockbroker, of Summit, New Jersey. There were several small bequests to charity and to servants, but the bulk of the estate, after payment of taxes, was to have remained together.

"Mr. Frank Osgood, interviewed at the offices of Cuthbert, Cuthbert, Rutherford, and Simes, where he is employed, stated that he had no knowledge of his cousin's marriage nor of the lady who claims to be his wife, but that it was his desire to see the estate distributed on strictly legal terms.

" 'If she is my cousin's widow naturally her claim comes first,' Mr. Osgood said.

"Mr. Gerald Winterbottom, counsel for Frank Osgood, said that 'of course' his client would defend the suit.

"Manhattan gossip columnists frequently linked the name of Charles Osgood with those of various young women of society and the stage, but no marriage has ever been reported. In 1939 his engagement to Sylvia Sylvester, the original debutante glamour girl, was widely circulated and never denied either by Mr. Osgood or Miss Sylvester. She subsequently married Evan Houston, widely known club-man and polo player.

"Miss La Verne has appeared in the chorus at the Club Imperial, La Playa, and the Three Queens. Her theatrical career began in 1937 when she was Miss Brooklyn at the Atlantic City beauty contest. She met Mr. Osgood at La Playa when he was entertaining a party there a few weeks before the alleged marriage. Miss La Verne was married in 1938 to Robert Gordon, stage-hand, and divorced the following year."

Miss Pomeroy read every word of it twice and then took the newspaper in to the office of her boss. Mr. Keene was a big, genial man with an easy, affable manner that often concealed from the unwary the sharpness of his twinkling eyes. He sat with his feet on his desk and his hat on the back of his head until he noted the approach of Miss Pomeroy, whereupon he hastily improved his posture very much in the manner of a small boy in the presence of a school teacher.

"I beg your pardon, Mr. Keene," she said sedately. "I've just noticed a story in the Times that may perhaps alter your plans on the Osgood case. I understand that Mr. Osgood is counting on his inheritance from his cousin to enable him to pay your fee, and this story says that there's another claimant for the estate."

Keene accepted the paper she held out and ran a practiced eye quickly down the column she indicated with a thumb. He paid the photograph the compliment of a soundless whistle, and over the contents of the article itself he briefly pulled the lobe of his right ear. Then he handed the paper back.

"I wouldn't worry," he said. "Osgood's not in very deep with us, and he's good for what he owes us all right. You're not running up much of an expense account, are you?"

"No, and I'm not getting any results either," she said. "The servants who were present say suicide was impossible, and the doctor who attended him says it would have been the easiest thing in the world, but you could never prove it. I'm not sure it would be suicide under the legal meaning of the term anyway for a sick man to overstrain himself deliberately in order to hasten his death. What do you think?"

Keene shrugged. "It's a delicate point. Anyway, if the doctor's straight you've proved that he got the insurance by fraud, and so our client doesn't benefit, and apparently that's what he's wanted all along. Funny duck, isn't he? Have you figured why he wants to do himself out of a hundred thousand dollars?"

"Yes, I think I have," Miss Pomeroy said, "but it's from things he told me in confidence. Is it all right if I keep it to myself?"

"Sure," he said, "sure. I've got enough on my mind. Use your own judgment. Just be careful never to keep anything to yourself that we might need to know here for your own protection—or for the client's, if anything should happen to you."

"I don't think anything will happen to me," Miss Pomeroy said, but she felt a faint cold chill chasing up and down her spine.

Frank Osgood at his desk in the offices of Cuthbert, Cuthbert, Rutherford, and Simes was rereading the same newspaper article for perhaps the tenth time that day. Each time he read it he enjoyed it a little more. It was nice of the reporter to have described him as "stockbroker" instead of "stockbroker's clerk" as he might equally well have done. Moreover the statement he had issued appeared, in print, both dignified and virile. Frank had worried about it ever since the previous day when a reporter from the City News Service had sought him out at the office, disturbing office routine and very possibly jeopardizing Frank's job in case any of the partners had noticed.

When he worried Frank's ulcers always took a decided turn for the worse, and he had been unable to eat any dinner at all the night before. Then this morning there had been the problem of keeping his mother from seeing the

newspaper; she was a worrier too, and a vocal one, and the
expression of her anxiety always increased Frank's own.
If she had any idea at all that they might not inherit
Charles's money she would be very badly upset. It was
only because he didn't want her to be upset, Frank told
himself, that he had so carefully concealed the paper at
breakfast. That was no easy task, for reading the news over
her morning coffee was one of his mother's major pleasures
in life. The story in the Herald Tribune had been shorter
than that in the Times and had not been accompanied by
a picture, but there was quite enough in it to worry his
mother. Keeping it from her had entailed getting downstairs early, bringing the paper in, and hiding it, folded into
a small wad, in the inner pocket of his overcoat. The bulge
was easily perceptible, and being normally a preternatu-
rally honest man, Frank had found it difficult to sustain
throughout breakfast the conversation on the subject of
the breakdown in the local news-dealer's delivery system.

However, since he had reached the office and read the
article in the Times as well, he was feeling more and
more pleased about it. The best thing that could possibly happen would be for the woman to establish her
claim and take all of Charles's money. Frank didn't want
a penny of it, but even if he had not quailed before the
thought of explaining such an aberration to his mother he
doubted whether his thrifty soul would have permitted
him to refuse so large a sum. If this woman took it, it
would solve everything. It would shock his mother, too,
possibly even jolt her a little out of her stubborn good
opinion of Charles. To marry Kay and live on Charles's
money was almost the worst fate Frank could imagine. He

loved Kay, he admired her, he trusted her. She had waited eight years for him, and the least he could do in return was to give her all his trust. He did give her all his trust; he never thought any more of the ugly suspicions he had once harbored as to the relations that might exist between Kay and Charles—well, almost never. At no time had he really believed it, but sometimes the suspicion had troubled him a good deal. He had never mentioned it to Kay—of course not, and he never would mention it, but if, in the years ahead, he must constantly remember that it was Charles's money that had bought her clothes, her furnishings, the little luxuries of the table in which she loved to indulge, it might sometimes be difficult. On his salary and their joint savings it would be a tight squeeze to get by sometimes, but how much better that would be than accepting favors from the dead hand of Charles.

His telephone rang, and when he answered a woman's voice spoke through the instrument.

"Mr. Osgood?" The voice was mellifluous, the accent just outside the bounds of his experience. It was British, tinged by California influences, and yet, even in the single short phrase there sounded the unmistakable twang of the Brooklyn "g."

"Speaking," he said.

"Oh," said the voice, still wearing the accent rather like a hastily donned hostess gown, "oh, Mr. Osgood, this is ah—Mrs. Osgood."

"What?" he asked inanely.

"Mrs. Charles Osgood. Your cousin Billie."

"Oh, yes," he said blankly. "Yes indeed. Of course. Certainly. Er—how do you do?"

"I've been reading your very kind and generous state-ment in the paper," she said, "and I can see you must be an aw'fly good sport. I thought maybe if I could talk to you without any lawyers or anything around we might be able to get things fixed up. Lawyers are so cold-blooded."

"Yes," he said, "yes, they are. But I really don't know anything. I mean it's out of my hands. Miss—er, Mrs. Osgood."

"Oh, please call me Billie," she cooed. "That's so formal between friends. Please, Cousin Frank."

"I'm at the office," he said stiffly. "I can't talk now."

It was a phrase he had heard other men say into the telephone with their faces suffused or debonair according to their temperaments, but he had never himself had occa-sion to use it previously.

"I could come down town and meet you," she said, "or you could come to my apartment. It really would save us a lot of time and money in lawyer's fees and things—a reasonable man like you. Couldn't you run up here and let me pour you a drink?"

"I can't get away during office hours," he repeated miserably. Mr. Donald Cuthbert was passing down the aisle directly behind his back. Frank was acutely conscious of his ulcers and of the fact that the back of his neck must be a bright pink.

Mr. Cuthbert had stopped and dropped a friendly hand onto his shoulder.

"Pardon me for eavesdropping," he said, "but if you want the rest of the afternoon off it's quite all right with the firm."

"Hold the line a minute," Frank Osgood said into the

instrument. He covered the mouthpiece and turned to Mr. Cuthbert.

"It's the woman who says she is my cousin's widow," he explained. "She wants to discuss her claim with me."

"Don't let her put anything over on you, my boy." Mr. Cuthbert's tone was still genial. "Better take your lawyer along. And you'd better watch yourself giving statements to the newspapers without his advice."

"Thank you," Frank Osgood said, and uncovering the telephone spoke into it again. "I can be there in about half an hour. Will you give me the address again, please?"

It was an address on Horatio Street, a thoroughfare with which Mr. Osgood had never been familiar. He tried first to look it up on a city map, but in the end he abandoned that attempt and confided himself to the escort of a highly self-confident taxi-driver. The self-confidence was justified; when, through a complicated maze of one-way streets, Osgood finally found himself safely deposited at the door of 17 Horatio Street he capped the extravagance of having come in a taxi by tipping the driver a quarter. It was, he reflected, undoubtedly a part of the effect of being heir to an estate of a hundred thousand dollars, exclusive of insurance. He was even cynical enough to reflect that the unaccustomed geniality of Mr. Donald Cuthbert might be another effect of the same cause.

Miss Billie La Verne, to use the name by which she designated herself on her mailbox, lived in a third floor walk-up apartment in a small house at the back of the garden of 17 Horatio Street. Frank Osgood rang the doorbell above the name La Verne, and the accent, issuing from the speaking tube, directed him to walk straight through

the hall to the back of the house, out the door, and across
the garden. He followed directions and was met at the door
of the annex by a girl who could not be anyone but his
soi-disant cousin-in-law. Her hair was of a peculiar shade
which he thought he remembered Kay having described
as platinum blonde, and there was a great deal of it dan-
gling on her neck and getting in her left eye. The visible
right eye was very large and very blue, with quite the long-
est eyelash Frank Osgood had ever seen. And, remarkably
enough, the eyelash was not platinum blonde like the hair
but very thick and dark. It looked almost, he thought, as if
it had been pasted on.

If there could have been any possible doubt of her
identity the girl dispelled it at once.

"Cousin Frank!" she said, holding out both her hands,
"I knew you'd come. I was sure you're the kind of a man
you really are. You can't fool me on men."

Frank offered her one niggardly hand, which she
promptly engulfed in her two and drew to her breast.

"I can't tell you what it means to me to find a man who
understands," she breathed. "This is all so terrible—so
heartbreaking."

Frank wondered if it would be polite to try to pull his
hand away.

"I'm afraid there isn't anything I can do," he said stiffly.
"Probably I shouldn't have come. It really is a matter for
the lawyers."

"Lawyers should never come between friends," she said,
smiling mistily. "Come upstairs and let's talk."

Frank followed her up two flights and into her one room
apartment. He had been in single apartments before, but

never in one furnished just like this. There was a soiled
white bearskin rug on the floor in front of the open fireplace; the fireplace itself was evidently used as a waste-
basket and was piled high with trash. The drapes at the
windows, the cover of the studio couch with its lavish
cushions, and the bathroom door were all vermilion. The
effect, in the confined space, entirely justified the word
"staggering." The screen which concealed the corner
kitchenette was covered with cartoons from Esquire,
mounted so that they overlapped here and there, and shel-
lacked for permanence. Frank glanced at them and hastily
averted his eyes. When Billie went behind the screen to
mix two drinks, however, he permitted himself a closer
look. He accepted the drink without a mention, or even a
thought, of his ulcers; he had never been so close to a
woman like this, and the experience was not in the least
like what he would have expected it to be.

He sat in the single easy chair the room boasted, and
Billie curled up on the studio couch with her feet beneath
her and held out her glass with a charmingly confiding
little gesture.

"Bottoms up!" she said, smiling.

Frank looked in alarm at the tall and generously filled
glass before he took one hearty swallow. It was by no
stretch of the imagination bottoms up, but it made him
feel relaxed almost immediately, and Billie did not criti-
cize the amount he drank although the contents of her
own glass were sinking much more rapidly.

"Isn't this cozy?" she inquired.

"You wanted to talk about my cousin's will," Frank reminded her.

"It's too bad to bring up business between friends."

"I hope you get it all," Frank said. "My lawyer wouldn't let me turn it over to you, but that's what I want to do. I don't want to touch his money. I hope you win the case and take every cent."

Miss La Verne's big blue right eye narrowed perceptibly at this unexpected approach to the problem, and she set down her glass.

"Why, darling, I wouldn't want to do that," she cooed. "I wouldn't dream of taking it all. If I was closest to him you were next. That's why I thought maybe we could talk it over and not have to bother with nasty old lawyers at all. If you feel that way it's awf'ly simple. Just give me half and I'll drop the suit right away."

"But if you're his widow you're entitled to a lot more than that."

"*If* I'm his widow? Where do you get that kind of stuff? Do you call it good manners to doubt a lady's word while you're drinking her liquor? What kind of a girl do you think I was to go on that cruise with him if we weren't married?"

"I didn't mean—I didn't know—of course I don't doubt your word."

"Then why don't you want to give me half instead of running the risk of me taking it all?"

"But I couldn't—I mean it's a legal problem. The widow's share is yours or it isn't. It's not for me to decide."

"All right, then, twenty-five thousand, and that's my final offer."

"But you're entitled to a lot more than that. I wouldn't

feel right to just give you such a little part of your own share."

"All right," she said, "I said that was my final offer and I meant it. I gave you your chance and you wouldn't take it, and now I'll take it into court and you won't get one red cent. You'll live to regret this, and don't forget it. Get out of here."

Frank Osgood set down his glass and left, quite honestly bewildered.

Chapter 6

FRANK's bewilderment at the attitude of Billie La Verne did not decrease upon consideration. She had been so friendly and cordial when she had invited him to call and even when she had greeted him that he had been entirely disarmed. And the change had come so suddenly and unaccountably as to baffle him altogether. Perhaps she thought that he hadn't been adequately appreciative of her generosity. If her marriage to Charles had been legal it certainly was big-hearted of her to offer to take only twenty-five thousand dollars. It would be difficult if not impossible to make her understand why he didn't want any part of Charles's money, why her appearance seemed to him like an answer to prayer. No mere division of the spoils could free him from the burden of being in Charles's debt; he wondered if he ought to go back and try to make her see that he wanted her to have all the money. But her attitude at the close of the interview deterred him; Frank

did not like scenes, and it would have taken a good deal
to lure him back to a place where he was likely to be forced
to participate in one.

And then there was her final remark. "You'll live to regret this!" What did she mean? What did she know? Had
Charles planned somehow to use her? When had she seen
him? What had he told her? Frank wondered if the best
plan might not be to speak to the detective agency about
Miss La Verne and have Miss Pomeroy try to see what she
could find out.

Then Mr. Cuthbert's advice returned to his mind with
greater force now that the interview had ended unpleas-
antly. Perhaps it would have been a good idea to consult
his lawyer first, and since he hadn't done so perhaps he
could repair a little of the damage by consulting him now.
He didn't like any lawyers, and Gerald Winterbottom in
particular always upset him. His eye was so piercing and his
manner so frigid that Frank always felt the man had seen
into his mind and passed judgment on what he found
there. The nice thing about that private detective woman,
Miss Pomeroy, was that she didn't make you feel that way
in the least. But Gerald Winterbottom was handling the
estate and would have the job of defending Frank's right
to it against Mrs. Charles. Frank found a public telephone
and called him up.

"Oh, hello, Osgood," the lawyer said. "I've been meaning to call you. I want to have a talk with you."

"Are you free this afternoon?" Frank asked. "I left my
office early to see this Miss La Verne or Mrs. Osgood or
whoever she is, and now I don't have to go back. I could
come in to see you now."

"Whatever you do, don't see that woman without counsel," the lawyer said sharply.

"Oh, but I have!" Frank regretted the admission as soon as it was out of his mouth. "She offered to take twenty-five thousand dollars and call off her suit."

"What did you tell her?"

"I said I wouldn't consider it, of course. If she's the widow she's entitled to the estate and I want her to have it all."

The lawyer chuckled. "Good for you. I didn't think you had it in you. What did she say to that?"

"Well, she got mad and ordered me out of the place. I don't quite see—"

"Maybe you don't need counsel after all, Osgood; you handled that all right. But you should never have given that statement to the newspapers without talking with me. If you could run down here now it would be fine."

Frank sought a subway for the trip back downtown; his extravagance had gone quite far enough for one afternoon. As he rode, his distaste for the approaching interview grew until by the time he had reached Winterbottom's office it amounted almost to terror. Damn it, he didn't want to talk about this business; he didn't want to think about it. Charles was dead; it was over; the sword hanging over his head had dangled by its thread for so long that he was beginning to believe it was anchored by a stout rope or even that it wasn't there. If he could be rid of the money and forget the whole thing, marry Kay, and settle down on his own salary!

He didn't have to wait in one of the big leather chairs in Winterbottom's outer office. The pretty little receptionist recognized him and waved him in at once with a flattering deference. She had never treated him that way before. Another of the effects of being heir to a hundred thousand or two! If he ever got the money into his own hands all life would be like this. But the price would still be too high. Frank Osgood didn't want to pay it.

There were two vertical creases down Winterbottom's commanding brow, and the manner of his greeting was definitely constrained.

"Does he think I killed him?" Frank thought suddenly, and he felt his heart pounding within his chest. Well, what if he did? Better to face it some day—better to face it right now than to live like this.

"You know, Osgood, I'm running into some mighty funny things trying to get this estate straightened out," the lawyer said, and his tone was apologetic rather than accusing. "Would you have called your cousin an eccentric man?"

"I certainly should." Frank spoke with fervor. "Very eccentric."

"Do you know of any reason why he should have deliberately concealed some of his assets?"

Frank thought that he did, but he couldn't admit it.

"Has he?" he inquired cautiously.

"I don't know what's the explanation, but there doesn't seem to be any money where we can easily lay hands on it. Oh, don't worry, don't worry, now. There's no question that your cousin had a very substantial fortune; it's simply a matter of unsnarling his accounts. For one thing, there have been enormous cash withdrawals from his bank accounts within the past year. Could you account for that?"

"He told me that he'd taken out a life insurance policy for one hundred thousand dollars in my favor. The premiums would have been pretty large, wouldn't they?"

"Yes, they would. That could account for a good deal of it. What company?"

"I don't know. He didn't say. I suppose the policy must be with his papers somewhere."

"Not in any of the usual places, because I've looked through all of them, but I'll look again. What would he have done that for, though?"

"I don't know," Frank lied awkwardly. "He told me just a few months before he died. We didn't talk much about it. We had other matters to discuss."

He was aware even as he spoke of how extremely improbable this sounded.

"It's funny," Winterbottom said, "very, very funny. The oddest thing about it is the inconsistency. It's not unusual to find a man who leaves his affairs in a mess, but the thing about this is that some of it is so meticulously correct. The will, for instance, was all shipshape. His accounts with his publishers were absolutely straight, and they say he was a first rate man to deal with—never asked for advances, turned in copy when he said he would, all that kind of thing. Same with the servants. And when you look over the accounts everything seems to be all right, but there just isn't any money. And this insurance policy—why should a man as businesslike as your cousin have taken out a big policy like that and not left any record of it or the policy itself where it could be found? Didn't you think it was funny when he told you?"

"Yes, I did," Frank said. "I told him I didn't want it. I—

well, to tell the truth, it offended me a bit. I'm planning to be married this year; it's as if he thought I couldn't afford it without his help."

"Did he think you'd collect on the policy sometime soon?" The lawyer pounced sharply. Frank blushed to the tips of his ears and swallowed hard.

"He—yes," he said. "He talked as if I might."

The whole story would be out in something less than a minute he thought, but Winterbottom tipped back his heavy swivel chair, put his hands behind his head, and scowled at the ceiling.

"It's very strange," he said, "very strange indeed, but I wouldn't go so far as to say it was unprecedented. Had your cousin been acting peculiarly?"

"We really weren't at all intimate. The last time I saw him was three or four months before his death; we had dinner together here in town then."

"Was he abnormal at that time?"

"Y-yes, I suppose in a way you'd say that he was."

"Do you want me to talk frankly to you, Mr. Osgood?" Winterbottom tilted the swivel chair forward again and regarded his client directly.

"Of course," Frank said miserably. "That is, naturally. Certainly."

"Very well. You understand I am not making any accusations; this is merely thrown off as random comment in the course of a general discussion. I have no idea what has actually happened, but the circumstances are strongly suggestive of a planned disappearance."

"But I saw him in his coffin!"

"You did? Actually? I mean literally, for of course if you

did there can't be any question about it. I mean we scarcely need go so far afield as to look for wax dummies and venial undertakers. If you saw him in his coffin that settles it. On the other hand, if you saw only the closed coffin—"

"I saw him in his coffin," Frank repeated stubbornly.

The lawyer shrugged. "That's that, then. No hard feelings I hope. Such things have happened in the best of families."

"No hard feelings at all, of course. Anyway, you could hardly insult me by anything you might say about Charles. I didn't like him."

"*De mortuis nihil nisi bonum*," the lawyer said sententiously, "especially when you are the residuary legatee."

Frank laughed politely. "Does this mean that perhaps I won't get any money at all?" he asked.

"No, indeed. You're not to worry, I assure you. It may take a little time, but I judge you're hardly the type to have splurged on your expectations. It's evidently all merely the result of carelessness and nothing to worry about. We'll straighten it out in time."

"What would happen if I were to refuse to accept it?" Frank asked.

"Well, there wouldn't be any legal way you could do just that. It's yours, and you can't refuse to accept what's yours. You could give it all to charity, of course, or just let it alone in the bank and wherever it is. However, that would be rather quixotic."

"To be quite frank with you, I hope this Billie person gets it," Frank said.

"I wouldn't be too hasty there if I were you," the lawyer advised. "It's one thing to think you don't want a hundred thousand dollars, and it's quite another to see it gone irretrievably into someone else's hands. I judge the woman hasn't much of a case if she's offering to settle for twenty-five thousand this early in the game, but you never can tell. It always pays to be careful in these matters. If I can get her down to ten thousand I think you might be well advised to buy her off."

"I don't understand. It's her money or it isn't."

The lawyer laughed comfortably. "An excellent line, excellent. I'm sure you baffled her completely. She'll be calling up here in the morning offering to take twenty thousand."

"You think it's just blackmail?"

"Sure of it, my boy. If she had a legitimate claim she'd never have presented it that way."

Frank thought of Billie's bright blue eye, of the charm of her friendly manner, of the pathetic aping of luxury in her squalid little apartment.

"I hope she gets it all," he repeated. She'd earned it if she spent two weeks with Charles on his yacht."

"There's another possibility there, you know," Winterbottom said thoughtfully. "She may have more than a nuisance value. This marriage was supposed to have been for a two-week period a year ago last summer, wasn't it?"

"I believe so."

"Well, then, how well did she know your cousin afterwards? Ever at his place? Did he visit her in the city?"

"I'm sure I don't know. I've told you I wasn't at all intimate with him. I never heard of her until yesterday."

"Is there any chance she might know where he'd hide important papers?"

"I shouldn't think so."

"It would explain her thinking she's worth twenty-five thousand dollars to you. The marriage story is pretty thin. But if she knew what he was up to—"

"She didn't intimate anything of the sort."

"It might be worth trying though. I don't want to alarm you unnecessarily, but I really seem to be at a dead end in my search for your cousin's assets right now. His safe deposit box was empty. I've already mentioned the recent enormous cash withdrawals from his bank accounts. The house in Connecticut is free of encumbrances, but that's absolutely all you can lay your hands on at present, except, of course, the income from royalties—not very large, but it will keep on rolling in for awhile."

"I suppose if people are foolish enough to keep on spending money for his books I might as well benefit as anyone else."

"He's cleaned up on all the movie rights. As far as I can discover those were all outright sales, and the money has been collected and disappeared. Unless you have a better suggestion I'm planning to go up to Connecticut next week and search that house from attic to cellar. It's the last chance."

"It might be a good one. He was always gloomy about the political situation. When he bought the farm it was with the idea of having a hideout from the Communists. I know he took a lot of money out of the bank in gold in 1933; he might have put it into jewelry or something he thought would retain its value, and hidden it against emergencies." But even as he spoke Frank thought of the will and the insurance policy and Charles' openly expressed intention of killing himself. He might have stored away jewels for himself, like a squirrel, but he wouldn't have done it for his heir.

"I have an idea though," Frank went on impulsively. "I've got a firm of private detectives working on this anyway—there were some things about the death that puzzled me. Why couldn't I send their representative up to search the house? She ought to be better at it than anyone who's not in the business."

"It's not just the sort of thing you'd want to entrust to a detective unless you were pretty sure of your man. What's to keep him from helping himself to what he finds, presuming it's marketable, and saying he didn't find anything?"

Frank laughed out loud and realized, checking himself spasmodically, that it was the first time since Charles's death that he had done so.

"You haven't seen Miss Pomeroy," he said.

"Don't judge people by their faces, my boy," the lawyer advised. "I'll talk to your Miss Pomeroy if you like, but don't you say anything about all this to her until I have."

"Why couldn't we all go up there?" Frank asked. "Everybody interested in the will, that is. All together we'd stand a lot better chance of figuring out where he might have hidden something than any of us alone."

"Who else is there? You're practically the sole legatee."

"You and I and Miss Pomeroy." Osgood ticked the party off on his fingers. "Miss Waterhouse, my fiancée—she knew Charles too." He flushed again and threw Winterbottom a fiercely vindictive glance. "The servants —they ought to know more about Charles than any of us, and probable hiding places. Miss La Verne."

"Come, come, come now!" Winterbottom was becoming slightly apoplectic. "You can't throw a bunch of people like that together."

"Why not?" Frank was suddenly intoxicated with the idea. For thirty-five years he had been careful, conventional, and correct. Charles's death had begun his transformation, and now he could feel himself bursting out of his chrysalis. "It's my house, isn't it?"

"Why, yes, I suppose—if the rest of the money can't be found it may have to be sold in order to pay the other legacies."

"Anyway, it's closer to being my house than anyone else's. Why can't I have a party in my own house if I choose? Why can't I ask anyone I like?"

"But, Mr. Osgood, women like this La Verne one—well, it pays to watch your step; that's all I have to say."

"If I choose to invite Miss La Verne to my own house is there anyone who is entitled to object?"

"No, of course not, but—"

"I'm going to do it," Frank said. "It'll clear the air. I'm sick of this uncertainty—sitting around waiting, wondering what's going to happen next. I want it all cleaned up. What day next week can you go up there?"

"I thought Tuesday, but—"

"Tuesday. Good. That will give me time. The furniture's all there, isn't it? Nothing been changed?"

"The house was closed just as it stood."

"That'll give me time to get some servants in and have the place cleaned—I'll have food in; by God I'll make it a house party—a wake for my cousin. Have you ever been to a wake, Mr. Winterbottom?"

Mr. Winterbottom was wondering whether perhaps his client had had a little too much to drink. He'd seemed perfectly all right when he came in, but it was always hard to tell with these quiet, repressed men.

"I wish you'd send your detective up to talk to me before you do anything rash," he said uneasily.

"I won't do anything rash. I'll get this damned mess settled and be done with it; you'll get your fee, and I won't have to talk any more about Charles Osgood. Let me use your phone."

He called the Keene Detective Agency and reached Miss Pomeroy almost at once. She listened to his plan without comment until he had finished and then said: "Richard Johnson's in the army, and Nora has another job. I don't think she could come."

"I'll leave it to you," Frank said crisply, in a tone of command quite different from the one she was used to associating with him. "Get Nora. Pay her a week's wages or whatever bonus you have to. If she loses her job she can get another. There are tenant farmers on the place— Mr. and Mrs. Munroe. There's a phone in their house. You can get her and have her start making things ready —party of five, tell her, plus the servants. Have her get the necessary food. Hang the expense. I'm depending on you to see that it all runs smoothly."

He hung up then and grinned a little weakly at Gerald Winterbottom. He had just realized that if he went away to the country for a couple of days in the middle of the week he would have to explain the action both to Cuthbert, Cuthbert, Rutherford, and Simes and to his mother.

Being masterful was all very well in its way, but there were penalties. His mother would think it very peculiar indeed for him to go on a houseparty with Kay when they weren't married. Kay probably wouldn't be able to get away from her school. If she could he'd have to ask his mother to go along as a chaperon. He began to wish that he had not acted quite so hastily.

But Mr. Winterbottom was looking at him with an expression that was at least akin to admiration. "Maybe you're right," he said. "There's nothing like taking the bull by the horns."

And he had no idea how large the bull was, nor how sharp the horns.

Chapter 7

THE Osgood farm was a place of considerable, if self-conscious, charm. The house dated from the eighteenth century, a square, sturdy box with walls of a thickness that had made the introduction of central heating a serious problem. Charles Osgood had knocked out half a dozen partitions to make the living room, which occupied one whole side of the remodelled dwelling. On both sides of it, built-in bookshelves ran the length of the room, filled with books in a pleasing confusion of sizes, shapes, and subjects. The windows, the couches, and the easy chairs were all low and inviting.

On the other side of the central entrance hall the rooms had been left unaltered to form a study, a dining room and a modern kitchen. Upstairs were five bedrooms on two floor levels, with sloping ceilings that could knock a tall and unwary guest unconscious. The beds were good, the decorations unostentatious, if just a trifle quaint, and the windows framed a charming vista of the Connecticut landscape.

Outside, in addition to the working farm, there was ample space devoted to the amenities of living—a flower bordered lawn where colored settees and vast sunshades sprouted in summer, a swimming pool walled with natural stones roughly cemented together, and a small grove, meticulously wild. Now in October the autumn landscape was breathtaking, and in June anyone—except possibly his cousin Frank—would have been delighted to accept an invitation to week-end with Charles Osgood.

And even now the big living room was inviting with a wood fire crackling on the hearth and bronze chrysanthemums blooming in a copper bowl on the center table. Frank Osgood, arriving with his mother and his fiancée ahead of the other visitors, as befitted the host of this peculiar party, looked about him with approval. Mrs. Munroe had done herself proud; the place looked quite as if she had prepared it for a really festive gathering. Nora was coming later in the evening; there would be no meals served until the following morning. The electricity had been turned off when the house was closed, and Frank had decided it was hardly worth the bother of having it turned on again to provide light for a single evening and the use of the electric refrigerator and stove. The effect of the light from the kerosene lamps was rather uncomfortably eerie, but they probably wouldn't want to read anyway. Get a good night's sleep and start searching early in the morning. Frank rather wished he had decided to wait until morning to come himself. The impulse to spend the night in the place was a curious one, difficult to explain and even more difficult to justify. Miss La Verne and the lawyer were coming early the following morning, and all of them would spend the day in an intensive search of the premises. Frank had told himself vaguely that he would like to have a night there first to get the feel of the place, not that he could actually start searching before morning, but in the surroundings likely hiding places were more apt to occur to him than if he pondered the problem from a distance. His mother, of course, thought it was only an excuse for an escapade with Kay. How curious that after eight years of waiting she should still regard them as two hot-headed children.

Kay herself had managed the time off from school with a minimum of difficulty; at least she had offered no objection when the arrangement was suggested. The three of them had driven out together from the home Frank shared with his mother; he was a careful man, and his gasoline ration for the past month was untouched. Miss Pomeroy and Nora were coming out on the train from the city and would take a taxi from the station, and Winterbottom and Miss La Verne would presumably use the same means of transportation the next morning.

Kay appeared to feel the strain of this intrusion into a dead man's house even more than Frank himself did. She was pale and silent, with a drawn look about her eyes. What was she thinking, Frank wondered, with a stab of the old jealousy. Was she grieving for Charles? Had she cared so much for him that the memories invoked by all his intimate possessions would overwhelm her? But, oh, hell, what was the use of going over that? It wasn't Charles she loved. She had chosen Frank while it was still possible to make a choice; if there were to be any jealousy it should have been the other way around.

His mother's thoughts were running along the same lines; she dabbed at her eyes with her handkerchief and said: "Poor Charles, doesn't this bring it all back?"

"The room is very like him," Kay said.

"I don't think so at all," Frank disagreed loudly and offensively. "It's a typical 1940 Connecticut farmhouse with literary trimmings. It's no more like him than Mount Vernon was like George Washington; he might have picked it out of a mail-order catalogue."

"I do think you might learn to speak a little more kindly of him now that he's dead, son."

"Being dead doesn't change what he was. I didn't like him; I don't like to think about him, and I don't like to talk about him. I'm sorry we ever came here."

"It's a good thing we came here," Kay said. "You had to do it sometime. The sooner the better. After tonight it will be over."

She spoke as if she struggled against the same dread that was oppressing Frank himself. They left their suitcases by the door and, walking toward the fire, held out their hands to the comfortable blaze. Mrs. Munroe spoke shyly from the doorway behind them.

"Is everything all right, Mr. Osgood? Mr. Munroe wanted to go in to town and see about the electricity for you, but you said—"

"It's fine, Mrs. Munroe, just fine," he assured her. "It

was mighty nice of you to bring up those flowers and start a fire. It could be a pretty cheerless place if you hadn't bothered."

"I didn't do anything in the study. I can't go in there any more without thinking of him lying dead on the sofa with his eyes popping out. I know it's foolish of me, but I can't abide going in the room alone now."

"It doesn't matter. We shan't need to go in there to-night. I'll have it dismantled very soon, and then it won't continue to have such unpleasant associations for you, I hope."

"Is there anything more I could get you or the ladies?"

"Nothing, thank you, Mrs. Munroe."

"Not a bite of supper?"

"No, thank you, we ate in town."

"There's no blackout curtains; in case of an alarm you'll have to put out all the lights. I've brought you all my lamps as well as what were here, but it's not a lot of light. Would you like some candles too?"

"No, really, we're quite all right, thank you." There was a note of strain in the courtesy of Frank's tone, and Kay hastened to make amends.

"Everything is lovely," she said. "Excuse us if we don't seem to appreciate it. We're tired and I guess we're a little nervous—like you about the study."

"I'm glad you've come, though. It's high time somebody went through this house. It's a shame to have it standing here shut up like this with all these things in it that people might use."

"Yes," Frank said. "It's time things were sorted out and disposed of. On the other hand we may decide to sell the place furnished, just as it stands. I'd like that."

"You don't plan to come here to live yourself, then, Mr. Osgood?"

"No," Frank said, and try as he would he could not altogether repress a shudder.

"I'd like it," his mother said obstinately.

"It wouldn't be practical for someone who works in the city every day like Frank," Kay put in. "It was all right for Charles; he did his writing here and didn't have to come in to town even once a week unless he chose, but even if it weren't for gas rationing it's too far for a man with regular office hours to commute comfortably."

"That hasn't anything to do with it," Frank said. "I don't like it. I wouldn't live in it if it was in Grand Central Station."

"It would look nice in Grand Central Station," Kay remarked. "Model Connecticut Literary Farmhouse. You could charge admission."

"I guess I'll run along if you don't need anything more," Mrs. Munroe said.

"I'll walk down with you." Frank buttoned the overcoat which he had not yet removed, and turned from the fire.

"Oh, there's no need. I run around the farm by myself all the time. Unless you'd like to have my flashlight. It might come in handy without any lights. If you'll walk down to my house with me you can bring it back. And I could send some cookies and a pitcher of milk too. It's gloomy going to bed in the dark with nothing to eat."

"That would be lovely," Kay said, although she wasn't hungry. A moment later, when the departure of Frank and the farmer's wife left her alone with the older woman, she regretted that she hadn't offered to go along. The two were always uncomfortable together, even in the presence of other people, and here, in this house with all its associations for them both, in the silence and the semidarkness each found the other's presence almost unendurable. Kay recognized it and thought that the other woman did too, but she did not expect a direct frontal attack. It came, therefore, with all the more force for being a surprise.

"This should have been your house," Mrs. Osgood said with undisguised bitterness. "If you'd married Charles we wouldn't be here like thieves in a house without lights."

Kay hesitated for the space of a full breath, uncertain whether to try to swing the conversation back to trivialities or to meet the issue squarely. She didn't want to be in the midst of an emotional scene when Frank returned, but the hostility of Mrs. Osgood's tone was too obvious to pretend to ignore.

"I didn't love Charles, Mrs. Osgood," she said at last, very quietly.

"There was a time when anybody'd have thought you did."

"Perhaps there was a time when I thought I did. But I was wrong."

"When I was a young girl it wasn't considered decent to experiment with your feelings like that. You loved a man or you didn't."

"And if you made a mistake?"

"You took the consequences."

"I'm taking the consequences, Mrs. Osgood."

"But what right do you have to marry Frank after what's

been between you and his own cousin? It's incest."

"Mrs. Osgood, I can't listen to accusations like that."

"Why did it have to be Frank? He's a delicate boy; he's not fit for the responsibilities of marriage. I've always known that, I've tried to protect him. Charles would have had you even after—"

"Mrs. Osgood, you'll have to stop." Kay was on her feet, her hands at her temples. "Believe me, I have qualms enough about marrying into your family. Nothing you can say will add to them. And if I decide to ignore them nothing you can say will make me change my mind either. Be quiet; there's Frank."

There was a noise outside the door, followed by a polite but firm pounding, but it was not Frank. The door opened before Kay had time to reach it, and Miss Pomeroy poked her head around the jamb.

"I thought we'd better just knock and walk in, since I could see you were already here," she said cheerfully. Nora Johnson behind her glowered at the two women in the living room and said "good evening" distantly.

"Good evening, Nora," Kay said, some of her relief showing in her voice. "It will be nice to have someone here who knows where things are."

"I wouldn't have come if I'd known I'd have to cook on that wood stove," Nora answered, "but since I'm here I suppose I may as well try to get a fire started. You don't want anything tonight, do you? I suppose you know if you want any hot water you'll have to heat it on the stove. The heater was electric too."

"Oh, heavens!" Kay said. "I guess we'll just have to get along with cold tonight. Please heat some in the morning for Mr. Osgood to shave—I guess the rest of us can manage."

"I shall require some tonight and some again in the morning," Mrs. Osgood said, in a tone which would have frozen any hot water that might have been available, and which clearly indicated her opinion of unmarried young women presuming to give orders about shaving water for their fiancés.

"Are you sure there's any water in the house?" Miss Pomeroy asked. "Aren't the pumps for these places generally operated by electricity?"

"There's an overhead storage tank," Nora said. "Mr. Osgood had it put in after the ice storm three years ago tore down all the electric wires and left him without any water."

"But weren't the pipes drained when the house was closed?"

"I don't think so. It was summer then. I know if there ain't any water but what I have to carry from the well, I'm going back to New York," Nora said, and no one doubted her ultimatum.

Miss Pomeroy moved toward the kitchen to settle the argument. Water ran from both faucets as she turned them, and Nora, behind her, snorted to express her satisfaction.

"Mrs. Munroe is sending some milk and cookies up with Frank," Kay said, "though I don't know how in the world he's going to carry them and a flashlight too. Perhaps when you've had time to get your things off, Nora, you could get us some plates and glasses."

"I see the flashlight coming," Miss Pomeroy said.

"I'm going to meet him," Kay answered. "He can't possibly get here with all that stuff."

Her only thought was to get away from Mrs. Osgood, but when Miss Pomeroy stepped outside the door with her she was glad to seize the opportunity for a word in private.

"Miss Pomeroy," she said, "I've been wanting to see you ever since that other day. I don't know what was the trouble with me. I must have been mad. I hope you didn't pay any attention to what I said."

"I don't think I paid too much," Miss Pomeroy answered. "I've been hoping you'd say more."

"There isn't any more to say." Kay laughed. She tried hard to make the laugh light and convincing; she tried to make her voice casual and easy, but she could see Frank's flashlight coming up the hill, and she had to talk fast in order to finish in the time at her disposal. "I thought it was awfully foolish of Frank to get a detective to stir up trouble about his cousin's death when it's all over and done with and well on the road to being forgotten. I still think it was, but I see now, of course, that it was even more foolish of me to take such a roundabout way to try to stop him."

"Then you're not ready to tell me what makes you think he killed his cousin?"

"I don't think he killed his cousin," Kay said, "and here he is."

Miss Pomeroy was not quite sure whether or not there was a faint emphasis on the word "think."

Frank Osgood's progress, impeded by a flashlight, a pitcher of milk, and a plate of cookies, was slow and awkward, but Miss Pomeroy could see that it embarrassed him to have a couple of women offer to help him. She therefore withdrew gracefully, but Kay insisted on relieving him of the pitcher. They walked the short distance to the house Indian file, with Frank carefully turning the light on the ground in front of the women's feet.

"It was awfully good of you to come, Miss Pomeroy," he said, "but already I'm regretting that I asked you. This place has a horrible effect on me. I haven't been in it half an hour, and already I'm suffering from the unreasonable depression it always causes. If I had any notion of being psychic I'd say something dreadful was going to happen before we're finished here."

"It's a good thing you're not, then," she said briskly. "Some people think it's fun to give themselves the horrors in a country house on a dark night, but I'm not one of them."

"It's natural enough," Kay said. "We're the first people who've stayed here since Charles died."

"Good Lord, Kay, must you talk about it?" Frank was ordinarily such a gentle, courteous little man that the savageness of his tone on this occasion made Miss Pomeroy jump.

"Why, Frank, it was you—" Kay said, and then stopped abruptly. Not very promising, Miss Pomeroy thought from her wide experience in observing married life. A little too ostentatiously tactful. It was, of course, Frank who had brought up the subject, but Kay should either have neglected altogether to point that out or have finished the sentence she had begun.

Back in the house they discovered that none of them

wanted any cookies or milk. Eventually Kay took the
pitcher to the back porch, Nora having retired to her own
old room over the garage after lighting a fire in the kitchen
stove and setting a kettle of water on it. Kay would have
been glad to follow suit at once, but it was still rather
ridiculously early for bed, and there would be no reading
lights in the bedrooms. She therefore proposed, half-
heartedly, a rubber of bridge, and found the suggestion
seconded with surprising enthusiasm. They were a
strangely assorted foursome. Miss Pomeroy and Mrs. Osgood elected to play against Frank and Kay, and the teams
turned out to be reasonably well matched. Mrs. Osgood
played with the enthusiasm and concentration of the
devotee; her comments on her partner's lapses were open
and caustic, and Miss Pomeroy, noticing Frank wince once
or twice, was glad that for once she had deflected them
from him. Miss Pomeroy's own game was conservative and
intelligent; she never opened on a count of less than three
and seldom redoubled, so that although her playing was
not brilliant her partner had little of which to complain.
Frank played like a conscientious and thoroughly well in-
structed dub, and Kay was brilliant and erratic, finessing
successfully when she had no business to have attempted
it and every now and again pulling her side out of a dismal
hole by winning a little slam redoubled. They played three
rubbers, but Miss Pomeroy thought the last one was rather
because no one wanted to suggest breaking up and scat-
tering to their separate bedrooms than because anyone
actually desired to play. At the end of the third rubber,
therefore, she made it her business to start the process of
getting to bed.

"We came out here tonight so we could get an early start in the morning," she said. "Don't you think we'd better get some sleep now and be ready?"

"Yes, you're right, of course," Frank said. "The bedrooms are all ready, Mrs. Munroe fixed them. I'm afraid Nora went to bed without turning down any beds or taking our bags up."

"Nora's really here to help just like the rest of us, not as a servant," Miss Pomeroy said. "We can perfectly well wait on ourselves."

"I hardly know about rooms," Frank said, "except that there are plenty. I suppose I'd better take Charles's—"

"Nonsense," Kay said sharply. "Don't try to be a Christian martyr, Frank. I'll sleep there."

"It would seem to me that since I'm the only one of the four for whom the place has no associations I'd be the logical one to sleep there," Miss Pomeroy intervened, and they all accepted the offer with obvious relief.

"We'd better just go upstairs together and pick whatever's comfortable," Frank said.

They were a rather pathetic little procession, Miss Pomeroy thought, as they went upstairs, clinging close together, each one carrying a lighted lamp and Frank burdened also by the teakettle full of hot water for his mother. You needed to move only a very little way from the lights and the machinery of a city, she thought, in order to realize man's helplessness in the face of any great natural force. It didn't take even a storm to make you feel it—just a dark night and loneliness.

Charles's old room was the first at the head of the stairs, a comfortably furnished, masculine one with sturdy, bat-

tered leather chairs and a good bed. Trust a man like
Charles Osgood to have a mattress it would be a pleasure
to sleep on. Miss Pomeroy set down her lamp and stood
in the door to watch the other three choose their rooms.
Mrs. Osgood ostentatiously selected one between Kay and
Frank, and the three lamps bobbed reluctantly to their
separate solitudes. Miss Pomeroy hoped devoutly that no
one of them would set the house on fire.

Chapter 8

MISS POMEROY set about her preparations for bed in her
usual calm and methodical manner. She was not a nervous
woman, and although the unusual circumstances did make
her a trifle uneasy about the possibility of the house burning down during the night she did not see any means of
avoiding the danger by altering her ordinary routine. She
undressed quickly and quietly, folding her clothes neatly
over the back of a chair before she slipped into her long-
sleeved blue flannel nightgown. Charles Osgood's room
had its own bath attached, where she was able to brush
her teeth and wash her face and hands in cold water without having to wait her turn. It was late in the year to leave
the water turned on in an unheated house, she reflected;
she had better speak to Frank Osgood or the lawyer about
it before they left the next afternoon. She brushed her hair
a hundred conscientious strokes, staring unheedingly at
the dim image of herself the wavering lamp outlined in the
mirror of Charles Osgood's dresser. Tomorrow would be
a strange and trying day. She doubted whether they would
succeed in finding anything of what the lawyer was looking

for, but the close proximity of such varied personalities might very well produce an explosion of some sort. Certainly if there were ever to be an opportunity to fulfill her own assignment, tomorrow should furnish it. If Charles Osgood had really planted any evidence against his cousin it must have been with one of those who would be present in the morning.

As to just how they would pass the day Miss Pomeroy had only a very hazy notion. The lawyer had already examined the dead man's safe deposit box, his desk drawers, and his files. As a professional detective she wondered uneasily whether she would be expected to take the lead in tapping the walls and measuring corners for hidden space. She had no idea how to do it; perhaps she should have suggested to Mr. Keene that he send an experienced man to direct a really thorough search. Of course if they failed to find anything tomorrow it would still not be too late to do that. Miss Pomeroy was not sure she knew even what to look for. How did one conceal a hundred thousand dollars? Would it be a wad of bills somewhere, or a small, square jeweler's box, or merely a sheaf of papers? It was appalling to think how small a space so much value could occupy when you set it against what it could mean in terms of human life. Miss Pomeroy imagined a hundred thousand dollars in terms of houses, in terms of motor cars, in terms of groceries piled high on the shelves of an imaginary super-market. It was a staggering sum taken in any of those ways. It was horrible that a selfish and irresponsible man could dispose of such a sum with the arrogant carelessness of Charles Osgood.

Miss Pomeroy sighed, turned back the covers of the bed,

and slipped between the cold sheets, every nerve of her body protesting bitterly. The mattress, however, was as good as she had judged it to be, and the blankets were warm but not too heavy. In a very few minutes a delicious warmth radiated from the center of her body to her cold limbs, and she succumbed to a creeping drowsiness.

She had slept for two hours, as the luminous dial on her wrist watch assured her instantly, when something startled her broad awake. She woke with the ease and quickness of the trained nurse, akin to that of a mother with a sleeping baby. Something, she knew, had disturbed her, but she did not know what it was. Her heart beat a little faster than usual, as though with fright, but she was not frightened. It took her less than half a minute to consult the watch and remember where she was. She lay very still listening and wondering. The moonlight was bright now; in the patch of whiteness from her window objects stood out more clearly than they had by the light of the lamp.

She sniffed for the odor of smoke, the anxiety with which she had gone to sleep reasserting itself, but there was no smoke. Neither was there anyone in her room, although she lay with her eyes closed and her breathing carefully regulated for several minutes until she could feel certain of that fact. No, whatever had disturbed her was outside of the room, and it was not fire. In all probability it had been someone going to the bathroom down the hall. Miss Pomeroy considered the propriety of falling asleep again. But her training in responsibility had been serious and was not lightly to be abandoned. As a detective she was responsible for the peaceful slumber of this household, just as she had often been responsible for the welfare of a dangerously ill patient. You couldn't take chances with a responsibility like that. Miss Pomeroy sighed and felt beneath her pillow for her flashlight. Having found it she directed its beam toward her slippers, neatly lined up at the side of the bed, and, sighing, swung her feet out of the bed and felt for their grateful wool-lined warmth. When her right foot was halfway in, she suddenly sat rigid, listening again with all her energy. Someone was moving about downstairs!

It was nearly two o'clock in the morning; there was no legitimate reason for anyone to be down there. Perhaps Frank or his mother was ill—the possibility that Kay might be so never occurred to Miss Pomeroy—and the other had gone for more hot water or whatever home remedies might be available here. Or Nora might have come in—but for what conceivable purpose at this time of the night? Miss Pomeroy finished putting on her slippers, picked up her dark blue flannel bathrobe from the chair closest to the bed and wrapped it about her, and tiptoed with catlike tread to the door. The knob turned soundlessly in her hand, and she was out in the passage. She stood for a moment listening to the sounds of the sleeping house and accustoming her eyes to the darkness. Now there were unmistakable sounds of someone moving about downstairs, but they were obviously not from someone moving about openly on an errand of mercy. They were stealthy, rustling sounds, and they came, Miss Pomeroy thought, from the study.

She did not venture to use her flashlight again, but guiding herself by the handrail felt her way cautiously downstairs. The stairs were solid in spite of their age, and didn't creak. The remains of the big wood fire in the fireplace were still smoldering, and the light flickered and danced on the hall at the foot of the stairs. Miss Pomeroy stopped cautiously just outside of the patch of light. After a moment she ventured to poke her head around the corner of the open door. The living room was deserted and in just the order in which they had left it at the end of the game. Mrs. Osgood had insisted on folding up the bridge table, and Kay had emptied the ash trays and put the cards in the drawer of the center table, but the room was still in a state of mild disorder. Miss Pomeroy did not think she was familiar enough with it to be certain that nothing had been moved, but to her at least it certainly looked exactly as it had two hours earlier.

Stepping softly around the patch of light from the fire, she went over to the closed door of the study just opposite. It had remained closed all during the earlier part of the evening; no one had stepped into the room. It was tightly closed now, and no ray of light was visible underneath it or through the keyhole. Miss Pomeroy stood very quietly, listening to her breathing and the beating of her heart. Both sounded extremely loud in the silence. But it was not a complete silence; unquestionably someone was moving about in the study. The steps were almost as silent as Miss Pomeroy's own, but she was listening for them, and presumably the marauder wasn't listening for hers, for the soft sounds continued. A drawer was opened and closed quietly; there was a rustling of paper and then a sudden and unexpected crackle. Miss Pomeroy was not certain whether she did or did not hear a muffled exclamation then, but complete silence followed. She could not hear footsteps nor any breathing except her own. She gripped her flashlight firmly in her right hand and waited for the door to open. She waited for what seemed to her an eternity, and for what she judged to be actually at least five minutes, but nothing happened.

So it was to be her move. Miss Pomeroy considered soberly what would be the best thing to do. If the searcher in the library were entirely unsuspicious of her presence it would probably be enough simply to swing the door open suddenly and flash her light into a startled face. But what face would it be? Miss Pomeroy didn't want to scare Mrs. Osgood into another heart attack; a second death in Charles's study would certainly do nothing to straighten matters out. If it were Frank or Kay or Nora she would be quite willing to take the risk for the sake of what she might learn. There was the possibility, too, that it was someone from outside the house, an armed intruder. Miss Pomeroy had never carried a gun; perhaps, as a detective, she should.

Again there was the cautious rustle of paper. Whoever it was hadn't heard her, then, and she still had the advantage of surprise on her side. But she couldn't use it unless she knew in advance who was in the room. Her grip on the flashlight relaxed, and she turned reluctantly toward the stairs. Very cautiously she started up again, feeling out each step with a slippered foot before she trusted her weight on it. She did not think she was a coward, but she didn't like the feeling that her back presented a perfect target to anyone who might step out of the library.

Safely at the top of the stairs she cast a longing glance at the door to her own room, standing invitingly ajar. But she could not go back to bed while work remained to be done. She padded softly past her own door and leaned down to listen at that of Mrs. Osgood. This proved to be easy. Unmistakable snores came from within, but they certainly could not have been faked. Mrs. Osgood was within the room, asleep or awake.

Frank gave her more trouble. She knelt down on the bare boards of the hall floor and put her ear against the panel of the door. Her hearing, fortunately, was unusually acute; it was a few minutes before she could distinguish anything beyond the subdued sounds of her own body, but in time she made out the rhythm of another's breathing. Frank was in his room too. Then it had to be Kay in the study! Miss Pomeroy pulled herself up stiffly and suppressed a small sigh. She had been afraid all the time that it was Kay; probably that was the reason she hadn't chosen her door at which to listen first. She moved over to it now and put her ear against the panel, but without kneeling down again. She could not make out a sound. She strained a little longer. Well, she would just have to be sure! In the unlikely event that Kay was in bed she would just have to make up an excuse—say she had lost her way returning from the bathroom. If Kay knew that Charles's room had its own bath so much the better; the excuse didn't need to be convincing.

She turned the knob very gently and very slowly. It yielded instantly to her touch. Stupid of the girl not to have locked it! Then she could have maintained that she had been inside all the time, unless, of course, she were caught somewhere else. The door swung noiselessly open and Miss Pomeroy stepped into the quiet room. At the first glance she saw that she had made a mistake. There was a figure lying in the bed. She moved softly toward it, and it stirred in sleep. It was Kay Waterhouse. Miss Pomeroy retreated in confusion, but without forgetting her caution. She backed out of the door and pulled it carefully to and latched it without disturbing the sleeping woman. But the intruder in the study was not any one of these three! That problem remained to be dealt with.

It was characteristic of Miss Pomeroy that she did not consider waking Frank Osgood to get him to go downstairs with her. Neither a nurse nor a detective claims the traditional privileges of a woman; this was Miss Pomeroy's problem, and she would solve it herself. This time she went downstairs with a firm although still not a noisy step; the advantages of surprise were considerable, but so were those of creating a sense of guilt in the prowler before confronting him. If it were Nora she would have a plausible story; best not to give her too much time to perfect it.

Miss Pomeroy seized the knob of the study door and turned it firmly. It also turned easily in her hand, and the door did not resist her push against it. She turned the beam of the flashlight toward the spot whence she had judged the sound came—and there was nothing there. She swung the light quickly from side to side of the room. Dim moonlight came through the uncurtained windows, so that the room was a place of shadows rather than utter darkness—and there was no one in it. For one horrible moment she felt panic welling up within her, and then she fought it back with grim determination and walked in to examine the room.

It was an attractive place to work. The back wall was

lined with bookshelves to the ceiling, all well filled. On the opposite side of the room one vast window overlooked the lawn and the approach to the house. A smaller fireplace than that in the living room occupied the wall opposite to the one in which the door was placed. There was only one entrance to the room; to get into the dining room behind it, it was necessary to go back through the hall. It must have been an inconvenient arrangement for the servants, but it would help to secure privacy for whoever worked in this room. There was a big flat-topped desk with nothing whatever on it; to the left stood a covered typewriter on a stand, and a rank of heavy steel filing cabinets was within easy reach. Miss Pomeroy stepped quickly to the filing cabinet and looked behind it, and on the floor behind the desk. She pulled back the drapes at the windows although they lay so flat that it was obvious no one could be behind them. She went over to the studio couch, where she remembered Charles Osgood had died, and put her hand on the cushioned surface. No one was concealed there. She pulled it forward, conscious even as she did so of the absurdity of the action. It stood flat against the wall, and no one could possibly be concealed behind it. Spiral whorls of dust fluttered in the light of her flash; there was no one behind the couch, and obviously it had not been moved for many weeks. Miss Pomeroy shivered; suddenly the room seemed very cold. Slowly and methodically she turned her flashlight all the way around the room, illuminating every corner. There was no possible place of concealment, and there was no one in the room. She had been upstairs how long? Less than ten minutes in all, probably not much more than five. And during all that

time her ears had been strained to their utmost; if anyone
had come out of the room into the hall she must certainly
have heard. There remained the time she had been in Kay
Waterhouse's room—certainly not more than a minute.
Could an intruder, by some incredible coincidence, have
chosen that moment to slip out through the hall? It would
have been possible, but just barely possible. There was
nothing for it, then, but to go out to Nora's room and see
if Nora were awake.

She went to the hall closet for her coat, but as she
opened the door she heard a step on the stairs. Whirling
instantly she flashed her light upward and illuminated the
startled face of Frank Osgood.

"Who's there?" he asked in a voice that quavered in
spite of him.

Miss Pomeroy turned the light away quickly to give him
time to recover himself before she looked at his face again.

"It's Miss Pomeroy, Mr. Osgood," she said. "I thought
I heard someone in the study, so I came down to see, but
I can't find anyone."

"You came down alone to see?" he inquired sharply.

"Why, of course." She was deliberately matter-of-fact.

"Why didn't you ask me?"

"You were asleep, and I thought I needn't disturb you."

"You mustn't take any such risk again. If you hear any
noise in the house at night, by all means call me."

"I will if you insist, Mr. Osgood," she said, realizing that
it was a point of pride with him and that she had hurt his
feelings. "I don't believe there was any danger, though. It
must have been Nora."

"Why should you say that? You aren't one of those

women who always blame the servants for anything that goes wrong."

"There's no one else it could be. I listened at your doors and made sure you were all asleep."

"Perhaps there was no one there at all."

"There was someone there. I heard something—I don't quite know what—from my room. I came down here and listened at the door, and I could hear someone moving about inside. There were papers rustling—"

"It could have been rats."

"I don't think so. The room doesn't look as if it were infested with rats." She stepped to the door again and swept her light around the room at the floor level.

"Was there a light?"

"I didn't see any."

"No one could have been looking at papers without a light. No one living."

Miss Pomeroy recognized the note of incipient hysteria and spoke sharply. "The noise I heard was made by someone living. Do you want to come out to Nora's room with me?"

"There's no use disturbing Nora. If she's been in here she's had plenty of time to get back to bed and pretend to be asleep. You couldn't learn anything, and if she's up to mischief you'd only put her on guard."

Miss Pomeroy had to admit to herself the justice of this observation. She hated to think there was nothing to do except go back to bed, but it seemed highly probable that that was the sensible procedure.

"Can you think of anything Nora might have wanted in this room?" she asked.

He shrugged. "We all want the same thing, which we presume is hidden somewhere in the house. That's why we're here. I don't know just what advantage Nora thinks might accrue to her from finding it before the rest of us do—but then, I don't think Nora was in here."

"Nora came along because she's anxious to locate the money and get her legacy," Miss Pomeroy said. "If she had some reason to think the money's in cash and hidden in here, would she have been tempted? Did your cousin consider her honest?"

"Of course she's honest. She wouldn't take a piece of jewelry from a guest's room, and I doubt if she even took a cut out of the housekeeping money. But a hundred thousand dollars could have quite an effect on a person's normal honesty. Did you ever read The Man Who Corrupted Hadleyburg?"

"Yes. Your cousin used the same idea in one of his books, did you know?"

"I never read Charles's books. I knew he had no literary integrity whatsoever; he'd pick up an idea wherever he could find it, and appropriate it."

"I don't think Mark Twain ever copyrighted the idea about human nature that he was illustrating in that book."

"I know. I'm never fair when I talk about Charles. Let it go; I'm not. I probably never shall be now. Even dead he can beat me."

"That's nonsense. Your cousin is quite beyond the ability to harm anyone."

"But you can't get an uninterrupted night's sleep in his bedroom, and something invisible is haunting his study and rattling his papers."

"The fact that I didn't move fast enough to see who was in here certainly doesn't prove that he was invisible, Mr. Osgood. I am really surprised to hear a man of your intelligence talking such nonsense."

"It's this damned house," Frank said, passing his hand wearily across his forehead. "I told you this evening I knew I should never have come. Something horrible is sure to happen here; it's already begun. I've a notion to go back to town as soon as it's daylight."

"You know that's foolish, Mr. Osgood, when it will probably take only one day to do what you want here."

"I'll stay through the day," he said, "but I'll be eternally damned before I'll spend another night in this place. Good night, Miss Pomeroy, and pleasant dreams."

Chapter 9

MISS POMEROY went back to bed and in due course of time to sleep. Her last waking thought was that she had failed to arrange with Frank Osgood as to whether or not they should refer to their nocturnal meeting before the others when they all reassembled in the morning. Better take her cue from him, she decided as she dozed off.

When she woke again it was nearly daylight, and the sky from her window looked gray and cold. There were no sounds from the other bedrooms; she lay still and dozed for a time until she heard the others stirring. Then she got up and dressed quickly. Halfway through the process she was interrupted by a knock at the door and Nora's voice saying curtly: "I brought you some hot water." She opened the door in surprise to find a steaming pitcher planted on the floor outside. Nora's bark quite evidently was worse than her bite. Grateful for the favor Miss Pomeroy washed with lingering pleasure. She would have been just as thorough if the water had been cold, but she was glad it wasn't.

She was the first one downstairs and proceeded at once through the dining room to the kitchen to thank Nora for the hot water and find out, if possible, whether she knew anything about the previous night's goings on. Nora was wrestling noisily and ostentatiously with the wood stove, but a big pot of coffee stood ready on it, and bacon sizzled in a skillet.

"Oh, Nora, that smells good!" Miss Pomeroy said quite without guile. She enjoyed good food and was not ashamed to admit it.

"I'd have made muffins if I coulda used my electric stove," Nora said. "I can't do nothing with that one. What's the use of having a good hot breakfast anyway if no one's going to be downstairs in time to eat it?"

"I think they're almost ready. It was wonderful of you to bring up the hot water. We don't want to impose on you, you know."

"I don't mind. If I get my money out of this a thousand dollars is pretty good pay for one day's work."

"Oh, but I hope you haven't gotten your hopes too high, Nora. Do you really think there's any chance to speak of that we'll find anything the lawyers have overlooked?"

"I don't know. Mr. Osgood and Mr. Winterbottom thought so, and it's more their business than it is mine."

"If he has hidden papers, where do you suppose he'd have hidden them?"

"Goodness alive, how should I know?"

"Well, you and your husband lived here with him; you knew his habits."

"That didn't include knowing where he hid things. Here comes somebody downstairs now; why don't you go have your breakfast while it's hot and not wait for the rest?"

Miss Pomeroy retired to the dining room defeated and met Frank Osgood and his mother coming in together. He looked at her significantly and raised his right eyebrow, a signal which Miss Pomeroy noted that his mother did not fail to take in. She judged correctly that he meant to say nothing about what had passed in the night, and also that his mother would worm the whole story out of him at her leisure. Kay's footsteps on the stairs headed off any further animadversions on the subject of people who were late to breakfast, and the four of them sat down around the table to enjoy the coffee and bacon and a plate of hot and fluffy scrambled eggs. Charles Osgood must have been a man who appreciated the creature comforts Miss Pomeroy decided.

Breakfast was on the whole rather more cheerful than the previous evening's bridge game. The night was behind them; they had to face only the day with its immediate and practical tasks, and before another night they would be back in the safe anonymity of the city.

"I think we'd better get to work right after breakfast, Miss Pomeroy," Frank said. "Mr. Winterbottom said he would be out here early with Miss La Verne—I never know whether to call her that or Mrs. Osgood—"

"Miss La Verne, of course," his mother said, "and why

you want her here is more than I can possibly understand. I won't say anything about asking decent women—your mother and your future wife—to meet such a creature, but in this case her interests are all opposed to yours. She doesn't know where anything in this house is anyway—she's never been here—and if she should find anything that'd do you any good she'd hide it. Or she'll turn up with a marriage certificate."

"Mother, if she was his wife I want her to have the money. I should think you would too; don't you believe in the sacredness of the marriage tie?"

Mrs. Osgood considered a snort an adequate reply to this question, and Kay said hastily: "I can hardly wait to see her."

"I expect you'll have a good deal in common," Mrs. Osgood said. Frank flushed angrily and started to speak, but Kay interposed quickly with a warning glance in his direction: "If we're relatives by marriage I hope we'll be able to find some common ground."

"Point to Miss Waterhouse," Miss Pomeroy thought, sipping politely at her coffee. It was unnecessary for her to underline her pleasure by choking or any other juvenile and uncontrolled display.

"The obvious place to start is the study," Frank said. "I thought perhaps if it would suit you, Miss Pomeroy, that Kay and I would start in the study after breakfast, and you could do Charles's own room—the one where you slept. Perhaps Nora would be good enough to turn out the kitchen for us after she's done with the dishes."

"And I am to be regarded purely as a supernumerary?" his mother inquired coldly.

"I thought perhaps it would be pretty strenuous for you, mother. If you like to start in the living room, though, we'll be delighted to have you, of course. Someone will have to go through all those books and shake out every one."

"Nonsense. Charles never left any money in a book."

"It isn't in any of the likely places, mother, so now we'll have to start on the unlikely ones."

Frank might be under his mother's thumb to a considerable extent, Miss Pomeroy thought, and yet he managed to assert himself with a rather surprising frequency. Eventually they distributed themselves for the search in exactly the order he had described. Miss Pomeroy had been hard at work on the bedroom desk for half an hour when a taxi deposited the lawyer and Miss La Verne at the front door. With unashamed curiosity she abandoned her task and hurried downstairs to meet the newcomers. They appeared to have arrived in extraordinarily good spirits and on excellent terms with one another. The girl was wearing a black wool dress with white accents and a tiny feather-trimmed black hat well over her left eye. Triple silver fox skins, elongated to an almost unmanageable extent, served her in lieu of a wrap. Miss Pomeroy thought it a chilly costume for this October day, but Miss La Verne didn't look cold. Her color was high, her eyes were sparkling, and her laugh rang out as she came into the house. Mr. Winterbottom looked as if he were trying to reassume the dignity appropriate to a lawyer in contact with the family of the deceased, but finding it difficult.

Everyone else had also stopped work and come out into

the hall, and Frank stepped forward bravely to make the introductions.

"Good morning, Mr. Winterbottom. Kind of you to be so prompt. And, ah, Mrs. Osgood, I'm glad to see you again. Mother, please permit me to present Mrs. Osgood."

"That remains to be proved," said the senior claimant to that name, yielding not a jot nor a tittle to the conventional amenities of greeting.

"Mrs. Osgood, Miss Waterhouse and Miss Pomeroy," Frank went on in a loud, commanding voice. "Mother, you are acquainted with Mr. Winterbottom. Kay, may I present him to you? Miss Waterhouse is my fiancée, Mr. Winterbottom. And, Miss Pomeroy, this is Mr. Winterbottom, my lawyer. Miss Pomeroy is the detective I mentioned."

Everyone said "how do you do" at once, except Miss La Verne, who managed to reduce the greeting by one full syllable, and who then added: "Please everyone call me Billie, and then there needn't be any argument. My lawyer didn't want me to come up here without him, but I said if you can't trust people what's the use of living? I'm on the up and up, and I like to think everyone else is too."

At this unexpected turning of the tables Mrs. Osgood, who had never been patronized in her life, looked completely dashed and took the first opportunity to retire from the scene. Miss Pomeroy felt it in her bones that she was going to like the show girl.

"We've already started to work," Frank said. "We didn't want to waste any time. Miss Waterhouse and I can't very well manage more than this one day away from our jobs. We're working in the study and Miss Pomeroy in the bedroom Charles used, and mother is starting through the books in the living room. Of course that will be an awfully big job. We haven't asked Nora to help because it seemed as if the housework would be all she could manage. The stove is giving her some trouble. Have you had breakfast?"

"Yes, thank you," said Billie and the lawyer almost in unison, and Frank realized that he had not phrased the question with the utmost possible tact. However he did not choose to press the matter; he wanted to get the work finished.

"Have you any suggestions about how to go about it?" he asked the lawyer.

"None beyond the application of the old adage, make your head save your heels," Winterbottom answered, smiling. "We have all the people interested in Charles Osgood's estate here or represented—wait a minute, let's have Nora in for this conference even if she is busy. After all, this is what we all came for."

Kay went for Nora, and Winterbottom turned back to Billie.

"It must be clearly understood at the start, Miss La Verne," he said, "that our inviting you to participate in this search does not constitute a recognition of your claim."

"I know," she said airily. "You told me that two or three times on the way out here. It's O.K. by me; anything we find is share and share alike, and I'll trust Cousin Frank to see that I don't suffer."

"At the risk of boring you by repetition I must say it here in front of witnesses," he repeated pompously. "We have asked you to come because Mr. Osgood thinks it possible that you may have known enough of the late Mr. Osgood's habits to be of some assistance to us in our search. Naturally, if that proves to be the case you will be suitably rewarded, and I think you are quite safe in your assumption that Mr. Osgood's generosity will not fail this test. On the other hand, if we find nothing your status is in no way advanced with any of us. We continue to reserve judgment on your claim to be Mrs. Charles Osgood. Is that clearly understood?"

"Oh, quite."

Kay came back from the kitchen with Nora, and the lawyer turned the full force of his personality on her.

"Mrs. Johnson?" he inquired.

"Yes, sir." Nora was more subdued than Miss Pomeroy had yet seen her.

"I wanted you to be here, Mrs. Johnson, while we discussed the provisions of Mr. Charles Osgood's will, since you are interested as one of the heirs. I think perhaps we all understand the problem that has arisen, but there can nevertheless be no harm in restating it. Will you sit down?"

They all sat down uneasily on the edges of chairs, and Winterbottom seated himself pontifically before continuing.

"The will of Mr. Charles Osgood included bequests to Nora Johnson and her husband, to Mrs. William Osgood, and a very substantial bequest—most of the estate—to Mr. Frank Osgood. Miss Waterhouse will share in that bequest when she becomes Mrs. Frank Osgood. No Mrs. Charles Osgood was mentioned in the will; therefore the lady who claims to be Mrs. Charles Osgood is suing to break the will in order to claim her widow's share. Is that quite clear?"

Considering that all of them had known it before he began Miss Pomeroy thought that it was almost unnecessarily clear, but she did not venture to do more than nod like the rest of them.

"Very well then. The will is perfectly clear and definite, but Mr. Osgood's assets cannot be found in the usual places. He has made large cash withdrawals from his banks recently; his cousin says that he spoke of insuring his life for a hundred thousand dollars, but at present we have not found a record of any such policy. What we are looking for, therefore, may be cash or jewelry or merely legal papers of no negotiable value. I should myself have preferred to put everyone not in the family under bond before commencing this search, but Mr. Osgood prefers to trust to your integrity, and I am following his wishes in the matter. We are here to search the house for the late Mr. Osgood's missing assets, but before we start I should like all of you to think carefully over what you knew of his habits and see if there is anything which may suggest a probable hiding place."

Everyone sat still and pondered, but no helpful suggestions resulted.

"Very well, then," the lawyer said. "We may as well go ahead and search."

"I suggest that you and Miss—er—Billie—start in here on the books," Frank said, "unless Miss Pomeroy has another idea."

"We'd finish faster if we each took a separate room," Billie said.

"But if we work in pairs we can sort of check up on each other and make sure we haven't overlooked anything," Frank explained, "and besides, we suggest ideas to each other as we go along."

The plan was agreed upon, and the senior Mrs. Osgood, who was getting tired of going through books, joined Miss Pomeroy in Charles's bedroom. Mr. Winterbottom appeared to be not too displeased with Billie as a partner, and the work progressed smoothly, if without much success.

By lunch time they were all dusty, dishevelled, tired, and cross. Nora produced more hot water for a pre-prandial wash up, and when they appeared in the dining room she was ready to refresh their spirits with a huge pot of baked beans with thick slices of Canadian bacon and a bottle of Charles Osgood's best claret. Everyone except the senior Mrs. Osgood brightened perceptibly at the sight.

"How in the world did you do it, Nora?" Miss Pomeroy asked. "On that dreadful stove and so soon? I thought baked beans took days and days."

"The wood stove's a nuisance, but I will say for it it bakes good beans," Nora replied, considerably mollified. "I started the fire last night and banked it so the oven would be hot to start them early in the morning, and of course I put the beans to soak last night."

"You didn't have to come back in during the night to tend to your fire, did you?"

"Certainly not. I guess I know how to bank a fire so it'll last all night."

Both Frank Osgood and his mother declined the claret which the rest drank with relish.

"I'll have a glass of the milk Mrs. Munroe sent up last night," Frank said half apologetically to Nora.

"I've always said baked beans without coffee are like apple pie without cheese," his mother remarked, at the same time setting to on the baked beans with an energy that belied her reluctance.

Nora did not deign to reply, but on her next trip from the kitchen she bore a steaming pot of coffee and an expression in her eye that seemed to say "find fault with *that* if you can." The chorus of delighted enthusiasm was even louder than that over the wine. Frank alone declined the brew. The rest drank in appreciative silence until Mr. Winterbottom remarked with a sigh that he supposed they'd have to tackle the cellar next.

"Do you really think he'd hide anything valuable down there?" Kay shuddered. Miss Pomeroy looked at her sharply. She was so pale that it appeared she might be on the point of fainting. The nurse in Miss Pomeroy promptly took precedence over the detective.

"You're tired," she said. "You must go and lie down."

"I'm all right." There was an edge of hysteria in Kay's voice. "We have to finish this afternoon."

"I've been thinking," Billie said. "Do you suppose there might be a hidden closet somewhere? You know, like you're always reading about in these old houses. Or a safe behind a picture?"

"I'm trying the walls behind all the pictures," Miss Pomeroy said. "I haven't found anything yet."

"If there had been such a thing you'd have thought he'd mention it to me when he had me draw up the will." Winterbottom's voice was fretful. His practice did not often entail searching through a client's dusty possessions for concealed assets, and he was glad that it didn't. He had thought this idea was nonsense from the beginning, and now he was sure of it and sorry he had consented to be dragged in on it. They would wear themselves out and not find anything. Billie was an amusing little piece for an hour or so, but a whole day of her company was altogether too much of a good thing.

Frank Osgood finished the milk, wiped his mouth off with a grimace, and pushed his chair unceremoniously back from the table.

"Excuse me," he said. "I don't know about the rest of you, but I, for one, will have to get back to work."

"Shall we put things back in the study?" Kay asked him.

"Not as far as I'm concerned. He's dead; no one will ever use those notes for his books; I say burn 'em up."

"Oh, no!" Miss Pomeroy protested. "I want all his notes."

"You'll need a trunk."

"I'll get a trunk, then. I want them."

"And the other stuff?"

"Burn it."

"Come along with me, Miss Pomeroy," Kay said, "and we'll sort over what to burn and what to keep. Where are you starting back to work, Mr. Osgood?"

"I'll go down cellar and see what I can find. I don't think it will be such a terrible job. As I remember, Charles kept his cellar fairly tidy."

"I'll come and help you as soon as we're through in the study," Kay said.

"I'm afraid that leaves the attic for Mr. Winterbottom."

Miss Pomeroy's voice was solemn, but there was a gleam of mischief in her eye. "I can come up there when Miss Waterhouse goes down cellar."

They separated again. At the door of the study Miss Pomeroy stopped short in consternation. Upstairs she had returned neatly docketed papers to their proper reposing places as soon as she had finished looking at them, but here manuscript, notes, bills, letters, and old wrapping paper had been indiscriminately hurled onto the floor. At a glance it looked as if simply sorting the trash from what should be saved would be a full afternoon's work.

"Do you really want all the notes?" Kay asked curiously. "That whole file was full of them. What earthly good could they be to you?"

"They might give me some ideas," Miss Pomeroy said, and set to work sorting. Kay carried piles of trash to the incinerator, and in much less than an hour the room had resumed some semblance of order.

"You might as well go down and help Mr. Osgood," Miss Pomeroy said then. "I can finish here."

She smiled to herself as Kay made hardly a proper show of reluctance before dashing into the cellar. What quality was it in a mousy little man like Frank Osgood that could inspire such devotion? She had scarcely had time to begin to phrase an answer to the question for herself when Kay was back, the dark eyes starting out of her dead white face.

"Frank," she gasped, "poisoned. Hurry."

Chapter 10

IN an emergency Miss Pomeroy reverted to the attitudes of her regular profession.

"Get Mr. Winterbottom," she said. "We won't be able to carry him up the stairs." As she spoke she was clearing papers and debris off the studio couch against the rear wall of the study.

"Not there!" Kay said wildly, "oh, not there!"

Miss Pomeroy did not bother to argue; she had silenced hysteria with a look before, and she did it now. "Get Winterbottom," she repeated, and departed for the kitchen as rapidly as she could move without running.

"Heat a lot of water," she said to Nora as she passed through the kitchen. "Have you any mustard?" She did not wait for an answer but hurried on down the stairs. Frank Osgood was sitting on a stool in the wine cellar with his head in his hands. He looked up at her approach and smiled wanly. His face was flushed except for pallid lines from the corners of his mouth, and his eyes were as bright as a cat's.

"Miss Apple," he said. "Greetings, Miss Apple of a King. I'm shick."

Miss Pomeroy cast a quick professional glance about the room. "What have you been drinking?" she asked.

"Never drink. Ulcers. Never drink, never drank, never have drunk; why should I have ulcers? Shome people get ulshers from drinking, and not drinking getsh ulshers for other people. Funny, isn't it? I feel funny."

There was no use questioning him, that was evident. And there was no time to try to make a diagnosis even if she had felt competent to make one. Perhaps he was only drunk; it would not be too surprising if the strain of this visit to his cousin's house combined with his mother's hostility had driven him to such a simple release. But she didn't dare assume that that was all that was wrong. She put a hand to his forehead and found it feverishly hot, but the hand he put up to push hers away was cold.

"Can you walk upstairs?" she asked briskly.

"Dowanna walk. Tired. My throat hurtsh. Better rest, dowanna walk. Charles can't rest; he was here last night; did you know? That detective woman heard him."

Miss Pomeroy put an arm about him, threw his left arm around her own neck, and started up the cellar stairs supporting the unresisting body, just as Kay, Mrs. Osgood, and Gerald Winterbottom appeared at the top of the flight.

"Will you take him, please, Mr. Winterbottom, and get him onto the couch in the study?" she asked. "I want to fix some mustard water."

"What is it? What's happened? Is he very ill?"

"I don't know."

"Hadn't we better call a doctor?"

"Of course, but we can't wait until he comes to do anything. We'll have to try emetics for the present; you can't do anything about antidotes unless you know the poison."

"Could you save him if you knew the poison?" Kay asked quietly.

"I'm sure I don't know. That depends entirely on what it is." Miss Pomeroy had the patient almost to the top of the stairs herself before the lawyer was able to shake off the numbing effect of the shock sufficiently to assist her. Billie and Nora were standing in the background of the little group at the head of the stairs behind Mrs. Osgood, who was wringing her hands and weeping.

"Can you find some hot water bottles, Nora?" Miss Pomeroy asked. "Fill all you can round up right away. You've got the mustard ready, bless you. Get him in there on the couch and lay him down, Mr. Winterbottom. Nora, call the doctor you called for Mr. Charles, please."

"No," Kay shrieked, her control giving way completely. "I won't let you. I won't have it. Charles died; you want him to die too. He can't get out from town for hours; call a doctor from the village."

Miss Pomeroy was busying herself with a pitcher of luke-warm water and the mustard. "Do you know the name of a doctor in the village?" she asked Nora.

"Yes, there's Doctor Jackson—"

"Call him, then."

"There's no phone connection," Mrs. Osgood sobbed. "Somebody do something. We're all just standing around here. He's dying and nobody's doing anything."

"Nora will have to phone from the Munroes'," Miss Pomeroy said. "Will you go down there with her, Mrs. Osgood, and be sure she gets the message straight? I'm a nurse; I think I'll be able to do all anyone could do for Mr. Osgood until a doctor gets here."

"Save him, Miss Pomeroy," Kay said. "For God's sake, save him. I'll do anything—"

"It will be messy," Miss Pomeroy said. "Have you a basin, Nora? Good. I'll need help. Someone with steady nerves."

"Let me," Billie said. "I can take it."

"I want to," Kay spoke at the same minute. "He's mine—"

"Miss La Verne, please," Miss Pomeroy said, and returned to the study. Frank Osgood was lying on his back on the couch, apparently unconscious; his stertorous breathing could be heard throughout the house. Miss Pomeroy shut the door and applied herself to business.

Billie La Verne was as good as her word; she came through the ordeal a bit pale and shaken, but entirely game.

"I think he'll live," Miss Pomeroy said at last. "We can't give him any medicine until the doctor comes. We'll need more blankets; he must be kept warm."

Kay was standing outside the door, her fingers clenched in the palms of her hands. "What?" she asked.

"I think he'll be all right," Miss Pomeroy said. "You may come in when we've cleaned up."

"I want to be with him," Kay said. "Is he breathing all right? If he's not you should get some strychnine."

"My lord!" Billie said. "Strychnine! Hasn't enough been done to the poor guy already? Whadda you wanna do anyhow?"

"No one but a doctor could prescribe strychnine," Miss Pomeroy said. "What makes you think—?"

"But if he needs it—if it will save his life—oh, what ridiculous nonsense!"

"He's going to live, Miss Waterhouse," Miss Pomeroy said, "and I'm going to have the doctor see you too when he gets here. I think you're in a very serious state yourself. Come upstairs and lie down."

She took the protesting but unresisting younger woman by the arm and walked up the stairs with her. When they were out of earshot of the others she spoke gravely.

"You'll have to pull yourself together, Miss Waterhouse. I realize that you're in no shape to be reasoned with now, but you must rest and control yourself. There's bound to be an inquiry about what has happened—"

"The police? But you said he was going to live."

"I believe he's going to live. I don't know whether police will be involved or not, but the doctor and the lawyer, if not the family, will certainly insist on an investigation. You've already talked very wildly and foolishly; they'll question you and they'll press you for true answers. You'd better tell me everything now, and I'll be able to protect you."

"There's nothing to tell."

"Why did you want me to give him strychnine? How did you know he was poisoned when anyone else would have supposed he was drunk?"

"Frank never drinks."

"Even then, when you found him like that in the wine cellar the normal assumption would be that the strain of the day had driven him to an abnormal action for the sake of relief. How did you know he was poisoned?"

"I didn't know. I only guessed. Let me alone; let me alone; you said yourself that I wasn't in a fit state to be questioned."

"If other people do the questioning it will be worse. You can trust me, I promise you."

"I can't trust anyone. Let me alone, can't you? Go back to him."

Miss Pomeroy gave up with as good a grace as possible.

"Lie down," she said. "You should have a hot water bottle yourself, but we can't spare any from Mr. Osgood. I'll give you some aspirin."

"I never take it."

"Nonsense. You need it and you'll take it."

"I have something much better." Mrs. Osgood spoke from the open door, and Miss Pomeroy jumped and turned about. How long had the woman been standing there? She must have come back into the house and followed them upstairs with an amazingly catlike tread for a woman of her size and weight.

"I'll get you some of my leaves," she said, addressing Kay where she lay on the bed. "There's nothing better."

"Oh, no!" Miss Pomeroy would not have supposed that Kay's deadly pallor could increase, but at this suggestion the last vestige of color fled from her lips. "No, no, no."

Miss Pomeroy was sorry that the first friendly overture she had observed on the part of the older woman should be thus rejected. Mrs. Osgood looked genuinely hurt as well as offended.

"They're from my herb garden," she said. "Soaked in wine vinegar. It's an old, old recipe—goes back to mediaeval times. I lay them on my forehead. Nothing's better to make you sleep."

"I'll take the aspirin," Kay said. "Please, Miss Pomeroy."

Miss Pomeroy gave her two aspirin tablets silently, covered her, and followed the older woman out of the room.

"You mustn't be hurt," she said. "She's upset; people

aren't reasonable when they're like that."

"It's always that way. She thinks I'm silly and old, a meddling, old-fashioned fool. My herb garden saves me hundreds of dollars in doctors' bills; nobody's ever found anything better than some of the mediaeval herbal remedies."

"I'm sure of that, Mrs. Osgood, but there's no point to arguing with her in her present state. I've been trying it myself, and I know."

"She poisoned Frank. It's no wonder she's upset, a murderess with her victim dying before her eyes. But you've saved him; you've foiled her, my boy, my boy. First Charles and now Frank. She'd have finished him off if you hadn't stopped her."

"Mrs. Osgood!" Miss Pomeroy found herself wishing for the cool head of Miss Billie La Verne. Respectable women did give way to their emotions so thoroughly. "You mustn't say such things. Let me put you to bed too; I know how dreadful this has been for you, but you mustn't say things that you'll regret all your life."

"I'll never be sorry I told the truth when no one else dared to."

"But, Mrs. Osgood, why should Kay try to poison Frank? She loves him; she's going to marry him; there wouldn't be any sense to it."

"She's afraid I'll succeed in breaking up the marriage. She'd rather kill him than lose him any other way. She killed Charles because he'd been her lover and she was afraid he'd tell Frank, and now she's killed Frank because she suspects that he knows anyway."

"Mrs. Osgood, you must stop this talk! No matter what

happens, if you start such gossip you won't be able to stop it. And if anyone here overhears you you'll start the gossip all right."

She persuaded her also to lie down and brought the leaves soaked in wine vinegar from a sort of glorified soap dish standing on the dresser. They were damp, dripping, and bedraggled, and looked unpleasant as well as ineffective, but Miss Pomeroy did not attempt to argue with Mrs. Osgood about their use. She laid them carefully on the wrinkled forehead and covered them with a damp cloth.

"That's wonderful," Mrs. Osgood said. "You must let me give you some, Miss Pomeroy. Better than any sleeping medicine I know."

"I should love to have some," Miss Pomeroy answered not altogether truthfully, and went back downstairs to her original patient. His breathing was quieter and reasonably even, and the flush had somewhat died out from his face. His eyes were open again, wide and feverishly bright. She felt his pulse, which was rapid and feeble but not alarming.

"You're going to be all right," she said, professionally reassuring.

"I'm thirsty," he said. "Thirsty. You think I killed him. Kay thinks I killed him, and Nora, and mother, and the lawyer. Billie doesn't think so. Nice Billie. Billie has a bearskin rug; have you ever seen a bearskin rug, Miss P.? Except, of course, in the movies. She should send it to the cleaners, but perhaps she can't bear to be parted from it. A pun. Did you get it? Bear—bear—I could always make puns when I was a boy, but Charles didn't think they were good. I'm thirsty."

Miss Pomeroy offered him more water, and heard with relief the pounding on the front door that indicated the arrival of more professional assistance. She liked Dr. Jackson, a country general practitioner of the old school, complete to the shabby black medicine case.

"Dr. Jackson?" she asked. "The patient is Mr. Frank Osgood, a cousin of the former owner of the house. He's been poisoned, we think; we don't know how. I'm a trained nurse. We've given him emetics and we're keeping him warm."

"Good," the doctor said. "Is he conscious?"

"Yes, he's rambling a little."

"Sleepy?"

"Not now. He was earlier."

"Any burns? Was it caustic?"

"No, nothing of that sort."

"Have you any idea of the nature of the poison?"

"Only from the symptoms I've observed."

"Yes?"

"I thought of atropine. His pupils are distended and he's thirsty, and his face is flushed. He could be drunk, but his relatives say he never drinks anything. He was found in the wine cellar."

The doctor nodded as he turned into the study. The man on the couch paid him no heed as Dr. Jackson set down his bag and bent over to make his examination. He pulled back the eyelids and looked carefully into the sick man's eyes, listened to his heart and his breathing, and tested his reflexes before he spoke again.

"What have you been drinking, Mr. Osgood?"

"Nothing. Let me alone."

The doctor felt of the heated bottles, turned away from the couch, and motioned Miss Pomeroy into the hall. But if he had hoped for a quiet conference there he was disappointed, for the entire house-party with the exception of the sleeping Kay was gathered in the hall outside. Mrs. Osgood couldn't have rested at all; her face was drawn and working with emotion, and she plucked at the doctor's sleeve with a clawing motion.

"Is he all right, doctor? Can he pull through?"

"He's resting very comfortably, and I think he'll be all right. Your Miss Pomeroy has done just the right thing. How did this happen?"

His inquiring glance took in Gerald Winterbottom and Billie La Verne, Nora, and Mr. and Mrs. Munroe hovering in the background.

"It must have been an accident," the lawyer said. "I can't understand it. He was searching the cellar, and his fiancée came running upstairs and said he'd been poisoned."

"Searching the cellar?"

"Mr. Osgood is his cousin's heir, and I am his lawyer. We—and these other people—came out here in an attempt to find some papers necessary for the settlement of the estate. We searched this floor and the one above it this morning, and this afternoon we had undertaken the cellar and the attic."

"I see. Now, which is the young lady who found him?"

"She's upstairs resting, doctor," Miss Pomeroy said. "She was in a state of shock, and I insisted on her lying down. I gave her some aspirin. I thought perhaps you would look at her when you'd finished with this patient."

"What made you think of atropine?" he asked.

Miss Pomeroy wished he had saved the question for a time when they were alone. "Well—the symptoms I mentioned—" she said uncomfortably. "Of course I didn't mean to attempt a diagnosis."

"Nevertheless it looks to me as if you'd hit on one. I suppose you know that atropine as a poison is seldom fatal, but why should he have taken it?"

"He was drugged," Mrs. Osgood said. "He never took it himself. Someone put it in his food or his drinks."

"But he didn't drink anything at lunch," the lawyer objected. "He was the only one who didn't. The rest of us had wine and coffee, and Osgood didn't take anything but a glass of milk."

"And where was the milk secured?"

"It was from the pitcher Mrs. Munroe sent up last night," Nora said. "Nobody wanted it then, and it was all left over to drink today, and then no one drank it but him."

"Do you have the rest of the pitcher?"

"I threw it out and washed the pitcher. They wasn't expecting to be here for another meal."

"And everything else that he ate the rest of you ate as well?"

"Everything."

"If you're going to pull him through, doctor, need we go into all this?" Gerald Winterbottom asked. "When he's better you can find out from him just how it happened. In the meantime I really don't think we can be much help to you, for none of us knows anything about the matter."

Dr. Jackson sat down on a chair in the hall and scratched his head.

"It's an odd case," he said. "Looks to me as if I'll have to report it to the police. A poisoning's a serious matter, you know, even if the victim doesn't die."

"But we can't take time for a lot of police questioning," Winterbottom protested. "We only came out for the day. There aren't even sleeping accommodations here for all of us. Put the thing down as an accident; it's bound to have been that."

"Some of you'll have to stay here overnight," the doctor said, "for Osgood can't be moved today. And I'll have to make a report to the police; you can talk to them about havin' to get back to New York. I don't believe they'll bother you any more than necessary." He turned to Miss Pomeroy. "I'll see the young lady now," he said authoritatively.

Miss Pomeroy had thought a little of warning him in advance that Kay was likely to talk wildly and irrationally, but she preceded him meekly up the stairs without comment. This was evidently a man who made up his own mind, and advance hints were more likely to make him stubborn and contrary than the reverse. She ushered him into Kay's room without knocking, and they found the girl asleep. He listened to her heart and her breathing, inquired in a low voice as to what sedatives she had taken, and then shrugged his shoulders.

"Let her sleep," he said. "She can talk later on."

Chapter 11

"Is there some place we can talk without all these people around?" Dr. Jackson inquired of Miss Pomeroy as soon as they were out of Kay's room.

"In here," Miss Pomeroy said, leading the way into Charles Osgood's bedroom. The doctor sat down on the chair in front of the dead man's desk and scratched his head.

"I hate to make trouble for all you people," he said, "but there's no two ways about it; I can't get out of having to report this to the police."

"Yes, doctor." Miss Pomeroy never argued with doctors. This one appeared to be more than a little surprised that she didn't. He was prepared with his argument and went on with it anyway.

"A clear case of accidental poisoning is one thing, but either attempted suicide or attempted murder is quite another. Now those people downstairs say this was an accident, but I can't find any reason to believe that they're telling the truth. In almost any case of accidental poisoning of an adult the poisonous agent, once the accident is over, is perfectly obvious. A man gets the wrong bottle from a medicine chest, and as soon as he begins to feel queer he goes back and looks at the bottle and sees what has happened. Or you look for the flour you made the pancakes with, and there's a box of roach powder instead. But here's a case of accidental poisoning, so called, and yet nobody knows where he got the poison, and the victim himself claims he couldn't have gotten it at all. That's no case for a doctor."

"I know," Miss Pomeroy said. "I've been trying to figure out how it might have happened. Of course we're all strangers here; wouldn't there be more chance of his having drunk something by accident here than in a house he was familiar with?"

"Less, I'd think. You don't go around drinking out of bottles in strange houses—it's only at home where you think you know the contents that you're likely to be careless. You haven't any theory about how it happened, then?"

Miss Pomeroy shook her head unwillingly.

"Well, could you get these people straight for me so I can make an intelligent report to the sheriff?"

"The sick man is the late Mr. Osgood's cousin and heir. The estate hasn't been settled yet, and it was his idea to bring everyone interested out here in an attempt to locate some missing assets. The elderly woman is his mother—you remember her?"

The doctor nodded.

"The girl—young woman—across the hall is his fiancée. They expect to be married very soon. Nora was the late Mr. Osgood's cook, and her husband was houseman. He's in the army now, and she has a job in the city. She got time off to come out here because she and her husband are in the will for a thousand dollars apiece."

The doctor ticked them off on his fingers as she spoke and nodded his head in agreement.

"Mr. Winterbottom is the lawyer who drew up the

will; he represents Frank Osgood now. And Miss La Verne is—that is, she says she is the widow of Charles Osgood. She's threatening suit to break the will, but of course there's no use her suing if there's no money to be had."

"But how would she happen to be here with these representatives of the family?"

"Mr. Osgood says that if she can establish her claim he wants her to have all the money. He'd prefer not to oppose her at all, but the lawyer insists that he must."

The doctor snorted. "Funny set up," he said. "What about you?"

"I'm a private detective."

"I thought you told me you were a trained nurse."

"I'm that, too, but I'm not working at it just now."

"You might have told me that before. What are you doing here?"

"Mr. Osgood has suspected foul play in connection with his cousin's death and retained me to investigate it."

"He has? Good Lord, woman, and you let me sit there and debate with myself whether or not this was a matter for the police?"

"I haven't found the slightest evidence that there was any foundation for his suspicions."

Although she had decided on the unequivocal truth, Miss Pomeroy did not feel it necessary to explain that she would have preferred to call Dr. James Laurence rather than the more readily available Dr. Jackson because she would have liked to see whether Frank Osgood's illness would remind him in any way of an earlier one he had been called to attend in that same room. After all, Dr. Laurence had given a certificate of death by heart failure and showed every indication of a stubborn determination not to change his mind. It might have been interesting to call him, but it could hardly have been helpful. There was no reason to expect anything but trouble from an insistence on calling him now.

"The cousin died of a heart attack, didn't he?" the doctor was inquiring.

Miss Pomeroy wondered that that information should stick in his mind so long about a man who had not been his patient. Perhaps there had been some professional jealousy involved. Did he believe that if he had been called instead of the doctor from the city he might have saved Charles Osgood's life?

"Yes," she said, "a heart attack."

"Well," the doctor shrugged, "it's not up to me to try to figure out a connection. I'll get the sheriff on it right away."

"I suppose I can let my investigation rest until he gets here," Miss Pomeroy said, "but if you wouldn't think it impertinent of me to inquire I'd like to know whether you think it possible that the Munroes might have had a grudge against Frank Osgood because he was his cousin's heir. Are they much afraid of being put off the farm, for instance?"

"You mean they might have poisoned him? Good heavens, no; I've known them for twenty-five years. Fine farming people, straight as they come. No, no, no, that's nonsense. Don't look to the natives of this place for your criminals."

"Blame it on any or all of the city people," Miss Pomeroy thought silently, "but of course nothing like this ever happens in Connecticut."

"I'll get the sheriff right out here," he repeated. "Of course none of you people can leave until he comes. Now about the patient—I think he's out of danger, but watch that respiration." He gave her instructions and medicines and told her where he could be reached in case of emergency.

"We have no telephone service here," she reminded him. "Any message would have to go through the Munroes."

"I'm not expecting an emergency," he assured her. "You should be able to take care of anything that occurs."

"Do you want me to let the sheriff question Miss Waterhouse and Mr. Osgood?"

"I doubt if he'll be able to make sense tonight. She ought to be able to talk when she wakes up."

Miss Pomeroy nodded and sadly watched the doctor walking down the stairs. She had no desire to follow him and be present when he told "those people downstairs" his decision. She waited until she was sure he had gone and then walked briskly down with an air of jaunty determination completely belied by her feelings.

Mrs. Osgood, Billie La Verne, and the lawyer were sitting in the big living room, three separate portraits of unrelieved gloom. A shrewd observer might perhaps have suspected Billie of sharing the prevailing mood merely to be obliging; a night in a comfortable country house with meals and shelter provided entirely free of charge was not an unmitigated disaster for her.

"Someone will have to see Nora about more food," Miss Pomeroy said firmly. "Mr. Osgood only bought supplies enough for lunch here, and now there'll be dinner and breakfast at least."

"You do it," Gerald Winterbottom proposed. "You know about food and things."

"Can you drive Mr. Osgood's car into town for supplies, Mrs. Osgood?" Miss Pomeroy asked.

"I don't know how to drive," she said.

"I can drive it," Billie volunteered brightly.

"It would look bad for any of us to leave here until the sheriff's been out," Winterbottom said heavily. "After that I could run into town. Maybe Mrs. Munroe can let us have some milk and eggs, or maybe the sheriff'll bring groceries if we ask him."

Billie looked at him uncertainly and then laughed. "You're such a joker," she said.

"I don't think the doctor knows anything anyway," Mrs. Osgood wailed. "I know Frank ought to be in a hospital; the very idea of leaving him out here with no telephone and no electric lights and nobody to take care of him!"

"I can take care of him, Mrs. Osgood, and he really is going to be all right," Miss Pomeroy said. "I think we'd all be happier now if we could keep busy until the sheriff comes."

"I'll talk to Nora and make a list if nobody else wants to," Billie said. "God knows I don't know much about housekeeping, but I guess I can write down a grocery list."

The afternoon shadows were growing long across the desiccated grass before the sheriff and his deputy arrived in an ancient Buick to investigate the poisoning. The sheriff was a large, stout, red-faced man with prematurely white hair; his age could have been anything from thirty to fifty. The deputy was thin, silent, and tired looking. They came into the house together after a perfunctory rap at the front door; plainly the sheriff considered the present occupants of the house to be trespassers and thought that amenities would be wasted on them. Gerald Winterbottom rose from a chair beside the fire and came forward to meet them.

"I'm an attorney," he said, introducing himself. "I think your doctor's getting a bit above himself sending you out here, but if there's anything you want to know I'll be glad to tell you about it."

"Yeah," the sheriff said, "we're funny out here. When there's a case of attempted murder we like to know what goes on."

"Yes. Well, your doctor says that Mr. Osgood can't be questioned tonight—or at least that you can't get an intelligible answer out of him—and none of the rest of us knows anything about it. For all I know he was merely drunk. And I might suggest that it would be wise for you to go a little easy; if you hold us all out here overnight and it turns out that he was merely drunk, I believe I can make things fairly unpleasant for you."

"Yeah," the sheriff said, "I expect you could, but I don't expect it's going to turn out like that. Maybe you didn't know the doctor took some samples of the bodily discharges in to town for analysis."

"Has he found anything?"

"I'm asking the questions today."

Miss Pomeroy didn't think Dr. Jackson had had time, even supposing he had facilities available, to test the specimens he had taken for atropine, but she refrained from interfering. She wished she had enough influence with Gerald Winterbottom to make it worth her while to try to persuade him not to antagonize the sheriff; at the very best it was bound to cause delay, and at the worst it could make very serious trouble.

"I wonder, sheriff," she said meekly, "whether you could release Mr. Osgood's car and someone to drive it in to town for more groceries. We hadn't planned to stay here beyond noon today, and we've run out of supplies."

"My name's Wentworth," he said. "I want to talk to everybody who's been in the house today, one at a time, and it'll save everybody time and trouble if you'll all tell the truth. Soon's I find one of you I think I can trust I'll let that one go in to town."

"Anyone being questioned on suspicion of having committed a crime has a right to legal representation," Gerald Winterbottom said nastily. "I shall insist on remaining in the room to hear all your questioning."

"You wanta represent all of these people, huh?" The sheriff turned a jaundiced eye on Winterbottom, who quailed a little before it.

"I don't suppose I could represent all parties here, no," he admitted. "There are conflicting interests. But I shall advise everyone that it is not necessary to answer your questions without legal advice."

"Do that," the sheriff said with heavy sarcasm. "That'll help a lot. All you want is to help us find out what really happened, but you're going to advise nobody to talk without a lawyer."

"I understand Mr. Winterbottom's caution," Miss Pomeroy said, "but I, for one, am quite willing to answer all your questions now." Again she admitted to herself that she was maintaining some mental reservations, but no more, she thought, than were justified by the strange professional ethics of private detectives. Sheriff Wentworth sized her up thoroughly and said: "I'll take you last. First I'd like to see the wine cellar where you found him."

Nora showed the way, and the two men remained in the cellar long enough, it seemed to those waiting above, to have dug up every stone in the foundation and then replaced them all. When they were finished at last, they established themselves in the dining room as an office and called Nora for the first interview. This proved to be short and, judging from Nora's appearance when she emerged, not too trying.

"They said I could go to town for the groceries," she informed Miss Pomeroy, coming into the study where the patient still rested on the studio couch. Miss Pomeroy wondered why everyone was assuming that she was in charge of this disastrous house party. With Frank Osgood incapacitated, the responsibility for running things should have devolved upon his mother, but Mrs. Osgood was obviously too shaken to assume it. Miss Pomeroy produced a ten dollar bill from the depths of her bag for Nora and tried to marshal her thoughts into reasonable order on the subject of supplies. She wished she had some uniforms with her; in street clothes it was hard for her to get into the proper frame of mind for looking after her patient.

Mrs. Osgood went into the dining room next, and just after the door had shut behind her Kay, pale but composed, stood at the open door of the study.

"May I come in?" she inquired softly. "How is he?"

"Resting quietly," Miss Pomeroy said.

"As well as can be expected?"

She looked up in surprise to realize that Kay was essaying a mild joke, her lips faintly curved upward.

"He *is* resting quietly," she said. "I think there's nothing to worry about."

"Will it disturb him if we talk?"

"Not unless we're very noisy."

Kay stood looking down at the sleeping man, the faint smile still on her lips, a trace of moisture in her eyes.

"I'm sorry I was so foolish, Miss Pomeroy," she said. "I want your advice before I go in there and talk to those men."

Miss Pomeroy's heart sank. She was a woman of the strictest rectitude; there would be no advice possible except to tell truth and shame the devil, and that being the case she wished she didn't have to be the recipient of Kay Waterhouse's confidence. But she gave no sign of her reluctance.

"Of course," she said.

"This is all my fault, Miss Pomeroy," Kay said. Miss Pomeroy glanced involuntarily at the sleeping man, and the younger woman added hastily: "No, no, I don't mean I did that to him. But what his mother says—all those dreadful hints—it's the truth. It was on my account that he hated his cousin. I was Charles Osgood's mistress.

That's the reason all this has happened."

"You mean you think your fiancé tried to kill himself?"

"No, no, not that. It's some horrible trap Charles laid. I don't see how, but I know that's what it was. And it was all my fault they hated each other. I should never have agreed to marry Frank."

"When—how long ago was this?"

"Fourteen years. It—you shouldn't speak ill of the dead, Miss Pomeroy, but it was mostly his fault. I was young—old enough to have known better, maybe, but pretty young and unsophisticated. He was a lot older, and dazzling and successful. It was in the late twenties when everyone was being a free soul—you remember. He persuaded me that a love affair was a necessity for my developing psyche. He—I'll have to give him that credit; he never pretended to be serious about it. But I couldn't control my emotions; I fell horribly in love with him. I—it's terrible to remember, Miss Pomeroy—I made scenes; I begged him to marry me; I humiliated myself. It's warped me for life; I'll never be quite a complete person."

"But it was over? It hadn't dragged on?"

"It was over. For more than thirteen years I've hated him. When Frank fell in love with me and I with him I was frightened at first—and then I thought I could live it down, that I'd forget it. Frank and I have been engaged for a long time, you know—eight years. He's had a hard struggle financially; the depression hit him at a crucial time. And all these years we've waited there's been Charles looking on and sneering and hinting. He held it over me and in the end he told Frank."

"Do you know that or only suspect it?"

"I didn't hear him, if that's what you mean, but I know it."

"And is that why you believe that Frank killed his cousin?"

She nodded wordlessly. "Believed," she said after a moment. "I don't think that any more. I don't know why I ever did."

"But you told me you *knew*—"

"I'm sorry, Miss Pomeroy. I've done a lot of wild talking these past few days. I've been upset. But there isn't much time; I need your advice now. Mrs. Osgood is in there; she's almost sure to tell them all this. I don't know whether Charles told her or whether she figured it out for herself, but she knows it and she'll tell them. And they'll think just like I did that it's why Frank killed Charles. Shall I tell them the truth or shall I deny it all? I'll do whatever you say, Miss Pomeroy."

"Tell them the truth, of course," Miss Pomeroy said, "but use discretion. Remember they're here to investigate your fiancé's poisoning; they're satisfied that his cousin's death was a natural one, and so is everyone else concerned. Why drag in a lot of past history? Just tell them what you know about what happened today—how you knew it was poisoning, for instance, and why you wanted me to give him strychnine."

"Did I say that? I haven't the faintest recollection. I must have been completely out of my head."

"And how did you know he was poisoned?"

"Anyone who knew him could have told. He didn't drink; it was unmistakable."

There was another knock at the front door, and Frank

Osgood groaned softly in his sleep.

"I'll go," Kay said. She drew the door from the study into the central hall almost shut behind her, but Miss Pomeroy could see the figure of Mrs. Munroe through the crack that remained open and hear her voice.

"I have to see the sheriff," she said. "I have a message from Dr. Jackson."

Chapter 12

MRS. MUNROE was closeted briefly with the sheriff, and when she emerged from the dining room she was accompanied by the sad-faced deputy, who escorted her to the door.

"Thank you, Mrs. Munroe," he said. It was the first time Miss Pomeroy had heard him speak, and the courtliness of the words astonished her. The deputy was evidently quite a different man from his chief. "I'm sorry you have to run errands for us like this. But that ought to clear up the case; I don't think we'll need to ask you to take any more calls. I may be down to your house in a little while to use your phone, though."

"I don't mind," she said, and Miss Pomeroy was quite sure she was telling the truth; this must be the most exciting day in her life since the death of the former owner of the house.

Neither the sad-faced deputy nor Mrs. Osgood returned to the dining room. The deputy went upstairs, and Billie La Verne went in to confer with the sheriff alone. Miss Pomeroy in the study could hear her voice raised in anger now and again, and upstairs the deputy's heavy tread went steadily from room to room. He was opening and closing closet doors and bureau drawers, obviously looking for something. When the dining room door opened at last to allow Billie to emerge she was in tears. The effect was altogether startling; the mascara had run down her cheeks, blotting the rouge, and the voice emerging from her nose had lost all trace of a British accent. Like Kay she turned at once into the study. Miss Pomeroy thought sadly of the days when a sickroom had not been considered the appropriate place for miscellaneous unhappy confidences.

"The so and so," Billie said, blowing her nose. "Just a hick policeman, and he tries to give me the works! Me that's been cross-examined by experts! Who does he think he is anyway?"

"He's not very polite," Miss Pomeroy agreed. "I'd try not to let it upset me if I were you. He treats us all alike."

"That's what you think!" Miss La Verne remarked, indicating, Miss Pomeroy gathered, that this was an erroneous opinion. "Give a hick like that somebody he thinks got no comeback, and he goes to town. Wait'll I get my hands on Charles's dough, and I'll show him."

"Has that fellow upstairs got a search warrant?" Gerald Winterbottom was inquiring in loud and distinct tones as he entered the dining room. The door closed behind him, and neither Billie nor Miss Pomeroy heard the sheriff's reply.

"That's the way to talk to a guy like that," Billie said.

"Oh, no," Miss Pomeroy disagreed. "I do wish he wouldn't antagonize him just before—" she meant just before Kay's interview, but she prudently changed the phrase—"just before he talks to me."

"You got nothing to worry about," Billie said, sniffing.

"He's just leaving you to the last because you're a disinterested observer."

Miss Pomeroy guessed correctly that this was a quotation.

"I don't know whether we're supposed to talk about what he asked," she hinted. "I suppose that's the reason he wanted to talk to us separately."

"He asked anything he could think of that might pin it on me," Billie said. "I tried to tell him about that milk that nobody else drank, but do you think he would listen? Not him. I ask you, Miss Pomeroy, you're an educated woman, if a guy drinks milk that nobody else drinks at lunch, and the guy gets sick and nobody else does after lunch, what does it look like?"

"It looks as if there was something wrong with the milk."

"Sure it does, but try to tell that wise guy in there! What am I doin' here, and when did I first meet Frank, and did he ask me to come or did I ask him to let me come?—I never knew a thing about it until he asked me to come along, and how could I? And where did I meet Charles, and when, and who married us, and where's the license, and why didn't we ever live together out here? And did I think if Frank was dead I'd be sure to get the money? As if I'd kill that little guy—" she looked with half contemptuous affection at the man on the studio couch. "Why, hell, I wouldn't need to. I can wrap him around my little finger. I could blink my eyes at him a coupla times, and he'd give me the money. Or I could marry him and have it all that way if I was mean enough to take him away from the schoolteacher."

"Oh, hush!" Miss Pomeroy glanced in alarm at the open door and the living room across the hall. "Don't let her hear you say such things. Of course it's not true, but don't let her hear you anyway."

"Don't worry. I wouldn't take him if it was a million dollars thrown in. He's not my type, and anyway I wouldn't be that mean."

Miss Pomeroy wondered. It was an entirely new idea to her, and a disturbing one. Kay Waterhouse was one of those quiet women whose quietness indicated banked fires; what she was likely to do if she had reason to believe that her possession of Frank's affections was in jeopardy was not a pleasant matter to contemplate. Miss Pomeroy could only hope devoutly that she had not overheard.

Gerald Winterbottom came out of the dining room red-faced and perspiring and definitely more subdued than he had been on entering. Kay came from the living room and crossed the patch of hall visible through the open study door. She seemed calm again, and she did not glance into the room. That was a bad sign, Miss Pomeroy thought.

She was closeted with the sheriff for a long time, longer than any of the others had been. Nora came back from town with the groceries and tiptoed noisily into the study to whisper that she didn't see how she could be expected to serve dinner if she couldn't get into the dining room to set the table; Gerald Winterbottom appeared at the door to announce that the sheriff was an officious fool but that the best thing they could do would be to cooperate with him, a conclusion at which Miss Pomeroy had already arrived independently; Mrs. Osgood came in to sit

for awhile with the invalid and offered to relieve Miss
Pomeroy for her own session of questioning, and still the
dining room door remained obstinately shut, and the little
quiet murmur of voices went on behind it.

At last the deputy came heavily downstairs and without
looking at any of the party went to the dining room door
and entered without knocking. A moment later the sheriff
emerged with a small bottle in his hand.

"I'm going to have to take this lady in for further questioning," he said, his voice oily with triumph, pointing at
Billie La Verne. Miss Pomeroy decided that she preferred
the brusqueness that indicated uncertainty.

"What have I done?" Billie's hands clenched at her
sides. "Oh, sure, pick on me, that's all right, but just tell
me what I done."

"That's yours, isn't it?" The sheriff held up the little
bottle. "Or will you attempt to deny that?"

"Sure it's mine," Billie said. "At least it's just like mine.
Only mine had a lot more than that in it. It must be somebody else's; it's to make your eyes brighter; everybody
uses it."

"That's right," Miss Pomeroy said, recognizing the
label. "You can buy it on any cosmetic counter in
America."

"It's got atropine in it," the sheriff said. "Says so on
the label. It's the only atropine in the house. And it was
in her handbag." He pointed again at Billie.

"But that's a very common drug," Miss Pomeroy said.
"You can't prove anything from that."

"I got time enough for my proof; I'm just taking this
lady in town for further questioning because Dr. Jackson

phoned out to Mrs. Munroe that the analysis showed the poison was atropine."

"He's quite right, Miss Pomeroy," the lawyer intervened. "We mustn't interfere. I suppose that leaves the rest of us free to go back to town whenever we like, sheriff?"

"I figure it does if you'll stay where I can lay my hands on you. I have your names and addresses, and I guess you know better than to try to run out on me."

"Of course we do, of course we do," the lawyer said. "None of us wants to do anything but cooperate."

"You're going to cooperate me right into a hick town jug and walk off and forget about me, aren't you?" Billie said. "All right, I've got nothing to say against it. I don't know anything about it, and you know I don't. I'll take the rap for you now because I can't help myself, but when I get hold of my lawyer and bring my case into court you'll wish you'd never been born, Mr. Gerald Winterbottom."

"Please be reasonable, Miss La Verne," he said. "If I could benefit you in any way by staying here I should be glad to do so, but I can't. You're not arrested; you're merely held for questioning. You should be treated with the utmost courtesy, and if you aren't, tell your lawyer about it and he can make trouble for these gentlemen. I can't possibly represent you, you know, when I'm already representing Mr. Osgood, but I shall be very happy to take any message you like to your lawyer in the city."

Billie's reply to this offer was pointed and unprintable. Winterbottom flushed angrily and cast Miss Pomeroy a glance that said as plainly as words "you see?" Miss Pomeroy flushed too, although in her work as a psychiatric nurse she was not unacquainted with obscenity and she did not feel as certain as Mr. Winterbottom that it necessarily indicated a guilty knowledge of murder.

"You'll wake Mr. Osgood," she said, and Billie at once moved farther from the study door with a muttered apology.

"I shall go back to town by the next train," the lawyer said. "You don't have the schedule with you by any chance?"

The sheriff didn't.

"It's no matter; I can go down to the Munroes' and phone. I have business in town and must be back at once. I shall be glad to escort any of you ladies who cares to return with me."

"Mr. Osgood can't be moved tonight, and I can't leave him," Miss Pomeroy said. "Perhaps Miss Waterhouse or Mrs. Osgood will take advantage of your offer."

"I won't leave my boy," the older woman said positively.

"I'll stay too." Kay spoke firmly and without hesitation.

"You're expected back at your work tomorrow," Mrs. Osgood pointed out.

"I'll telephone from the Munroes' too and have them keep my substitute another day."

"There's no need for you to stay. Miss Pomeroy and I can do everything necessary."

"I'm staying," Kay said.

"May I suggest, ladies," the lawyer intervened, "that we're all tired and overstrained? We really ought to try to avoid any discussion at this time."

Billie opened her mouth to answer him, and Miss Pomeroy spoke hastily. "If you really want to escort someone into town, I expect you ought to take Nora. I'm sure she's expected back at her job, and it's hardly fair of us to keep her here—"

"I'll stay here as long as the rest of you do," Nora said. "If I lose my job I can get another."

"Then it really looks as if you'll have to go back to town alone, Mr. Winterbottom," Miss Pomeroy said.

"Are you ladies afraid to stay here without a man?" the sheriff inquired.

"Dear me, I hadn't thought of that." Winterbottom had the grace to blush. "Of course it will be the same party that was here last night, but then Mr. Osgood wasn't ill— of course if you ladies desire me to stay—"

"Not in the least." Miss Pomeroy addressed the sheriff rather than the lawyer.

"I suppose I can go upstairs and fix my face?" Billie asked sullenly.

The sheriff nodded to the deputy, who turned without a word and followed her upstairs.

"Don't you want to talk to me?" Miss Pomeroy asked him when they were gone. He shook his heavy head and grinned at her.

"The doctor told me what you said," he answered. "He figured nobody'd get anything out of you that you didn't want to let them."

"I'm certainly anxious to see justice done in this case, and I'd do anything I could to help straighten it out. I really think you have the wrong person, sheriff. Of course I can see that Miss La Verne's background might make her seem the most likely person in this house if you were looking for a criminal, but I don't think she'd have poisoned Mr. Osgood. And she was nowhere near him all day. I remember especially at lunch—she was across the table and at the opposite end. And she was the last one into the dining room. There wasn't any possible way she could have slipped anything into Mr. Osgood's food or drink. And she gave me splendid help afterwards when I was taking care of him; a nurse couldn't have done it better."

"That don't prove anything except that she's smart," the sheriff said. "Nobody says she did it, but atropine did it and she had atropine. That's two and two enough to start me lookin' for four. If you change your mind and decide you want a man in the house tonight you call me up at the jail and I'll send you somebody."

He went out to the car without further farewell, and Winterbottom said: "You shouldn't try to argue with a man like that, Miss Pomeroy; it never does any good." This was exactly the advice she had been aching to give him, which made it none the more palatable coming from him.

"It's an awfully little thing to go on," she said. "I'll bet I could search any house in this town and find at least one bottle of that stuff or something else of about the same composition. The only wonder is to me that he didn't find any here except the one in Billie's things. It's almost as common a cosmetic as cold cream."

"He had his knife in Billie before he started looking for the poison," the lawyer said. "Osgood was paying some attention to his daughter, and he's sore as a boil because Billie claims he was a married man. He had his mind made up she was an impostor before he knew anything at all about the case. And the chances are that she is, too, you know. You really shouldn't get too much wrought up over the business, Miss Pomeroy; I doubt if it will be the first time she's seen the inside of a jail. I never wanted her brought here in the first place."

"Nevertheless you were pretty chummy with her when you both got here this morning," Miss Pomeroy thought, but she had the tact to keep silent.

Billie came back down the stairs.

"Forgive us," Kay said impulsively, stepping forward as she reached the bottom of the flight. "This is all our fault. It's a dreadful thing we've done to you. Please forgive us."

"You get me out of jail before you start talking about forgiveness," Billie said. "I'm not sore at anybody except that Winterbottom and these hicks, and believe me they'd better keep out of my way when I'm outta this."

She swept regally out toward the car, a tragedy queen with the sad-faced little deputy as her entourage, and Miss Pomeroy went back to her patient. Half an hour later the taxi came for Gerald Winterbottom, and the four women were left alone with the invalid to face the approaching night. Not for the first time Miss Pomeroy considered the problem of where Frank Osgood would sleep. She could have asked the doctor or the lawyer or the sheriff and his deputy to move him upstairs to a more comfortable bed, but she hadn't felt like asking favors of any of them, and now she was going to have to spend the night in the study. It would be unthinkable to go upstairs and leave the invalid alone, and yet even Miss Pomeroy's excellent nerves felt a little thrill of uneasiness at the prospect of spending the night in the room with the sounds which had disturbed her slumbers the night before. The thrill was on the patient's account, she told herself. It certainly wouldn't be good for a man to be waked up by mysterious sounds in the night after he had been through what Frank Osgood had been through today. But it was too late now to do anything, unless she wanted to ask Mr. Munroe to come up and help her move the invalid.

Nora was making comfortable, familiar noises in the dining room. The clatter of dishes and silverware, the odor of roasting meat were friendly and reassuring as the cold, hostile shadows lengthened in the study and the sick man breathed thickly and now and again moaned in his sleep. Across the hall the two women in the living room were so silent that Miss Pomeroy could hear the click of Mrs. Osgood's knitting needles as well as the crackle of the logs in the fireplace. Five lonely, inimicable people in a house that none of them liked or trusted. Not one of them liked or trusted another; the five of them stood each alone against the encroaching darkness and terror.

Miss Pomeroy sat up straight and mentally shook herself. This wouldn't do at all. There was work to be done —two jobs now, and the nursing left her ample leisure to devote her mind, if not her physical energies, to the problem that had brought her here. The thing to do was review the salient features of the case, trying to eliminate everything irrelevant, and see if there weren't any overlooked clues inherent in the facts themselves.

First, then, whom could she trust of the four human beings enclosed by the walls that surrounded her? The sick man? He wouldn't be much good in an emergency, of course, but on the whole Miss Pomeroy thought that

he meant well and that he would be honest with her. In
any case this was getting the cart before the horse, for she
was here to serve the interests of Frank Osgood, not he
hers. Nora? Miss Pomeroy was inclined to like the dour
and capable servant, as she generally liked competent people who did their work. Nora complained a good deal, but
the complaint was only a sort of running commentary on
what she was doing, and that was almost always unexcep-
tionable. Why was Nora here? It didn't really seem very
probable that she liked the Osgoods, and as for her avowed
reason, she had spent all her time over the housework and
hadn't joined in the search for missing papers at all. Well
then, supposing one couldn't trust Nora, what followed?
Had she poisoned Frank Osgood with the atropine from
the bottle in Billie La Verne's bag? Putting aside all personal prejudices and regarding the problem as a purely
intellectual one, it seemed unlikely. Nora was not a woman
to half poison anyone; if she had wanted to dispose of
Frank Osgood she would have done it in a way that would
have finished him off without a doubt.

Kay? Miss Pomeroy sensed the reserve untapped beyond
the confession the girl had made that afternoon. The confession itself might or might not be true; it fitted well
enough with what Miss Pomeroy knew of the characters
of Charles Osgood and Kay Waterhouse, and with the
hints Mrs. Osgood had dropped so freely. But if it were
true had it left no deeper mark on Kay than the girl was
willing to admit? Was she a woman who could love and
hate with such facile superficiality? Was it not more likely
that Charles Osgood had been able to instil into her
something of the deviltry of his own character? Could a

woman possibly engage herself to a rabbit of a man like
Frank Osgood for no purpose but to harm him? Could
she have been Charles Osgood's tool, and from impatience
or hysteria or fear have tried to poison Frank and be done
with it instead of waiting for the slow working out of
Charles's more elaborate scheme? She was certainly an
enigma, an unknown quantity in the problem.

And Mrs. Osgood herself? One could scarcely suspect
a mother of poisoning her son, and yet the attempt had
more of the marks of her bungling, feeble hand than of
any other there. Or could the poisoning have been deliberately unsuccessful? Was it perhaps intended to warn
Frank away from his current undertaking? Or was it—Miss
Pomeroy sat up straight—could it be that Frank had somehow stumbled across his cousin's carefully planted evidence against him and disposed of it by the simple
expedient of swallowing it?

Chapter 13

It was quite dark now, and the sounds from the dining
room indicated that Nora was about ready to announce
dinner, when the lights of a car coming up the driveway
swung across the study windows. Miss Pomeroy hoped
it was the doctor coming back and not the sheriff again.
The motor was switched off; there was the sound of a
door banging and footsteps on the flagged walk, and then
someone knocked at the front door. Not the sheriff then;
he didn't wait to be let in. Nora came from the kitchen,
and Miss Pomeroy wondered whether a second visit from

the doctor boded ill for her patient. Had the analysis showed something worse than they had suspected? Nora swung the door in and blocked the opening with her body. The voice that came from the darkness was a man's, and unfamiliar. Miss Pomeroy listened as hard as she could but was unable to make out any words. After a brief parley Nora carefully shut and latched the door and stepped from the hall into the study.

"It's a man come to spend the night," she said.

"To spend the night?"

"He says the sheriff told him a bunch of women was alone out here with a sick man, and he thought someone ought to stay but he couldn't, and the doctor can't because he dassent be away from a telephone, so they asked him to come."

"But who is he?"

"Says he was a friend of Mr. Osgood's."

Miss Pomeroy hesitated. There was no sound from the room across the hall except the click of knitting needles; the responsibility of decision was obviously to be left to her.

"Bring him in here," she directed.

Nora unlatched the door again and admitted a tall, dark young man with a pleasantly saturnine expression. His quick gaze flickered about the room and took in the confusion of papers, the open, empty drawers of the filing cabinet, the seated woman, and the sick man on the couch before she had a chance to speak. For the first time since the discovery of Frank Osgood's mishap she was conscious of the untidiness of the room and remembered the purpose of their journey out here.

"I'm Adrian Perry," the man was saying in a pleasant and reassuring voice, "one of your neighbors here. Sheriff Wentworth was telling me about your troubles and thought that perhaps I could be of some assistance."

Miss Pomeroy looked at him coldly.

"Come, come now!" she said. "You're not trying to tell me that this town harbored two noted mystery novelists."

"Oh, you know my books?" He seemed inordinately pleased.

"I'm a great admirer of your books if you are Mr. Perry, but your appearing on the scene here just at this time is a little too much of a coincidence for me."

"As a matter of fact it's not a coincidence at all. Osgood bought this house because I liked the neighborhood so well. I bragged about what a fine place it was to work— very foolish of me, and I'll never do it again. So he took over my territory—if you call that a coincidence."

The pleasant voice was still pleasant, but there was an edge to it that contributed toward the convincing of Miss Pomeroy that it told the truth. It was the sort of thing Charles Osgood would have done.

"Hasn't he ever mentioned me?" the strange young man asked with a faint note of injury as well as surprise in his tone.

"None of us knew him well," Miss Pomeroy found herself explaining. "It's very kind of you to come, but really we're quite all right. If we need any help there's Mr. Munroe. I'm sure he and his wife would be glad to come up here to sleep if we'd ask them."

"But someone has to be at their house to be within reach of the telephone, haven't they?"

"Well—" how did you tell a strange and obliging young man that you didn't trust him, that you preferred to take your chances with the unknown terrors of the night rather than confide your safety to his doubtful protection?

"I really don't know anything about you," she said. "I don't want to be rude, but you know if we were to take in just anyone who came to the door and said he wanted to protect us—"

"Of course. I see your point. Would you want to telephone Dr. Jackson or Sheriff Wentworth?"

"That won't be necessary," Mrs. Osgood said from the doorway. "We're very grateful to you; it's extremely kind of you. I'm afraid Miss Pomeroy is inclined to be too cautious."

Miss Pomeroy said nothing. After all this was the Osgoods' house, and Mrs. Osgood could offer hospitality to whom she chose. It was conceivably Miss Pomeroy's business to see that they weren't all murdered in their beds, but she would have to manage it without assuming the prerogatives of a hostess.

"I have my driver's license and my social security card," Mr. Perry said—"and of course my draft registration and my sugar and gasoline ration books. I'd been about to say that I hadn't thought in advance of the need for credentials, but these days we all carry them all the time, don't we? I remember how that impressed me about Russia as a child; I read somewhere that everyone had to carry an identification card at all times, and that the police knew where every man, woman, and child in the country was every night of the world. The idea fascinated me. Times change, don't they?"

Ignoring the chit-chat Miss Pomeroy coolly held out her hand for the cards. Mr. Perry looked startled, but after an uncomfortable instant he produced them one by one from an inside pocket. She looked them over carefully and returned them one by one without comment. They tallied with the information he had given about himself.

"Miss Pomeroy!" Mrs. Osgood said. "Mr. Perry, will you please let me have your hat and coat?"

"I can go down to the Munroes' and phone about him," Kay offered.

"The cards seem to be all right," Miss Pomeroy said, "and if Mrs. Osgood is satisfied I believe we may be too. I'm very sorry if I have appeared to be rude, Mr. Perry. It's been brought home to us here today that we can't trust anyone entirely."

"We are deeply obliged for your kindness," Mrs. Osgood said. "Kay, tell Nora to set another place for dinner."

There was no denying that Mr. Perry exerted an ameliorating influence on the dinner party. Nora had secured a better than passable steak, and as she had counted on the presence of both Billie La Verne and Gerald Winterbottom, there was quite enough to go around. Adrian Perry managed to produce a steady flow of light chatter, a rather remarkable feat under the circumstances, even though none of it was particularly brilliant. Thinking back to the last meal eaten around this table Miss Pomeroy found it almost impossible to believe that it had been only six hours earlier, so much had happened during the afternoon. So far as she could observe everyone was eating and drinking quite freely, without any fear of being poisoned as Frank Osgood had been—was it at this table? Nor did the absence of the chorus girl and the lawyer appear to cast any shadow over the spirits of the other two women. Miss Pomeroy wondered what Billie was getting to eat and whether the county jail would provide a decent place for her to sleep. She ventured to say as much during a brief and discouraged pause in Mr. Perry's light badinage, and to her surprise it was Kay and not Mrs. Osgood who turned on her.

"I do wish you could stop thinking about her, Miss Pomeroy," Kay said, "especially when you're taking care of Frank. It's going to upset him awfully if he hears about her just when he's coming to; he's so horribly chivalrous. Please try to avoid mentioning her."

"But perhaps he knows something about how it happened that would help to get her out of jail."

"Miss Pomeroy, I don't see how you can talk so. If he'd known he was being poisoned would he have kept on eating or drinking whatever it was? And if he'd known it in time to give the alarm, wouldn't he have done that instead of just sitting there in the cellar suffering?"

"I really think Wentworth will be as decent to her as he possibly can, Miss Pomeroy," Perry said. "He's not a bad sort, and he knows he hasn't much of a case against her yet. He'll watch his step I promise you."

"I don't think he had any business holding anyone until he could get a statement from Mr. Osgood," Miss Pomeroy answered with gentle obstinacy. "It couldn't have done any serious harm for all of us to wait here overnight, and it would have been better than taking the poor girl to jail if she's innocent."

"Even if she doesn't know anything about the poisoning, she's definitely a gold digger, isn't she?" Perry asked.

Miss Pomeroy withered him with a glance.

"Precisely. And it is on just such assumptions that justice too often operates in this country, and that's what I'm objecting to. Do you suppose if atropine had been found in my room or Mrs. Osgood's we would have been arrested?"

"Well, but there's a certain justice in that policy too," the man argued. "It's based on a loose generalization, perhaps, but on one that's grown out of generations of human experience. People do act in character more often than not. There are exceptions, of course, but we all know that criminals are more likely to commit crimes than respectable citizens; that's why the respectable citizens make headlines when they do it. You have a man poisoned in a house with five self-respecting, self-supporting, conventional people and one who lives on the fringe and has a grudge against him besides, and practically any policeman in the world will pick on the one, even if he doesn't find poison in her handbag. Ninety-nine times out of a hundred he'll be right, too."

"But the American legal system is supposed to be based on the idea that it's more important to protect the hundredth one than to catch the other ninety-nine," Miss Pomeroy went on, "and I suppose it's because of the exceptions that there are private detectives like me to help guard against the mistakes the police make."

"I don't think the police have made a mistake this time," Mrs. Osgood said coldly.

"And I still think you ought not to discuss it in front of Frank," Miss Waterhouse added. Fnding herself hopelessly outnumbered Miss Pomeroy subsided, silenced but not convinced.

"Please don't go to any trouble whatever for me," Adrian Perry said over the demi-tasses which Nora had somehow managed to produce. "I think it would be best if I were to sleep on the couch in the study and leave the rest of you undisturbed upstairs. That way I'd be within call but not in the way."

"But Mr. Osgood's in there," Miss Pomeroy said. "I'm expecting to sit up with him."

"I'll help you get him upstairs," Perry offered. "Surely he'll be much more comfortable in a regular bed."

"I shouldn't think of moving him without doctor's orders," Miss Pomeroy answered positively.

She thought Mr. Perry looked a little dashed, but he did not argue the matter further.

"Surely, though, he's not sick enough for you to have to surrender your whole night's sleep?" he added after a brief pause.

"I can sleep sitting up," Miss Pomeroy explained. "I often have. I expect to wrap myself up well and doze most of the night."

"Couldn't you let me relieve you for a part of the time? Of course I'm not a nurse, but if you could tell me the symptoms to watch for—"

"It's out of the question," she said firmly. It was good to be on familiar ground, issuing orders with no private uncertainties. Mr. Perry, looking at Mrs. Osgood, suggested a shrug of the shoulders. Miss Pomeroy affected not to notice.

After dinner she returned to her patient; this evening

there was no pretence of games or the ordinary social amenities. Mr. Perry went into the living room with the other two ladies, where Miss Pomeroy could hear him making himself agreeable to the best of his ability. He brought in fresh logs and built up the fire, admired Mrs. Osgood's knitting, and chatted with Kay about the book she was reading, but his efforts did little to relieve the ominous sense of waiting for something to happen that hung over the house. When he gave up at last and lapsed into silence Kay suggested almost at once that they should all retire.

"It's ridiculously early," she said, "but we're all dead— we're all worn out, and tomorrow is another day."

"Not another day like this, I hope," Miss Pomeroy thought. She wondered whether they would resume the interrupted search for the hidden assets of Charles Osgood; nothing whatever had been said about the matter since Frank's attack.

Mr. Perry came to the door to inquire whether she had changed her mind about allowing him to relieve her, but he did not press her when she refused again. The extra bedroom was made up and ready, Nora reported; he might retire when he chose. Miss Pomeroy suggested that Nora herself might prefer Charles Osgood's bedroom or the one Frank had occupied on the previous night to the privacy of her own room above the garage, but Nora declined the offer with scorn.

It cost Miss Pomeroy a not inconsiderable amount of cogitation to decide which of the others to ask to sit with her patient while she went upstairs long enough to make the necessary preparations for the night. Perry she did not even consider; the Osgoods might welcome him if they chose, but in her eyes he was definitely an interloper and his good intentions not to be trusted. Kay was eager for the privilege, and it was natural enough that she should want to do something for her fiancé, but her anxiety to be alone with him was so exaggerated as to be vaguely alarming to Miss Pomeroy. The mother was certainly the obvious substitute, but without trying to explain the choice to herself Miss Pomeroy finally asked Nora to remain in the study for twenty minutes while she was upstairs. Nora consented with her customary ungraciousness, which bothered Miss Pomeroy less as she encountered it more. Nevertheless she hurried the rites of bathing as best she could with a pitcher of hot water, cleaning her teeth, brushing her hair, and conscientiously applying and removing cold cream from her petal-soft and apple-pink cheeks. The sense of impending disaster that had bothered her on the preceding evening was stronger than ever now. In vain she told herself that it was absurd, that she was foolish as a girl, that she was acting like a probationer on her first case. In spite of all she wished that she had insisted on the doctor's removing Frank Osgood to a hospital. Trouble had started from the moment they had set foot in this house, and it wouldn't end until they were well out of it.

In the morning, as soon as she decently could after it was light, she would go to the Munroes' and phone the doctor. She could tell him the atmosphere of the house was having an adverse effect on the patient without, she thought, overstepping the limits of professional accuracy. If the place weighed so on the spirits of those who were

well—even her own equable nerves—it was certain to be
bad for the sick man who hated it more than any of the
rest. In the midst of a stroke of the hairbrush her arm
hesitated. Would it be too ridiculous to put her clothes
back on and go down and phone now? It was still early;
the doctor would certainly be up, and it should be possible to send an ambulance and get the sick man to a
hospital within the hour. The face looking back at her
from the mirror in the dim, uncertain light was pale, with
hollows under the eyes accentuated by the shadows of the
room. It looked so unlike the placid, wholesome, unlined
one to which she was accustomed that Miss Pomeroy suddenly laughed out loud. This was what came of giving way
to fancies. She finished brushing her hair promptly and
efficiently, pinned it into a neat roll at the back of her head,
and put on her blue flannel bathrobe and plain, low-heeled
black slippers. So accoutred she was ready for the night and
anything it might bring forth.

She went downstairs with her flashlight and a pocket
edition of an anthology of American poetry under her arm.
When she had to spend the night sitting up with a patient, she had found that the best way to insure getting
some sleep in her uncomfortable position was to provide
herself with a book. As soon as she began to read she in-
variably fell asleep, although she could woo sleep in vain
for hours in a soft chair with nothing to occupy her mind.

She had been gone from the study for scarcely twenty
minutes all told, but when she came back into the room
her patient was awake for the first time since the vigorous
treatment following the poisoning. While she was still on
the stairs Miss Pomeroy recognized from his voice that he

was talking coherently with Nora, but silence fell abruptly as she entered the room.

"You're feeling better, Mr. Osgood?" she asked.

"I'm all right," he said. "It was that damned Pernod of Charles's."

Miss Pomeroy did not follow up the lead. It was not her place to question the patient, nor did she believe it could profitably be done tonight. Besides, she was not entirely certain that he was not wandering mentally. Could it be that he thought Charles was still alive?

"Thank you, Nora," she said. "We'll be all right for the night now."

Nora volunteered no explanation of what they had been discussing just before Miss Pomeroy came in, and Miss Pomeroy asked none. Nor did the patient show any curiosity as to where he was or why Miss Pomeroy was obviously preparing to spend the night in the room with him. He lay with his eyes wide open and watched her as she arranged her pitcher of water, her book, and her flashlight on a table conveniently placed at her right elbow and settled herself in an easy chair for the long vigil. When she had finished he spoke abruptly but listlessly.

"Am I dying?"

He asked the question as if the answer were a matter of complete indifference to him, but Miss Pomeroy answered with the conventional heartiness and good cheer appropriate to such questions from the sick.

"Mercy, no!" she said. "You'll probably be up and around tomorrow."

He smiled the shadow of a smile.

"Not I," he answered. "This is the night. Charles is coming back."

Miss Pomeroy didn't answer. Nothing was worse for a man in Frank's state than to argue with him.

"This is what Charles planned," the sick man said. "I was looking for a different sort of a trap, and I walked right into the one he laid for me. He'll be back tonight to take his revenge."

"I'll be right here with you all night, Mr. Osgood," she said. "I won't let him come back."

She had made such promises to her patients hundreds of times in her life, but never before had she felt the flesh on her back crawl as she spoke. Frank Osgood did not answer her; from the expression on his face she could not tell whether or not her words had penetrated to his consciousness.

The back door slammed as Nora went out to her room. From upstairs came the sounds of a household preparing for bed—water running, footsteps moving about, doors opening and shutting. Miss Pomeroy felt herself growing tense as she listened for the creaking of bedsprings that should put a period to all the activity. When it came at last she drew a long breath and relaxed for the vigil ahead. She did not expect to sleep.

Chapter 14

MISS POMEROY did not expect to sleep, but the day had been longer and harder than she realized. She leaned back in her chair and relaxed into a comfortable doze in which she remained conscious of the sleeping man's breathing and of the flickering light on the floor from the fireplace across the hall, but entirely oblivious of the passage of time or the discomforts of her position. When she woke to full consciousness next she was stiff and cold. Her watch said it was after midnight. Frank Osgood was sleeping quietly; his breathing was normal and when she slipped silently to his side and found his pulse regular and even she did not disturb him to take his temperature. Most of the unwelcome attentions nurses usually insist on inflicting upon their patients during the night sprang, she thought, from an unacknowledged jealousy on the nurse's part of the patient's comfortable sleep.

And now temptation presented itself to Miss Pomeroy in a particularly virulent form. Immediately above her head was a comfortable bedroom with a soft and well-blanketed bed. It was scarcely possible to doubt any longer that Frank Osgood had cast off all the effects of the poison; the doctor had not been even sufficiently concerned to make a second visit. Tomorrow the patient would in all probability get up and go home, and on the following day he would be conducting his normal business. Why, then, should Miss Pomeroy sacrifice another night of much needed sleep? Supposing she did go to bed, she would be sure to sleep lightly; her training made that certain. If Frank Osgood were to waken and need her attention she could hear him as well from upstairs as from here. The doctor hadn't even asked her to sit up all night; it had been altogether her own conscientious decision.

As a nurse she would be entirely justified in going to bed, she decided. As a detective she was not quite so sure.

But even on that field she had provided pretty thoroughly against trouble. Everyone in the house had gone to sleep in the belief that she intended to spend the night sitting up in the study, and that was almost as much protection as she could give by actually remaining there. Moreover, it hadn't taken much of a disturbance in the study to awaken her on the previous night, and tonight certainly it would take even less. Miss Pomeroy knew perfectly well that all of her arguments were specious; she was cold, stiff, and sleepy, and therefore she wanted to go to bed. She could save a larger share of self-respect by admitting it to herself than by trying to justify the action. She would go to bed, and she would be thoroughly ashamed of herself tomorrow; having struck this bargain with her conscience she tiptoed to the door with her watch and flashlight, leaving the blanket and the water pitcher to indicate that she had only stepped out of the room for a moment. She left the door slightly ajar to make more certain that she would hear any sound from within the room, and tiptoed guiltily up the darkened stairs.

The bed was cold, and as she climbed into it, it squeaked and creaked as if determined to shout her guilty secret to the sleeping household. She lay rigid, encased between icy sheets, listening to discover whether she had disturbed the sick man. There was no sound from below. She strained her ears for the faintest whisper of sound, and after a time was conscious of the fact that she was still straining although the bed was coming to be faintly warm. Perversely she was much wider awake than she had been in the chair downstairs. She made herself relax one set of muscles at a time, beginning with her toes, but by the time she had reached the neck her feet were rigid again. She watched the pattern of the moonlight on the floor and half-heartedly counted a few sheep. They all had sad, reproachful faces resembling Frank Osgood's, and they "baa'd" at her in almost human bleating tones. When number twenty-seven bleated: "Charles is coming back tonight," she realized that her conscience had belatedly won the battle. With a sigh she sat up in the bed, now comfortably warm, and noted with grim irony that she began immediately to feel drowsy. Whatever she may have been, however, Miss Pomeroy was not wishy-washy. Her good angel was victor and had no intention of permitting the argument to be reopened. Miss Pomeroy put on her slippers and her robe and went back downstairs, making no particular effort to be quiet.

Three quarters of the way down she stopped short. The door to the study was closed! She was absolutely certain she had not slept an instant; she would have sworn it was impossible for anyone to close the door without her hearing the click of the latch. She moved forward as swiftly and silently as she could, seized the doorknob, and pushed as she turned it. The knob turned in her hand but the door did not open. It was locked from inside. She fought down panic that struck her like a bucketful of cold water and left her shivering and ineffectual. Should she knock, scream, rouse the rest of the household, go for Nora? Within the room the silence was deathly, and the comparison shook her anew. She rattled the knob and called out: "Mr. Osgood, are you all right?"

There was no answer.

She called again, urgently but still softly, rattling the

knob continually. It pleased her to realize that her voice was as firm as ever in her life.

"Let me in, whoever you are," she said. "I must be with Mr. Osgood."

The silence continued undisturbed. She looked about the hall wildly. The table with a card tray and a dead telephone instrument on it was too flimsy; it would splinter against the door without making any impression on it. The poker in the living room would be better. She had never tried to batter down a door, and she hadn't much idea as to how to go about it, but in the movies it looked fairly easy. She started across the hall to get the poker from its place with the other fireplace tools, and her eye fell on the barred front door. Instantly a better plan suggested itself to her. The french window opening onto the front lawn would be much easier to break through than a door. Thought followed action immediately; this time she would not allow the intruder to escape while she fiddled around with irrelevant matters. She unbarred and opened the front door and was out into the frosty October night before she had time for a second thought. She was hardly conscious of the bite of the cold ground through her thin slippers. As she ran she picked up a stone from beneath the shrubbery. She remembered exactly where the latch was placed inside the french window; it was the work of a moment to smash the pane of glass closest to it and reach her hand in, with care for the jagged glass, to turn the latch.

As she groped for it a hand seized hers in an iron clutch.

Miss Pomeroy stood still on the frosty ground. There was no point in trying to wrest her hand away from the one that held it. She was not conscious of terror. "This is what comes of going to bed when you should be sitting up with a patient," was what she thought.

"Stand still, you old fool," a masculine voice said. "You'll cut your jugular vein."

The marauder, then, was someone who didn't know his anatomy.

"I'll turn loose your hand and let you in," the voice went on, "if you'll promise to be careful getting it out and not try any more fool stunts. Do you think I want to be responsible for killing you?"

"I don't know," she said reasonably. "Don't you?"

For answer the hand gripped her wrist even more tightly. "Watch out," the voice said. She felt the latch being turned, and the window in which she was impaled drifted slightly outward; its fellow swung wide open, and then her wrist was tenderly relinquished.

"Come in," the voice said, "or will you go around to the door like a sensible woman?"

Miss Pomeroy did not deign to answer, but clambered stiffly over the window sill and into the study. Adrian Perry stood just inside the window. She did not stop to observe whether or not he was armed, but hurried over to the couch. The sick man still slept undisturbed. She felt his pulse quickly and quietly, timed his respiration, and then turned to the other man.

"You haven't done him any harm?" There was more surprise than accusation in her tone.

"Of course I haven't done him any harm, unless you've scared him to death, making all that noise. I suppose I should beg your pardon for calling you an old fool, but really you gave me a terrible turn."

This didn't seem quite the tone a criminal caught in the act should take, and Miss Pomeroy was somewhat at a loss as to how she should answer. She decided to ignore the apology and stick to the subject in hand.

"What are you doing here?"

"I suppose I'll have to tell you now, though it's really none of your business. Sit down and be as comfortable as you can. It's going to be infernally cold in here with that window broken."

"What did you mean by locking me out of the room where my patient was?" Miss Pomeroy flashed back, tired of being on the defensive when she was altogether in the right—except of course in having gone to bed when she should have sat up.

"I'd have let you in the minute he showed signs of needing you. I tried to get you to put him to bed somewhere where I wouldn't have to disturb him."

The cool effrontery of this attitude took Miss Pomeroy's breath away completely. She sat down and stared at Adrian Perry without any reply. She noted now for the first time that he was completely dressed; he had made no preparations for bed whatsoever. He carried a better flashlight than Miss Pomeroy's own, and a brief case that had not been there when she went upstairs leaned against Charles Osgood's desk. The confusion of papers in the room was such that it was not easy to tell at once which ones had been disturbed, but there was a pile on the desk that had also not been there earlier in the evening. There was no sign of a gun.

"If I assure you that the matter that brings me here is

none of your business, will you let me go back to bed in
peace?" he asked.

"I don't see how I can stop you."

"And promise not to tell anyone I was here?"

"Certainly not. I shall take the first opportunity in the
morning to notify the sheriff as well as the doctor. I have
only your word for it that you haven't harmed the patient,
and your word hasn't counted for much so far."

"Ouch," he said. "You believe in straight talk, don't
you, Miss P.?"

She did not answer.

"All right," he said, "I'll tell you all about it, and then
I suppose you'll notify the sheriff anyway."

"I am not asking for your confidence," she reminded
him.

"Suppose you'd come in here and found a real desperado
with a gun?" he inquired curiously. "What would you have
done with him?"

"I should have had to allow circumstances to guide me."

Mr. Perry laughed. "I'd enjoy putting you in my next
book," he said, "but nobody would believe you. All right,
here's my story, and, believe it or not, one reason for my
reluctance to tell it to you is that it proves your client's
cousin was a louse."

"I don't get emotionally attached to the cousins of my
clients," Miss Pomeroy said primly. She had been tempted
to say: "I know it," but after all she didn't know very
much about Adrian Perry yet, and none of what she did
know was good. It certainly wouldn't be wise to be indis-
creet with him.

"Very well," he said. "I'm here to secure the return of

something that belongs to me."

"I believe there are legitimate channels for that," she replied. "Had you notified Mr. Winterbottom or Mr. Osgood that there was some of your property here? We could have been looking for it along with the other things we were searching for."

"Will you please let me tell you this in my own way?" he asked violently. "If you interrupt again I shall go directly back to bed and take the consequences."

Miss Pomeroy, whose curiosity was as highly developed as that of any member of her sex, remained silent.

The man also was silent briefly, obviously searching for words. They were a strange pair in the cold moonlight, shivering in the draft from the broken window, looking defiantly at each other from easy chairs some three feet apart, and conversing in tones which remained just above a whisper even when they grew strained or angry.

"Charles Osgood was a plagiarist," the man said. "Now wait a minute; I know all the things that can be said in his defense, but in this case they don't apply. Certainly it's possible for two men to get the same idea at about the same time; certainly it's true that all mystery plots are essentially the same anyway and vary only in their twists; certainly it's true that every good idea is in the public domain by this time. Nevertheless the guy was a plain, unadulterated thief, and if you weren't so obviously a lady, Miss Pomeroy, I could make my adjectives a good deal stronger."

It occurred to Miss Pomeroy that for a man caught at midnight in his rival's study this was a rather remarkable example of the pot calling the kettle black, but she said nothing, not wanting to interrupt the flow of the narrative.

"I never knew Osgood until a couple of years ago," the pot went on. "Then I ran into him at a literary tea, and he rather played up to me—seemed to want to cultivate me. I dare say I was flattered. The first thing I knew he'd bought a farm here in my neighborhood—not that I have a monopoly on this part of Connecticut, of course; plenty of other people own farms around here, but it did seem a bit thick. Of course we ran into each other all the more then, and naturally we talked shop some. About a year ago I told him about a plot I was working on—not in detail, you understand, just sketched in the idea in casual conversation. I was sorry as soon as I'd done it, but not because I distrusted him; it's just that it's always bad luck to talk about a thing before you've finished it. I had the devil's own time with that book. But I got it done at last and shipped off; the publishers liked it, and while it was in the process of manufacture, damned if Osgood didn't come out with the plot!"

"No!" Miss Pomeroy did not quite know why she should have said that when the end of the story had been obvious well in advance, but some sort of exclamation seemed to be called for, and "no!" was adequately brief and pointed.

He laughed mirthlessly. "You haven't heard anything yet. I was pretty much upset when I read it, as you can imagine. Mine was due to be published in six weeks. I—at first I actually gave the guy the benefit of the doubt and thought it might be a terrible mistake. It had been a casual conversation, you know; I thought perhaps the thing had just sunk into his mind and he'd really forgotten where it was he'd picked it up. I went up to town and saw my publishers, and they decided to go ahead. Hardly any reviewers noticed the similarity, and it looked as if it were going to blow over with nothing worse than the loss of a few sales of my book. And then—", he paused at this most annoying moment, and Miss Pomeroy leaned forward in her chair for what should come next. Perry laughed again.

"Then damned if he didn't have the nerve to sue me for plagiarism."

Miss Pomeroy heard something like a chuckle from the couch where the sick man was sleeping. She hurried over to his side, but it must have been her imagination for he had only stirred in his sleep.

"But how could he?" she asked then with a note of awe in her voice.

"Don't ask me that. He did. Of course he had the advantage in that his book had appeared first. I came over here and tackled him, and he had the unrivalled gall to admit the whole thing. He said a schoolboy should have had better sense than to give away a valuable property like that idea of mine and that he intended to teach me a lesson. He wouldn't be specific, of course, but he indicated that he had notes and synopses dated to prove that he had started work on his book before I had. I don't know why a judge should believe the date he chose to put on a bunch of notes, of course; he could write any one he chose. But it sounded as if he could make something of a case. He had me worried. The money involved wouldn't be negligible for me, and in addition to that it would wash me up forever if he'd gotten a judgment against me."

"But he's dead," Miss Pomeroy said. "He can't do it now."

"But I haven't been able to find out whether his lawyers or his publishers plan to go on with the suit. It had gone far enough to be out of his hands, you see. He intended to accuse me of rifling his study, and when I got to worrying over the thing it struck me I might as well be hung for a sheep as a lamb; if I came over here and actually *did* rifle the study and take away all the manuscript and notes I could find for his last book I couldn't be in a worse position than I already was, and I might be in a considerably better."

Miss Pomeroy thought that over.

"But why choose a night when the house was occupied?" she asked.

"I'd been fiddling around with the idea, doubting if I'd ever get up courage actually to carry it out when I found you people were coming out here looking for something— a lawyer and the heir and a bunch of assorted people. Maybe it was foolish, but I jumped to the conclusion that what you wanted was evidence against me and that I'd have to hurry up if I wanted to get it first."

"And so you came last night?"

"And would probably have found what I wanted and been done with the matter if it hadn't been for you."

"But how did you get out?"

"That french window you came in. If you pull it just right behind you the latch falls back into place. I learned the trick when Charles and I were pals."

"But if you and he were pals why didn't Nora know you?"

"I never used to see the servants when I came here. He'd open the door to me himself, and he never asked me to stay for a meal. I don't know whether he was up to something or just didn't like me well enough."

Miss Pomeroy drew a deep breath and looked at the disarray of papers. "Did you find what you want?"

"I have some manuscript," he said. "There's no way of telling whether it's all that I want. The evidence he's manufactured against me may be in the hands of his publishers or his lawyers for all I know. Well, now you've caught me red-handed, what do you want me to do with the loot?"

He held out a fairly bulky fistful of dejected looking manuscript.

"Keep it," she said without hesitation.

"And what are you going to tell the sheriff?"

"Nothing. As far as he's concerned I sat here all night, as I should have done, and no one came in. You'll have to think up a story to account for that windowpane though."

"Gosh," he said, "that's mighty white of you, Miss Pomeroy."

"Go on to bed where you belong," she said wearily.

Chapter 15

WITH the windowpane broken it was bitterly cold in the study. Miss Pomeroy made another trip upstairs for an extra blanket for the patient. When she returned he was sitting dizzily on the edge of the couch.

"Here, here!" she said with unaccustomed sharpness, "what are you doing?"

"What are you doing?" he countered.

"Taking care of you. The doctor thought you were too ill to be moved tonight."

"What's the matter with me?"

"No one knows exactly. Don't you?"

He lifted his head from his hands where it had been resting, his elbows upon his knees, and looked at her sharply.

"How should I?"

"Miss Waterhouse found you acting very peculiarly in the wine cellar and jumped to the conclusion that you had been poisoned. We cleaned out your stomach at once, and the doctor thinks you are on the road to recovery. He's waiting for your own statement about what happened."

"It must have been the Pernod," he said, rubbing his forehead wearily.

"That's what you said before," she answered. "Lie down now and let me cover you. You mustn't get chilled."

He submitted to her ministrations without protest, the puzzled frown still creasing his forehead.

"You drank some Pernod in the wine cellar?" she ventured to go on with the subject when she had made him comfortable. "Have you ever had any before? Do you suppose you might have some special sensitivity to it?"

"No, it wasn't that. I've had some before—some of Charles's own supply, too. He's the only person I know who drinks it—drank it. He's had the devil's own time getting it lately, too. It was all imported, you know. As far as Charles was concerned all Europe could have starved, but when the war started interfering with his supply of Pernod he got really worked up."

"Your mother and Miss Waterhouse said you never drink."

He shook his head impatiently. "They know almost everything about me, between them, but I still have a few secrets."

"Did you leave any in the bottle?" Miss Pomeroy asked, wondering what the sheriff had found.

"I don't think so," he said. "I'm a little vague about it all."

"Well, whatever it was, you're getting well," she consoled him. "So you needn't worry any more."

"I feel a little rocky," he admitted, "but not sick enough to keep you sitting there. Go on to bed."

Miss Pomeroy smiled and shook her head. "I tried that once," she said, "and I couldn't sleep. Bad conscience. I may as well stay here now."

"If you do you'll keep me awake with a bad conscience."

"Better yours than mine," she answered lightly. "Go on to sleep. After all, you're paying me."

"I can't sleep," he said fretfully. "If you insist on staying, we might as well talk."

"Very well," she agreed. "I'm willing. What about?"

"I'm sorry I dragged you into all this," he said. "It was absurd of me. Just a childish attack of nerves. Do you know that so far I've done just exactly what Charles must have foreseen all along? He had the most damnable understanding of human nature."

"He couldn't have known you'd come to me," she argued.

The sick man laughed. "That's right. I do believe you'd have been entirely outside Charles's ken, Miss Pomeroy."

Miss Pomeroy was puzzled and on the verge of being hurt. This was almost exactly what Adrian Perry had said. What was there about her that was so out of the way? But she kept her mind, nevertheless, to Frank's problem, with the theory she had worked out earlier in the evening foremost.

"I don't see how you can say that he could have foreseen your hiring a detective and coming out here to his house," she argued. "Perhaps I'm prejudiced because I'm a detective, but it seems to me that was a very sensible thing to do. Whatever evidence turns up now you have my testimony that you expected it before it turned up."

"But don't you see how that cuts both ways?" he asked impatiently. "If I had killed him and knew that I had left some damning evidence against myself where I couldn't destroy it, I might have been clever enough to figure that going to a private detective with a story like the one I told you would be my best defense. The police are bound to think I was that clever. Charles had it all worked out, like a chess game."

"Do you have it all worked out now?" she asked.

He was silent for a moment. At last he said in a subdued tone: "Yes, I think I do."

"The drink that poisoned you was the same that had poisoned him?"

"Doesn't it seem reasonable?"

"And you found the evidence against you? But why didn't you just destroy it? Why—if you'll pardon my asking—did you have to drink it?"

He laughed again. "If I'd just destroyed it I'd never have been sure. By drinking it I made certain."

"But, good heavens, Mr. Osgood, at what a fearful risk! And not just to yourself! Think of the people who might have been accused of your murder!"

It was on the tip of her tongue to tell him then about Billie, but she decided it would be better to let him have his night's rest if that were possible. They couldn't get Billie out of jail before morning now anyway.

"But now I know," he said.

"And a lot of good that would have done if you'd died! How could you be so sure you'd pull through?"

"I wasn't sure I'd pull through. I didn't much care. Charles has done that to me."

"But what was the evidence?"

"There's a case of Pernod down there with the label still on it. It came by express, and it was addressed in my handwriting."

Miss Pomeroy sat very still in the cold room and thought that through. Had the sheriff found that case, and if so had he noticed the address? He certainly had taken nothing as large as a case of bottles away from the house. But a single empty bottle? Why, oh, why hadn't she had the sense to search the wine cellar before the sheriff did? Of course she had been bewildered in that first hour, and it hadn't occurred to her that the sheriff would turn into an enemy instead of a friend, but she would be in so much better a position now if she could only know exactly what the sheriff had found down there and what he had made of it.

"I have no right to scold you at least until you're well,

Mr. Osgood," she said at last, "but in my opinion what you did wasn't so very far from attempted suicide. I certainly can't go on with the investigation you've asked me to make unless you're willing to promise me not to make such an attempt again."

"I can't promise anything," he answered querulously. "I agree with you that the investigation should be dropped. Let's wait until morning to talk about it, shall we?"

"Of course," she said, and settled herself as comfortably as she could in the chair. But even before Frank Osgood fell asleep she knew that as soon as his breathing was regular she was going to leave him again. She was no longer afraid of Adrian Perry; Osgood himself was obviously on the road to recovery, and there was no better time than the silent middle of the night to remedy her carelessness in having failed to inspect the wine cellar.

It was a long time before the breathing lengthened and steadied; Miss Pomeroy felt her own head nodding and her lids dropping over her eyes more than once before a faint snore assured her that the patient was unconscious. Even then she did not leave at once; she did not want Frank Osgood waking up and asking her where she was going. She sat still until she was stiff with cold; the creeping paralysis from her toes had reached her knees before she ventured on a sharp movement that might be expected to disturb a light sleeper. There was no change in the smooth rhythm of Osgood's respiration. She stood up, not cautiously, flashed on her light, and moved about the room. It was rather foolish to bother with such tests; if Osgood had slept through her encounter with Perry he might certainly be expected to sleep through anything else

that might occur that night. When at last she had convinced herself that he was sleeping soundly again she
stepped quietly into the corridor and back through it to
the dining room, flashing her light before her. The odor
of the sheriff's cigars still lingered from the afternoon. She
wrinkled her nostrils in distaste and went on into the spotless white kitchen. The door to the cellar was locked. She
repressed an exclamation of annoyance and looked about
her. A key hung on a nail above the sink. She took it down
and fitted it into the keyhole, and it turned without a
squeak. With her hand on the knob of the door, she hesitated. The locking of this door might mean that the outside entrance to the cellar was left unlocked, and by going
down she would perhaps offer a means of ingress to another
marauder. But no, Nora would certainly have locked the
outside cellar door after all that had happened, if not before. And if she waited until morning she would have no
opportunity of investigating the cellar uninterrupted.

She opened the door, turned her flashlight down the
stairs, and began to descend. The cellar was even colder
than the cold house she was quitting. The chill struck
through her heavy robe and made her shudder involuntarily. The silence of the cellar, too, was different from the
silence of the house; here there were no slight creakings
and groanings and cracklings of fire and wood settling to
relieve it. The cellar was hushed with the silence of a tomb.
Miss Pomeroy slightly hastened her firm pace.

It was an admirably kept cellar, clean, dustless, with the
screens and the out-of-season furniture neatly covered and
tagged. An open door gave a glimpse of a well equipped
laundry room; ahead she caught the gleam of chromium

in the game room, unused since she had been in the house. She turned to the right, into the room where she had found Frank Osgood, and flashed her light along the racks of bottles lying neatly on their sides.

It was the cellar of a connoisseur; the selection was not large, but even without any special knowledge of the subject Miss Pomeroy could see that each kind of bottle was stored in its own particular way. Every section was neatly labelled in a meticulous hand.

The stool on which Frank Osgood had been sitting was pushed back into a corner. There was no sign of an empty bottle or a glass. She flashed the light very carefully all around the room to make certain on this point; then she turned it toward the ranks of bottles and read their labels and descriptions. Everything appeared to be in place and undisturbed. Dust was thick on many of the bottles rather to her surprise; everything else in this cellar was so clean. There were three shelves stacked with bottles of Pernod standing upright. On a lower shelf, by itself, stood an opened case. She moved over closer and flashed her light on the label. She did not remember ever having noticed Frank Osgood's handwriting, but she could well believe that this represented it. It was neat and precise. It bore a distinct resemblance to the hand that had labelled the wine bins, but a moderately attentive examination showed readily that it was not the same. The sheriff, then, hadn't recognized this as evidence and commandeered it.

She flashed the light into the case. Plainly it had held a dozen bottles, and there were ten in it now, all unopened. She pulled one out and held it up, turning it around and around and flashing the light on it. The seal showed no signs of having been tampered with. She tried the other bottles; all of them seemed to be as they had come from the maker. And there was no empty or half empty bottle anywhere. Well, undoubtedly that would have been too much to hope for. She sighed and started to put the bottle she was holding back in the case. Then she hesitated. The sheriff had taken the evidence he wanted; was there any reason she might not do the same with what he had left? She was an accredited investigator on this case, and the content of this bottle of Pernod had certainly become a matter of vital importance. Of course there was the possibility that the sheriff would come back in the morning for the rest of that case. If he did would he know how many bottles it ought to contain? Even at the worst, though, she could simply hand back her bottle and explain why she had abstracted it. And supposing he didn't come for the case, or even that he didn't miss one bottle, she would have acquired some valuable evidence. Miss Pomeroy tucked the bottle under her bathrobe and started back upstairs.

She mounted the steps firmly and without haste; the feel of the darkness pressing against her back was a challenge to her dignity, and she would not hurry. She had closed the cellar door and locked it and hung the key on its nail before she noticed the smell of smoke. The fireplace had been drawing perfectly all day; it was odd, she thought. Then she heard the crackle of flame, and terror this time lent wings to her feet. She was down the hall before the fear was fully formulated in her mind, and had flung her full weight against the closed door of the study. It gave at her touch, and because she had flung herself against it with such force she fell into a room full of flame and smoke. She slammed the door shut behind her, remembering what a draft could do for such a fire, and ran across to the couch before she thought of trying to extinguish the blaze. Frank Osgood still slept. She shook him and dragged him awake and across the room, choking and gasping as she did. At the door she hesitated momentarily. Could she risk opening it again? But a glance across the room to the window, beyond what looked like an acre of blazing rug decided her on that point. She pulled the door quickly open, shoved her patient through it, and pulled it to behind her. So far the fire was confined to the study. She paused long enough to shout "fire" at the top of her sturdy lungs, and then lugged the sick man across the hall and dropped him into an easy chair in the living room. He was wide awake now and hard to control.

"I'll have to get Kay," he said, struggling to rise to his feet.

"I'll wake them all," Miss Pomeroy promised grimly. "Sit still. You'll only make more trouble if you interfere."

She returned to the foot of the stairs and shouted "fire" again lustily. She could go up and waken them, but she wanted time to get back into the study and remove the bottle of Pernod if she were unable to put out the fire. An unexplained bottle in the ashes would be a complication with which she didn't feel capable of dealing.

Perry came into the hall first, and she called: "The study's on fire; wake the women," and then to Osgood: "Do you know where there's an extinguisher?"

"Landing of the cellar stairs," he answered.

She ran back through the kitchen, cursed herself for her carefulness in locking the door, got down the key, unlocked it, and looked into the blackness of the cellar. Somewhere, in the confusion, she had dropped her flashlight. She plunged grimly into the darkness, trusting to her sense of direction and the fresh memory of traversing these same stairs. She lost a horrible amount of time groping on the landing; just as she had determined that she must go back for a light her hands encountered the firm, rounded, metallic contour of the extinguisher. Then she lost more time finding, in the dark, how to get it off of its hook. When she reached the hall again a tongue of flame was licking beneath the door of the study. Adrian Perry took the extinguisher competently from her hands. She was grateful even in the midst of her bitter anger. What a reckless young man he was to be the first to answer her call, to have the effrontery to pretend he was helping put out the fire he had set! Perhaps it argued a certain virtue in him, though; if he had been a really hardened criminal he would have pretended to sleep through it all. And no doubt he really wanted to put out the fire now that all the incriminating papers were burned.

"I'll get Nora," Miss Pomeroy said, and turned away, leaving him to deal with the fire as he might.

"Closest water's in the kitchen," she said in passing to Mrs. Osgood, who stood on the bottom step of the stairs wringing her hands. As she passed through that room she turned both taps on full in the hope that the sound might remind the hysterical women that they could help. Unlocking the back door delayed her for another minute; then she ran through the covered passageway to the servants' quarters above the garage. Flame would spread through here as through a well-laid nest of logs.

Nora woke quickly when Miss Pomeroy pounded on her door. "What is it?" she called. Her voice now, when she was suddenly awakened from sleep, sounded just as it did in the daytime, querulous and aggrieved.

"The study's on fire," Miss Pomeroy said. "We're afraid for the house. You'd better dress." Then she went back in to help Adrian Perry put out the fire. She stopped in the kitchen this time for a bucketful of water, but when she reached the study the flames were already under control. The room was a mess, sodden, charred, and full of smoke, but the damage had not been very considerable. The rug and the drapes were gone; the desk was scarred, but beyond that nothing had been destroyed except papers —the papers that Adrian Perry feared.

"I'm going home this minute," Mrs. Osgood was sobbing. "I shan't stay in this house another hour to be roasted alive or poisoned."

"Where's Kay?" Miss Pomeroy missed her for the first time.

"Gone down to the Munroes' to phone for the fire department."

Fire department—that meant that the sheriff and his deputy would be back among them very shortly. He certainly wasn't going to overlook a fire following so closely upon a poisoning. The bottle of Pernod lay plainly visible on the drenched bed. Miss Pomeroy walked over and picked it up.

"What's that?" Mrs. Osgood demanded.

"Something of mine," she answered calmly. She caught

Adrian Perry's eye as she spoke, and the young man was —yes, undeniably—grinning at her. Perhaps he was a more hardened criminal than she thought. Miss Pomeroy felt worse about his crime than about all the damage the fire had done. She had trusted him. Moreover there was very little time to plan what she would tell the sheriff. If he didn't actually come with the fire department he would be certain to follow it very closely. The fire had taken care of an explanation for the broken pane of glass; that much was all right at least. But could she be expected to hold to her agreement not to tell about Perry's search of the study now that he had added arson to his other crimes? He could hardly expect it, and she certainly didn't expect it of herself. But if she told about that he would be sure to say something about her bottle. And Miss Pomeroy ached to get that bottle back to town and have its contents analyzed.

"We'd better get Mr. Osgood to bed," she said.

"No use," Perry answered, and it was plain that the reins of authority had passed into his hands. "Here comes the fire department, and the law is sure to want to talk to him."

Chapter 16

THE hours from the arrival of the fire department until dawn always remained an unhappy blur in Miss Pomeroy's memory. She had never in her adult life told a lie, and she didn't intend to let the tangled affairs of the Osgood family start her on such a course now, but she had no qualms of conscience about withholding from Sheriff

Wentworth any items of information which she believed
would do him more harm than good. However, sorting
out such items of information from the tangle of events
that had occurred during the thirty-six hours she had spent
in Charles Osgood's house was a task almost beyond her
powers at the present moment of confusion. And there
was the ever present fear that, if someone else told him
something she had left out, his suspicions would be
aroused against her. Of her conversation with the sick
man in the night she intended to tell him only that Frank
Osgood had drunk from a bottle of his cousin's Pernod;
she thought that the address in what appeared to be Frank's
own writing and Frank's awareness of the risk he was taking were matters for her own private investigation. Billie
La Verne had demonstrably never been near the wine
cellar, so that it was not necessary to tell all of Frank's
story in order to clear her of suspicion. Of Kay's confession
she intended to repeat nothing at all, nor of her conversation with Adrian Perry unless she were asked point-blank
whether she had spent an undisturbed night in the study.
And she certainly did not intend to tell about the bottle of Pernod she had abstracted from the wine cellar.
She had managed to conceal that in her suitcase before
the sheriff arrived, some ten minutes behind the fire department. Since the luggage had already been searched
once she trusted that it would not be again, and fortune
favored her.

What she actually did tell the sheriff she was never
quite able to remember, but it must have been satisfactory,
for at 9.00 a.m. she found herself on a commuting train
enroute to New York, her bottle safe in her suitcase and

the rest of the party off her mind. She was just a little uneasy as to whether she should have gone to the jail first for Billie; perhaps riding into town alone might look as if she were trying to avoid the chorus girl's company, but it was such a relief to be alone that her generous impulse was smothered at birth.

Frank Osgood was pronounced out of danger, and his mother and fiancée were driving him home this morning. They had offered Miss Pomeroy a ride which she had refused with a fervor of which she was a little ashamed. Nora alone of the party which had come up from town so blithely only day before yesterday was remaining at the house. Miss Pomeroy wouldn't have minded her company on the return journey, but Nora had offered to stay over and close things up; it was not unlikely that she would do a little further searching on her own hook. Of the purpose which had brought them here they had accomplished exactly nothing. They had found no hint of any concealed assets, nor had they searched thoroughly enough to be able to say with certainty that there were none.

On Miss Pomeroy's private line of investigation there was a little more progress. The case of Pernod addressed in Frank Osgood's handwriting was definitely a clue, and if it should turn out that every bottle in the lot contained atropine it would be almost certain that here was the evidence Charles had planted against his cousin. But it seemed an awfully slight bit of evidence for a man of Charles's cleverness to have left with any idea that it would be certain to send an innocent man to the electric chair. There was every chance that it might be overlooked, as it had been for so many weeks, or that it could be explained away or proved to be a forgery. Miss Pomeroy was not very familiar with the work of handwriting experts, but it was her opinion that they were able to pronounce with certainty on the authorship of any given sample. And then there was the baffling, confusing, altogether illogical and inescapable fact that Charles Osgood hadn't died of poison at all, but of a chronic heart disease of long standing. If Dr. Laurence had been a different sort of man she would have planned to go back and talk to him now that she had more information, but, he being the man he was, it seemed to her quite out of the question.

In spite of all the excitement of the past twenty-four hours, it appeared that the county officials intended to let the matter pass as an accident. Thinking of the sheriff Miss Pomeroy snorted aloud, and then look guiltily about the train, fairly well filled with late commuters and early shoppers. No one appeared to be paying any attention to her, and she drew a notebook and a pencil out of her handbag. It was easier for her to think in silence with such tools at hand.

The sheriff's insistence yesterday on assuming that Frank's poisoning must have been a crime was outdone only by his serene and imperturbable certainty this morning that the fire had been an accident. A house with the electricity turned off, heated by open fires, lighted by kerosene lamps, and cooked for on a wood stove was so obvious a fire hazard that he refused to open his mind to the facts. In vain had Miss Pomeroy assured him that there had been no light in the study except her flashlight and that the fire had been confined to the study and could not possibly have originated in another room. He was so airily sure of himself that he did not even bother about where she had been at the moment when the fire broke out—either that, or he was in the pay of that young man. Miss Pomeroy wrote "Adrian Perry" in her notebook and underlined the name three times, not because she had anything to write down about him but because the thought of him made her so angry that she had to express her emotion in some kind of physical action. It wasn't his breaking into the study the first night that she resented, nor even his coming into the house like a wolf in sheep's clothing to repeat the attempt. She could grant that there was provocation enough for all that. But after she had trusted him, after she had given her word not to betray him, to come back down and burn the papers, callously indifferent to the possibility of roasting the sick man alive or burning down the house with all of them in it—that was beyond forgiveness. She had been worried for a little while about what the law might do to him, arson being a crime that country police were likely to regard rather more seriously than murder, and when the sheriff airily refused to consider the possibility of arson having been committed, she was perversely the angrier at the man she knew to be criminal, for having worried about him. Anyway, she would never buy or rent another one of his books.

Tired as she was, Grand Central Station gave a lift to her spirits as it always did. A cup of coffee, a baked apple, and a corn muffin restored her serenity to the point where she was able to contemplate the idea of calling the detective agency and reporting her return. Mr. Keene listened to her account of the events of the two nights and a day during which she had been away without any apparent

surprise. Miss Pomeroy edited a little. After the sheriff
and the doctor and the warring elements within the Osgood family she was becoming, she realized, appallingly
adept at such editing. Mr. Keene, however, was her boss,
and she left out nothing except the handwriting on the address label of the case of bottles of Pernod.

"Yeah?" Mr. Keene said. "Well! Quite a night! Anybody arrested?"

"No," Miss Pomeroy said. "They took the chorus girl
who says she's Mrs. Charles Osgood down to the jail last
night on suspicion, but of course they had to let her go
when Mr. Osgood said it was an accident. And the man
that set the fire must be in league with the police out
there."

"Be careful who you say that to," he cautioned. "You
better go home and get some sleep. I don't see what more
you can do today."

Miss Pomeroy thanked him and took the shuttle train
across town and then the west side subway uptown to her
apartment on 116th Street near Columbia University. It
was a quiet and dignified neighborhood, and she liked the
proximity of the students. She smiled at two or three of
them sauntering along the street hatless in the chill
October sunlight as she turned into her own block and
then up the brownstone steps to her own front door. The
click of her key in the lock, the familiar weight of the
doorknob, the warm, slightly musty air of the quiet, empty
hallway soothed her, welcoming her back to the orderliness
of her own life, her own possessions. She climbed a flight
of stairs and opened the door of her own apartment, so
happy she could hardly keep from singing like her canary

in his sun-flooded cage. Everything was in order; Willie Mae had remembered to feed the bird and water the flowers; the chintz cushions and curtains were just as bright and cheerful and homelike as when she had left them. Miss Pomeroy sat down in her wing chair and offered a brief prayer of thankfulness that she was Miss Grace Pomeroy living on West 116th Street instead of Kay Waterhouse or Martha Osgood or Billie La Verne or any of the excitable, unpredictable, unhappy females she might have been.

Her next act was not, as might have been expected, to unpack or cook herself a more substantial breakfast or undress and get into bed. Instead she hung up her hat and coat, washed her hands, ran a comb through her tidy hair, and, going to the maple bookcase, selected a fat volume. It was the old Materia Medica of her student days, and although much of it was out of date she still used it as a faithful standby. She turned to Atropine and read with intense concentration, skipping here and there. It was as she had remembered it—"botanically known as atropa belladonna, and is official in the form of the root (Belladonna Radix U.S. and B.P.) . . . belladonna contains an active principle in the form of an alkaloid known as atropine . . . should be kept in amber-colored, well-stoppered vials . . . full medicinal doses produce flushing of the face, dilated pupils, sometimes an erythematous rash over the skin, rarely diplopia and delirium. . . . Poisoning by atropine is an exceedingly common occurrence, but death is rarely produced by it, partly because its influence is not very actively exercised on vital parts, and partly because it is eliminated by the kidneys almost as rapidly as it is absorbed by the stomach. Recovery has occurred after

as much as one grain of atropine has been taken by a child
of three years. Severe poisoning is characterized by deep
sleep, preceded, it may be, by convulsions, violent delirium,
blindness, and sometimes loss of speech."

That was that. She laid down the book, leaned back in
her chair, and put her hands to her temples. There had to
be an answer if she could only find it. Why should anyone
try to commit murder or suicide with a poison which rarely
produced death? Ignorance? But anyone who knew enough
of the poison to procure it and mix it with liquor should
know that much more about it. It was the sort of a poison
a man—or woman—might use to fake a suicide, to frighten
friends or bring a recalcitrant lover to his knees. Could
Charles Osgood have taken atropine with some such notion and been tricked to his death by his unreliable heart?
No, that wouldn't fit with his threat to Frank. Miss Pomeroy remembered the story of a farmer she had heard of
years before who had been driven to plan suicide because
of constant quarrels with his son. The old man had decided
to frighten the boy into a proper filial respect, and with
that aim in mind had gone out to the barn, slung a rope
across a rafter, and arranged the end in a noose around
his own neck, and stood on the edge of the corn-crib waiting for the boy to come and stop him just in time. Almost
before his preparations were completed the boy appeared
in the open door saying in a tone of some amazement: "I
believe the old fool's going to do it." The farmer jumped.
Miss Pomeroy thought she remembered that the end of
that story was that he had been cut down in time and lived
to quarrel with the son again. Perhaps most suicides followed the same pattern. But that was an unfruitful line

of inquiry, for Charles Osgood, to the best of her knowledge, hadn't committed suicide, and Frank's impulsive swallowing of the remainder of the bottle of Pernod could scarcely be described as a suicide attempt. Miss Pomeroy looked at her own bottle and struggled with an almost irresistible impulse to taste its contents. She was sorry now that she hadn't taken it to be analyzed even before coming home; she doubted whether she could make up for her lost sleep until she knew what it contained. But that was nonsense; she did know what it contained; analysis would merely confirm her knowledge. Her trouble was not uncertainty as to the contents of the bottle but an inability to figure out how her knowledge of its contents was to be interpreted.

She got up with a sigh, carried the bottle to the kitchen where she set it well back in the darkest cupboard, and then, returning to her bed-sitting-room, she took off her clothes, removed the daytime disguise from the studio couch, and turned back the cool and inviting sheets. Finally with a little sigh of complete satisfaction she got into a hot bath. But she had hardly settled herself to enjoy it when a new thought struck her; with a muttered exclamation she got out, dried herself, and pattered out to the kitchen. There she took a package of labels from the left rear corner of the upper right drawer, marked one neatly and conspicuously POISON and affixed it to the bottle of Pernod. After that she went back to her bath. She was not expecting any callers in her apartment that morning, but Miss Pomeroy had always been a careful woman.

Meanwhile Kay, Frank, and Mrs. Osgood, having gotten a somewhat later start, were motoring home together. Kay drove, and Mrs. Osgood sat on the front seat beside her, with Frank half reclining in the rear in a nest of cushions. A casual observer might have been pardoned for thinking that Kay and Frank had their roles reversed, for she was much the paler of the two. There were lines of strain on her face, and she drove with a passionate attention to traffic conditions that left her unable to join in any conversation. Frank, on the other hand, looked rested and relaxed, as if the poisoned Pernod had been a medicine that had done him more good than anything he had taken since his cousin's death.

"I never thought we'd get out of there alive," Mrs. Osgood said. "I've never in all my born days passed such a day and night, and I never hope to again."

"I'm only sorry the place didn't burn down so we could be done with it," Frank said. "I'd be thankful if I never had to hear of it again."

"You shouldn't talk so, son." His mother was reproachful. "A lot of people might think that all this that's happened was a judgment on you for the way you've talked. Charles was your own flesh and blood, and mighty good to you too, and you never have a kind word for him."

"Charles was a fiend," Kay said in a low voice without taking her eyes off the road. "I firmly believe he was the devil incarnate. No human being could be so evil."

This direct frontal attack left Mrs. Osgood gasping and momentarily without a reply. "I shouldn't think you'd want to marry into the family of the devil incarnate," she said when she was able to say anything.

"Mother, stop it." Frank spoke with a note of authority that was not often heard in his voice. "Charles is dead;

the harm he's done ought to be dead too. He set us all quarreling while he was alive; we mustn't keep on with it now."

"I'll not have her talking that way of your family that's going to be her family too," Mrs. Osgood said. "What if you have children? Have you thought of that? First cousin to the devil incarnate the father of your children! Have you thought of that?"

"I've thought of it," Kay answered in the same low voice.

"Please, mother!" Frank's voice was querulous now, not commanding. "I'm not in shape to stand this."

"Are you all right?" She turned in the seat solicitously. "Ought we to stop somewhere? Do you want anything? Are you feeling faint? I knew we shouldn't have let that nurse go off on the train and leave you. I don't think that doctor knew anything anyway; you ought to be in a hospital; I never heard of anyone getting over being poisoned in just one night, and with a fire in the bedroom too."

"I'm all right, mother," he said patiently. "I'll go to bed when we get home, and you can call Dr. Smith, but I know I'm all right. There's a load off my mind that was worse than the poison."

"I don't see what it could be. We didn't settle anything. We haven't found the money, and have you given a thought to how much we're spending, running around like this looking for it, with detectives and lawyers and things? You'll probably have to sell the farm to pay your bills—if that woman doesn't get it."

"Look at that cow," Kay said.

"What about her?"

"The markings on her side look just like a map of the United States."

"Humph," Mrs. Osgood said, and even Frank objected mildly: "I don't see it."

"It looked like the map in my school geography," Kay repeated stubbornly. "Shall we cross the river on the bridge or go down town and through the tunnel?"

"The bridge by all means." Mrs. Osgood did not wait for Frank to attempt a reply. "I never go through the city traffic if I can help it."

Kay opened her mouth to reply that city traffic was no longer a problem, and then closed it without having spoken. They drove in silence then for a time, each one busy with his own thoughts. It was past noon when they finally drove up to the house in Summit, New Jersey.

Kay stretched her cramped muscles and looked anxiously around to see how the sick man had stood the journey. He smiled at her, but her answering curve of the lips was only a stiff grimace.

"Good driver," he said. "I feel as rested as if I'd made the trip in an ambulance."

"Thanks," she answered. "Do you need me to help you get settled inside? For if you don't I'd like to take a turn around the garden and then get started home. I've still got a long trip."

"You should have let us drop you off. I could have finished driving home."

"Nonsense. You go to bed and stay there."

"Whatever do you want in the garden this time of year?" Mrs. Osgood asked curiously. Kay did not answer, but her eye caught Frank's, and he paled at her look.

"I'll come with you," he said, however, quite steadily.

"Please don't be a damned fool, Frank."

"Need you talk like that chorus girl in jail back there?"

"In jail where?" Frank was clambering stiffly out of the car, but he stopped abruptly and turned on his mother a look of complete dismay. Kay sat down on the running board and groaned.

"That's torn it," she said. "And all because I said damn. After the way I drove and talking about cows and—"

"In jail where?" he demanded. "You mean Billie? What for?"

"The sheriff took her into town last night on suspicion of having poisoned you," Kay said. "They'll let her out now you're all right."

"But why didn't you tell me? You let me do that to her?"

"They found a bottle of some eye stuff with atropine in it in her handbag," Kay said wearily. "You were poisoned with atropine. Can you prove she didn't put it into something you drank?"

"You know damned well I can," he said violently. "You knew it all the time. That poor kid—let me get at a telephone."

"Frank," she said. "Frank! Call if you must. But stop and think what you're doing first. They'll let her out in a little while. Oh, Frank, be careful."

Chapter 17

IT took half an hour for Frank Osgood to convince himself that Sheriff Wentworth could not be reached by telephone. While he cursed, jiggled the receiver futilely, and tried out helpful suggestions from the long distance operator, Kay sat woodenly on a bench in the hall listening in silence. Mrs. Osgood paced up and down the hall, alternately arguing, cajoling, and weeping. No one had bothered to bring in the suitcases from the car, which stood at the curb with the doors open.

"You'll kill yourself," Mrs. Osgood sobbed. "You're not responsible. Kay, can't you make him go to bed? Let me get at that telephone and call a doctor. Frank, please go to bed. What can you tell him if you get him?"

"That's right, Frank," Kay agreed. "What will you tell him?"

"You know what I'll tell him," he said with a look that brought color into Kay's pale cheeks. "Kay, I wouldn't have thought you'd let me come away from there without knowing that."

"But I thought you *did* know," his mother said. "All the rest of us did; we were talking about it all around you. And she did have the atropine; how can you be sure she didn't poison you in order to get the money?"

"She didn't need to poison me to get it. I told her if she's Charles's wife she can have it."

"A woman like that probably wouldn't believe you. She's probably never known an honest man."

"Oh, don't, mother," he said. "Please don't. This is bad enough for me anyway."

She stopped her pacing and looked at him and then, with a visible effort, controlled herself.

"Of course," she said quietly. "I'm sorry, Frank. I'm afraid I wasn't thinking. You know best."

Kay looked up and opened her mouth to speak, but the sudden dignity of the older woman's manner silenced her.

"I'll have to go back," Frank said. "There's nothing else for it."

"You can't get the gasoline," Kay pointed out.

"I'll have to go on the train then."

"I'll go along," Kay said, but he shook his head.

"This is something I have to do by myself."

"Frank," she said in a low voice. "Please don't go. I beg you not to."

"I must, Kay. I have no choice."

"Please. For my sake."

"Kay, how can you? For your sake leave that poor, innocent girl in jail? What kind of a woman are you?"

"You have the effrontery to talk like that to me?"

"I don't know what you mean, Kay, but I gather that you admit you deliberately kept the news from me so I'd come away and not try to do anything for her. I find that hard to forgive."

"I'm not asking your forgiveness. If you go back up there you may consider our engagement at an end."

He shrugged his shoulders helplessly, and turning back to the telephone called the railroad station. Kay stood up and pulled the ring from her hand in a single gesture. She dropped it on the telephone stand as she passed.

"Goodby," she said. "Goodby, Mrs. Osgood. It's been nice knowing you."

"He has to go, Kay. It's what he thinks is right."

The younger woman did not answer again. She walked out to the car, took her small suitcase from the rear seat, closed the door, and walked stiffly down the street without a backward glance. Neither of the Osgoods made any attempt to stop her.

"Thank you, mother," Frank said. "There's a train in seven minutes. I'll have to take the car to the station."

"All right," she said. "Bring me my suitcase first, please."

When he had brought it in she put her arms around him briefly and touched her lips to his cheek.

"Be as careful as you can, son," she said. "Kay will be all right in a day or so."

He picked up the ring from where it had lain untouched on the telephone stand, tossed it into the air once or twice, and thrust it loose into a pocket. "She didn't go into the garden, did she?" he inquired irrelevantly.

"Frank, you're not thinking she had anything to do with it?"

"Mother, please! I'll tell you all about it when I come back."

"Come as soon as you can, son."

He kissed her again, and was gone. Not until he was out of sight did she begin to cry once more.

As he put the car in motion Frank realized that Kay would be going to the station too. He would have to pick her up if he passed her; it would be too ridiculous not to, and besides it was a long walk to the station. As he rounded the corner he watched for her, but she was nowhere in sight. Perhaps she too had recognized the awkwardness of riding to town on the same train and had deliberately spared him. He couldn't keep his eye open for her at cross streets and watch traffic too, but he tried to see out of the tail of his eye, and she was nowhere in evidence. There wasn't really time to be concerned about it, but after he had parked the car, bought his ticket, and boarded the train Frank began to wonder. There was no alternative way to the station; either she had turned away to avoid an encounter with him or she had changed her mind and gone back to the house. He felt the ring in his pocket. Eight years ago he had bought that. The touch of it even now brought a faint, gnawing sensation to the pit of his stomach, reminiscent of all the lunches he had foregone for it. And the shabby suit he had worn a whole season after it was definitely disgraceful. If anyone had told him then that someday he would be Charles's heir, owner of a hundred thousand dollars exclusive of insurance, and still wouldn't be happy, how he would have laughed. Lack of money wasn't the worst thing in the world, but it was near enough to it.

Then he gave himself up to contemplation of what he would say to Sheriff Wentworth.

It was a long and exhausting journey back to Connecticut for a man who had yesterday been on the verge of death from atropine poisoning. In the taxi crossing the city from one station to the other Frank wondered seriously whether he might collapse before he had accomplished his purpose. In Grand Central Station he felt so dizzy and ill that when at last he was settled in a train again he drew out a notebook from his pocket and wrote a statement.

"To whom it may concern: I, Frank Osgood, being in my right mind, do hereby declare that Miss Billie La Verne, otherwise known as Mrs. Charles Osgood, is altogether innocent of any complicity in an attempt to poison

me on October 23rd at the home of the aforesaid Charles
Osgood, deceased."

It sounded rather silly and not very convincing. He tore
up that sheet and started again.

"Billie La Verne did not poison me. I know this because—". The man sitting in the seat next to him was
looking over his shoulder curiously. Frank shut the notebook with a snap and became engrossed in the scenery
outside the window.

It was late afternoon when he reached his destination.
He took a taxi at the station—what had he spent in taxi
fares today?—and asked to be driven to the jail. The driver
was inclined to be facetious until he recognized him.
When this occurred he turned squarely around in the seat,
without slackening the pace of the vehicle, and remarked:
"Say, you're Mr. Osgood's cousin, aren't you? I heard you
was dying."

"That was yesterday," Frank said. "I'm all right today."

The remark sounded more like Charles than like himself. Well, that was all right too. He was heir to Charles's
fortune, and in a curious, diabolical way he was heir to
Charles's character too. It would be like Charles's sense of
humor to send the La Verne girl to jail on a charge of attempted murder of which he knew she was innocent. It
wouldn't be for much longer though. He was himself, not
a weak copy of Charles, and in a few minutes the world
would know it.

The county jail was a gloomy structure of gray stone
with the sheriff's offices just inside the front door. Frank
walked up the steps with a dignity somewhat impaired by
his having forgotten to pay the taxi-driver and being pur-

sued and dunned. Business attended to, however, he
squared his shoulders and walked into the office where
the sheriff sat with his feet on his desk, puffing a large
cigar. Frank was glad there wasn't to be any to-do with
secretaries. Wentworth removed the cigar from his mouth
with an expression of amazement at the sight of Frank,
and opened it as if to speak, but the visitor rushed to bring
out his words first.

"I've come to give myself up for the murder of my
cousin."

"Huh?" said Sheriff Wentworth.

"I murdered my cousin Charles and yesterday attempted to commit suicide by drinking some of the poison
I had previously sent him; I demand to be arrested, and
that you free anyone else you may be holding in connection with the case."

Sheriff Wentworth stood up. "Hey," he said, "you better lay down. There's a couch in there. Who let you out?"

In the course of the long, wearisome journey Frank had
imagined a good many receptions for his announcement,
but not this one.

"I'm not sick, you fool," he said angrily. "I'm telling you
I killed my cousin."

"All right, now, keep cool, keep cool. You lay down
and I'll call the doctor. Nobody's saying you're cra—nobody's saying you're sick. Where's that nurse?"

"I demand that you put me in prison and release Miss
La Verne."

"Her?" the sheriff said. "Oh, she's been out since noon."

Frank sat down abruptly; more properly speaking, perhaps, his legs gave way beneath him.

"That atropine in the stuff you drank wasn't like the atropine in her eyewash," the sheriff explained. "That is, the eyewash had a lot of things in it that wasn't in the liquor, so it couldn't have been from that, could it? I'm going to call the doctor."

"Where is Miss La Verne?"

"She's gone back to New York. And I've done you a good turn that's worth being poisoned for. Before I let her out of here I got her name to a paper says she's no more Mrs. Charles Osgood than I am. I knew he wasn't the marrying kind."

Frank felt dizzy and ill. How long would it be before what he had said would penetrate into the mind of this yokel? What evil fate had prevented him from completing the telephone connection this noon? It was said now, irrevocably, and it need not have been. Nothing could call back the words; his mother would have to know—wasn't that fool ever going to get it through his head?

"Just a gold digger," the sheriff said. "I know her kind. But she didn't put anything past me. You just lay there on the couch and let me call the doctor. Where'd you come from anyway? I thought you'd gone home to New Jersey."

"I did," Frank said. "I came back when I found out you were still holding Miss La Verne unjustly."

"Unjustly!" The sheriff laughed briefly. "Listen. She went on that cruise with him like she said, but she was no more married to him than—than I was." His command of similes, Frank noted, was limited. "She cooked it up with the skipper to get hold of some money; they were going to split even. Well, young man, you have me to thank for getting you out of that."

"Thank you," Frank said, resting his head in his hands.

"Thank you! Huh! I guess your lawyer'll have more than that to say; he knew what you were up against there if you didn't. You can't never trust that kind of a woman, son."

"Aren't you going to arrest me?" Frank asked dully.

"You just lie there and rest until the doctor comes."

When the words had been said and he had first realized that they were unnecessary, Frank had longed bitterly to have them back again, unuttered. But now perversely he felt a mounting rage at the stupidity of this man who would not believe him. His head ached, though, and he was tired; if the doctor was coming there would be no use in arguing. What would he tell the doctor, anyway? A man couldn't be Sir Galahad for nothing. Billie was free. And then suddenly a great light burst over him. He had discovered the way to circumvent Charles's plot. If he confessed to the murder and no one would believe him, then surely when Charles's carefully planted evidence turned up it would be worthless. If he could only make the doctor react as the sheriff had reacted! He revolved the idea carefully in his mind and then spoke to the sheriff again.

"If you've let that girl off and you don't believe I took it on purpose, who do you think poisoned me?"

"You're not dead," the sheriff said. "Looked yesterday as if you might be before this thing was finished. Long as you're all right and the whole crew of you cleaned out of that house, I guess we don't need to worry."

"And the fire? Suppose I tell you I set that too?"

"Look, now, the doc's going to be right over. You just take it easy."

Frank sat quietly with his head in his hands and took it easy. It was ten minutes before the doctor arrived looking harassed and more than a trifle annoyed.

"Good lord, man, I thought you'd be in the hands of your own doctor in New Jersey long before this."

"I came back as soon as I heard about Billie La Verne being in jail."

"Didn't you know it before you left?"

"No one told me, and I supposed she'd gone back to town."

"Well, she has now; what's your trouble?"

Frank laughed ruefully. "I spoke a little out of turn. I didn't wait to find out she'd been released; I went right ahead and told Wentworth that I murdered my cousin and tried to commit suicide yesterday. I don't think he believes me."

The doctor snorted. "I suppose you want me to believe that you expected him to. What's the big idea? Does your mother know where you are?"

"She knew I was coming back here, but not what I was going to confess. I wanted to keep it from her as long as I possibly could."

"And where's that nurse?"

"She's gone back to town. Nursing's not her regular job any more, you know. She just looked after me to be accommodating."

"She should have stuck around a little longer. Does she

know you murdered your cousin and tried to commit suicide?"

"No, she doesn't. No one knew it until I told the sheriff just now. It's not the kind of thing you go around boasting about, you know."

"It isn't, eh? Well, and how did you kill him?"

"I sent him a case of poisoned Pernod, a drink of which I knew him to be very fond. I chose it because I thought there was less danger of his sharing it with friends than if it had been any other sort of liquor."

"Where'd you get your atropine?"

"If you doubt my word you can have the contents of the remaining bottles in the case analyzed."

"That case that was open in the wine cellar with the one bottle gone?" the sheriff interjected. "We had a bottle of that analyzed. It was all right."

"I must have missed one," Frank muttered. "Try the others. If you don't believe me why don't you have my cousin's body exhumed?"

Was he saying too much, going too far? It was hard to judge. He felt himself being carried away by his role into a genuine eagerness to convince these men that he was telling the truth.

"Let's get that blood pressure," the doctor said. "We're not getting any place talking this way."

He went methodically and with obviously mounting indignation through the ritual of medical examination—blood pressure, heart, respiration, pulse, reflexes. At the end he said irritably: "As far as I can see you're perfectly all right, but you plainly ought not to be running around loose. I don't know what sort of after-effects to look for from this stuff; it's clear outside my experience. But my advice to you is to go home and call your own doctor and stay in bed until he tells you it's all right to get up."

"But, doctor, suppose I'm not suffering from any after effects at all? Suppose I'm telling you the truth? Won't you admit at least that it's possible?"

"No," the doctor said. "Your cousin died of a chronic heart condition. The stuff you drank wouldn't kill anybody. You weren't a very robust specimen to start with, and look at you. If you'd meant to poison yourself or anyone else you'd have had sense enough to use something that would finish the job."

"You mean, then, that you and the sheriff are going to let this whole matter drop, not even try to find a culprit? Suppose whoever did try to burn down my cousin's house —my house—last night finishes the job tonight."

"To be quite frank with you, Mr. Osgood," the doctor said, "all I want is to get you out of here. You upset us all. And now I'm darned if I know how to do it. I can't send you back to New York alone in the shape you're in, and if I let you sleep up at that house again something will happen just as sure as—"

"As the sheriff isn't Mrs. Charles Osgood," Frank finished, observing that the doctor was at a loss for a way to complete the sentence.

"I could send you to the hospital," the doctor said, "but I don't want you telling your crazy stories to the nurses and starting any more gossip around here, as if we didn't have enough already."

"Perry'd put him up for the night," the sheriff sug-

gested. "He went up there last night to sleep on his own
hook, just to be accommodating. Or the Munroes could
bunk him in the farmhouse."

"I believe that would be best," the doctor agreed,
"though they've put up with an awful lot these last few
days. And I'll have to send word for someone to come out
here and get you in the morning. Who shall it be? Your
girl or that nurse? I don't suppose you'd want me to drag
your mother clear out here again?"

"That's nonsense," Frank said firmly. "If you don't
intend to arrest me for the crime to which I have confessed
you'll just have to let me go. I assure you I'm entirely
responsible."

"I'll put you in jail if that's the only place you'll stay
quietly," the doctor said. "It's pretty clean, for a jail, but
I hear they get bedbugs every now and then. Will you give
me your word to stay at the Munroes' and make no trouble, if they'll have you, or do you choose the bedbugs?"

"If the Munroes are kind enough to offer their hospitality I shall have to accept," Frank said reluctantly.

"You promise not to run out on them, then?"

"I promise."

Chapter 18

THE MUNROES not merely agreed to furnish their land-
lord a bed for the night, but volunteered to drive down to
the jail and get him. Waiting for their arrival Frank reflected bitterly that Billie had not had her choice of a
pleasanter haven in order to escape the bedbugs. He won-

dered whether they had bothered her. The bitter unfair-
ness of the whole proceeding appeared to worry no one
but him. Now the matter was to be allowed to drop; no
one was going to prosecute anyone, and that an innocent
woman had spent a night in jail over a crime of which she
knew nothing was a trifle. And the method which the
sheriff had used to insure the county and the Osgood
family against a suit for false arrest was neither more nor
less than blackmail. He held Billie's confession of attempted fraud as a weapon against her.

Frank's hand encountered the ring lying loose in his
pocket, and quite suddenly his resolution was taken. Kay
had jilted him; he was free to make what restitution lay
in his power to Miss La Verne. If she wanted Charles Osgood's estate there was one way he could make certain
she would receive it. As soon as that fool of a doctor should
release him he would go directly to the Horatio Street
apartment and offer his hand in marriage to Billie La
Verne. It wouldn't be the first time he had taken his
cousin's cast-offs.

He drew a deep breath preparatory to speaking and
then thought better of it. If he told the doctor his idea
and asked permission to go back to New York tonight the
man would merely be all the more certain that he must
be completely off his head. Better to wait overnight and
make sure he could carry through his scheme without
interruption.

The noise of the Munroes' car coming down the street
announced their arrival ahead of time. Frank stood up and
put on his hat and coat.

"Remember your promise," the doctor warned.

"I shall keep it. But I am to understand that I am *not* under arrest for my cousin's murder or for attempted suicide?"

"I've never heard of a prosecution for attempted suicide," the doctor said. "It's a crime on the statute books all right, but I guess most prosecutors figure it's generally its own punishment."

"And the murder?"

"Forget it," the doctor said patiently. "In fact I'd advise you to say no more about it to anyone; it could get you into serious trouble."

Frank laughed briefly and turned to meet his tenant, who regarded the tableau with a lively and unconcealed curiosity. As he was about to leave the room with the farmer he suddenly remembered his mother waiting anxiously in New Jersey. His marriage to Billie would be a terrible blow to her. She hadn't been too enthusiastic about Kay, but this would be many times worse. At least he mustn't leave her in suspense now.

"I'll have to call my mother," he said, turning back. "She'll be anxious about me."

"Run along and get some rest," the doctor said. "I'll call her."

"You'll frighten her. She worries about me anyway."

"I'll be careful. You'd frighten her worse than I could, the way you've been carrying on."

This was so patently incontrovertible that Frank could not pretend to argue. He turned away with Mr. Munroe and walked out of the jail a free man. It was more than a little ignominious after the confession he had just made.

The Munroes' cottage, he thought, was really a pleasanter place to live than Charles's arty house. The kitchen, dining room, sitting room was clean and warm, rich with the odors of good food. The same stove served for cooking and heating. With the orange glow through the draft holes it was as cheerful, he thought, as Charles's fireplace, and much more effective on a chilly evening. Since he absolutely refused to turn the Munroes out of their bedroom, he was to sleep on a decidedly bumpy day bed in the cold and cheerless parlor. After a supper of fried ham, roasted sweet potatoes, canned corn, and tomatoes, which he ate with a superb disregard of his ulcers, he sat in the kitchen with his hosts, hoping to put off the unpleasant moment of retiring as long as possible.

The Munroes were friendly and companionable people; it grieved him that he had waited so long to know them. They talked about the problems of farming, so suddenly reversed. The men who for ten years had been trying to avoid producing too much were trying frantically now to increase their output to the maximum, with all their help drained away to the cities or to the army. Bill Munroe had gone to an agricultural college and looked forward to better things than being a tenant on the farm of a gentleman amateur.

"I'd been thinking about asking you whether you'd like to sell me the farm," he confided abruptly when the conversation had reached the pitch of intimacy. "I figured maybe you'd like to keep the house with an acre or so for looks and I could start buying the rest."

"But I thought it wasn't making any money anyway. Where could you get the cash?"

"It'll make money the next few years, and I can borrow

at the bank. Maybe I'd work it harder if it was mine."

Frank opened his mouth to say: "I'll give it to you," and shut it again. Things weren't that simple. It would be like his confession of murder, too outrageous to be believed. This man was discussing a business proposition; he didn't want charity. And besides, he had already decided to give the estate, with himself included, to Billie La Verne, and if, as began to appear probable, there wasn't any estate except the farm, she would need the income from it to support the house. On the other hand Frank believed that land should belong to the man who could work it. It was a dilemma.

"Yes, I'd be willing to sell," he said. "I haven't much idea about how to set the price, but I think maybe we could make a deal."

"I couldn't make much of a down payment," the farmer said.

"You don't think any of those stocks Mr. Osgood gave you might turn out to be good after all?" his wife put in timidly.

"No," he said impatiently. "He told you they weren't worth the paper they're printed on; he just gave 'em to you as a curiosity."

"Could I see them?" Frank sat bolt upright in his chair. He had never suspected a streak of generosity in his cousin's character; could it be that he had simply given away his money to these nice people?

"They're in the bureau drawer," Mrs. Munroe said. "He told me to burn them, but I couldn't bear to. You're always hearing about old stocks that suddenly turn out to be worth a lot of money."

"That's just in the movies," her husband said, but there was a not completely repressed eagerness in the look with which he followed her. She was gone only a moment; the two men heard the scraping of a recalcitrant drawer, and she came back with her hands full to overflowing of stock certificates. The hands trembled with excitement as she gave the documents to Frank. He turned them over one by one, at first slowly, then with mounting speed and astonishment. The stockbroker's clerk had never seen such an array in one place in his life. For the first time it occurred to him that his cousin must really have been insane in the last months before his death. The plot involving suicide and murder he could accept as characteristic of Charles, but no sane man, Frank was certain, had ever spent his money on such a weird array of worthless stocks and bonds—gold mines, banana plantations, repudiated municipal issues—hardly one of the lot had ever been listed even on the Curb Exchange. Where in the world had Charles found them, and how had he managed to acquire such a collection of them without making his name notorious throughout Wall Street? He must have bought through a number of scattered brokers; no respectable one would stand for handling all those.

He looked up and met the concentrated gaze of his host and hostess; their expressions told him that they had read his.

"I'm afraid you're right," he said. "Have you any idea in the world why he bought all this stuff?"

Mrs. Munroe shook her head. "He said it was bad investments," she said. The dull bitterness of her tone pierced the insulation of Frank's concern with his own affairs. He looked at the documents again and then turned them over, now and again choosing one out of the pile to put in a smaller pile at his right hand. He was careful to match those he chose so that it would look like genuine sorting.

"There's nothing here worth anything like its face value," he said, "but we might be able to realize something on these—the lot, I think, would cover the down payment on the farm."

But Bill Munroe shook his head.

"They're yours," he said. "Your cousin told her to burn 'em; he didn't give 'em to her."

"All right then, I'll have them valued and the farm valued before we try to talk business," Frank agreed. "However I certainly owe you something for saving them for me; the estate couldn't be settled until we found what had happened to all the assets, and this will account for most of them. You can't refuse to accept a commission on that. Half of what these are worth would be fair, I think."

Half of what the documents were worth would be exactly the same figure as their total worth, but it would be a comparatively simple matter to deceive the farmer with a valuation approximately double a fair down payment on the farm. Then the payments for ten or fifteen or twenty years ought to be enough to pay taxes on the house and run it. At the end of that time he and Billie would have to sell it, unless he'd struck it rich in the meantime. It wasn't much for Billie in comparison to what she had gambled for, but it was better than the room on Horatio Street. Maybe she'd prefer to sell the house and have the money. He could hardly wait for morning to get back to New

York, tell Miss Pomeroy of this discovery, and propose to Billie.

The couch in the Munroes' parlor did nothing to aid his impatience in speeding the night away. If he hadn't given the doctor his solemn promise he would have slipped away in the darkness and taken a train to New York. As it was, he made up his mind that in the morning he would insist upon being either released or arrested. The insistence proved unnecessary, however; in the morning the doctor gave a reluctant consent to his returning alone to the city.

"And don't turn up here again," he growled. "I wash my hands of you now, and if I find you back on them I'll pop you into a hospital where you'll stay for awhile."

Frank accepted the permission eagerly, and with the certificates stuffed into his suitcase he shook the dust of the town from his feet—forever, he hoped. All the way in to town he debated with himself as to whether he should go first to the detective, the lawyer, or the chorus girl. Eventually he arrived at a reasonable compromise; he would telephone Miss Pomeroy and Gerald Winterbottom as well as his boss at Cuthbert, Cuthbert, Rutherford, and Simes to explain his continued absence, and then he would go to see Billie. He made the calls from the station. Gerald Winterbottom was frankly perturbed at the information about the stock certificates.

"Try checking through the shadiest brokers you can think of," Frank advised. "Nobody respectable would touch these with a ten foot pole. There's not enough here to account for all the money he should have had, but if he bought these he probably bought more of the same."

"At least you can get something out of the house if it

doesn't burn down before you get a chance to sell it," the lawyer said gloomily.

Mr. Cuthbert continued genial on hearing the news that Frank was ill and would remain away from the office at least one more day. In order to spread the geniality out as far as possible Frank did not enlighten the boss on the current standing of the Charles Osgood estate.

Miss Pomeroy, at the Keene agency, was more interested in Frank's health than in what he had to tell her.

"You've been to New Jersey and all the way back up there alone?" she said incredulously. "But you should be in bed."

"This has done me more good than going to bed," he assured her. "I tell you I'm all right. But I'm going home as soon as I've seen Billie, and then I'll go to bed and stay. But listen to what I'm trying to tell you. All the time we were turning that house upside down what we wanted was in a bureau drawer in the farmhouse. He's been throwing his money around like chicken feed on the most outrageous collection of worthless junk that ever masqueraded as investments. He must have been crazy."

"Maybe," she said cautiously. "Maybe not. Anyway it gives me a new idea. Now for heaven's sake go home and go to bed."

Frank took a taxi to Horatio Street and ran impatiently up the front steps to the doorway. He pressed the buzzer labelled Billie La Verne and waited for a long time, but there was no answering click of the lock. He had just turned away in disappointment when another tenant came up the steps with his key in his hand. Frank hesitated an instant and then followed him into the house, feeling, and if the truth be told looking, a good deal like a sneak thief. It would be an anticlimax to write out his proposal to Billie and slip it under her door, but it would be better than going away without having made it at all.

But when he reached the third floor of the little house behind the garden the door was ajar, and Miss La Verne herself was curled up in the middle of the day bed reading *Variety*. She looked up at him in mild astonishment. For a moment he thought she was disconcerted by the untidiness of the room in which he found her, which was certainly marked enough to distress a man of Frank's orderly habits in connection with the woman he hoped to make his wife, but after tentatively fluttering her eyelashes she suddenly laughed and spoke in what he had come to recognize as her normal voice.

"I hope you're not going to behave the way you did the last time I saw you."

Frank was afflicted with a vague and yet too distinct recollection of her having assisted Miss Pomeroy through some very unpleasant ministrations to him. It was an unfortunate recollection for a man on the verge of a proposal. He blushed and gulped.

"I want to apologize for—everything you had to put up with up there," he said awkwardly. "I—if I had known—it was all my fault. I went back to tell them as soon as I learned they were holding you, but by that time you were already gone."

"It wasn't your fault," she said. "Skip it."

"Oh, but it was," he assured her gravely. "That's why I had to—I felt it was necessary—Miss La Verne, will you do me the honor to become my wife?"

"Is this a gag?" she inquired, rising. "Because if it is I'd like you to know that I don't consider it a very funny one. And you can just—"

"Please," he said, raising his right hand, "please listen to me. It is quite true that I am not in love with you, and I don't mean to insult you by pretending to be. You know that I was engaged to Miss Waterhouse; my feelings for her are unchanged, but she has returned my ring. I think you are woman of the world enough to realize that love is not the only basis for a successful marriage. I wish to share my inheritance with you, and if we start without pretence on either side we should get along as well or better than most couples."

He stopped abruptly. He was only just reaching a proper oratorical swing, but he had finished what he had to say. Billie did not reply at once. She stood looking at him, frowningly at first, then calculatingly. Then she sat down on the day bed and lit a cigarette, still without speaking. She took two puffs, flung it away from her, and burst into tears without preamble.

"Honey," she said when she could speak, "that's the sweetest thing anybody ever said to me."

Frank approached awkwardly, assuming that an accepted lover ought to claim a kiss. She went on talking, however, apparently unaware of his intention.

"But I wouldn't take you away from Kay even if I could. You go on back and make up with her; she's just the wife for you, and she's probably tearing her hair out because she gave you back that ring."

"I don't think so," he said. "She's not a vacillating character."

"You listen to your Aunt Billie," she said. "Don't talk: just go put that ring on her finger and see what happens."

"There's more to it than I can explain to you now, and in any case I've just asked you to marry me."

"Darling, I'm glad I don't have to stand up to that temptation, for I'm not sure I could. I'm married—been married over a year to the skipper of your cousin's yacht. We cooked up this idea together, because if Charles Osgood didn't marry me he ought to've."

There was no reason for it, but Frank Osgood felt a great weight lifted from his heart.

"I'm going to give you the house for a wedding present," he said, "and I'd like to see anybody stop me."

"Oh, Frank—oh, gee—honestly, it's too much."

"It's not too much at all. If Charles hasn't sold the yacht I'll give that to your husband for a wedding present. No, I'm not crazy and I'm not sick. I never wanted his house or his yacht or anything of his, and I don't know anybody better entitled to 'em than you are."

"Oh, gee, honey," Billie said. "How did you and him ever come out of the same family?"

Chapter 19

FRANK OSGOOD's telephone call had caught Miss Pomeroy at a moment of profound depression. A day's and a night's sleep and fresh clothing had refreshed her and sent her back to Keene's eager to go on with her investigation of the Osgood case, but once back on the job she had run up smack against a stone wall. The first blow was that the bottle of Pernod contained Pernod and nothing more. She had been so certain of finding poison in it that the discovery was like a rebuff. The second blow was that her boss, having listened to an edited version of the affair— for Miss Pomeroy did not feel free to tell even Mr. Keene the full story of Charles Osgood's threat without her client's permission—advised her to make out her expense account and abandon the matter.

"The cousin's dead and the guy is nuts," he summed up the situation. "You can't prove he committed suicide, and this Frank Osgood is liable to get us mixed up in something serious going around drinking out of strange bottles."

"I've had a notion in the back of my mind all along that maybe the cousin isn't dead at all but has just staged a disappearance," she said.

"Well, what if he has? He hasn't absconded with anybody's money, has he? If we prove he's alive it only makes him mad and doesn't do anybody any good. You type out your report and turn it in, with itemized expenses, and I'll put you on something else."

"But I hate to fail on the very first case I've tried."

"Good lord, lady, you'll fail on plenty. This business is mostly just standing outside of hotels to notice when people go in and come out and who with. I haven't unravelled anything myself since 1937."

Miss Pomeroy felt that no further argument was possible. In a sense Frank had stumbled on the answer to his own question; the case of Pernod must have been the manufactured evidence, and by drinking the remainder of the contents of the poisoned bottle Frank had successfully destroyed it. It was a heroic method in more than one sense of the word. And yet the solution left so many odd discrepancies. Why, for instance, should Frank have felt it necessary to drink the poisoned Pernod instead of merely pouring it down a drain? How had Kay known the nature of the poison so promptly? And what had Charles been thinking of to die with all the symptoms of a heart attack if he intended to have Frank accused of poisoning him?

Miss Pomeroy sighed over her neatly typed report, revolving all these questions in her head. It was at this point that the telephone rang with Frank Osgood's report about the worthless stocks and bonds. Miss Pomeroy left the typing at once and sought out Mr. Keene, whose face fell perceptibly at the information that the money was largely squandered.

"He'll still be able to pay us," Miss Pomeroy interpolated hastily, correctly interpreting the look. "There's the house and the farm, and there should be insurance, though they haven't located it yet. But what I was thinking is that this looks like deliberately throwing the money away—as if it had been intentional, I mean. And if he did that with investments, wouldn't it be logical to think he might have done it in his private spending too? Could that be traced—stores and restaurants and clubs and so on?"

"Yes, it could," he said, "and quite easily too. It's a good idea. I'll put a man on it that knows the ropes; it won't cost enough extra to worry Osgood, and I expect he'd be glad to have the question cleared up. I guess that puts the kibosh on your disappearance theory."

Miss Pomeroy was a little sorry that she was not to take

care of the new line of inquiry herself, but she admitted that there must be people in the office better equipped than she to interrogate head waiters and credit managers. She put her report to one side until this last item of information should come in to complete it and devoted herself again to pondering the many curious aspects of the case. She wished, as she had many times before, that she might talk it over with Dr. Owen. She felt convinced that the clue that would ravel out the whole tangled skein was within her grasp if she could only seize upon it. She shut her eyes and leaned back and went laboriously over every conversation she had had with Frank Osgood, with Kay Waterhouse, with Mrs. Osgood, everything that had happened during the memorable two nights and a day in Connecticut. The idea that came to her at last was so horrible that she continued to sit with her eyes shut, waiting for her heart to resume its steady beating. It was more than horrible; it was fantastic, but it sent Miss Pomeroy back to the Public Library.

There she asked for a book about herbs, and having secured it sat uncertainly wondering how to go about looking up in the index a leaf that could be soaked in wine vinegar and laid on the forehead to induce sleep. The answer was so apparent that she refused to consider it. If she looked up atropine and found that the herb which produced that drug could also be used as a soporific—. Miss Pomeroy summoned all her courage and opened to the index. It was as she had half remembered, half suspected. "Atropine," the index said, "see nightshade, deadly, p. 119." Miss Pomeroy turned to page 119. Opposite it were two fine colored engravings of the familiar plant, one as it looked in summer with its graceful purple flowers and shiny green leaves, the other barren except for clumps of glistening red berries. The lower leaves, she read, are solitary, and the upper occur in pairs. They emit a characteristic bitter odor when crushed. The plant prefers a light, permeable soil and a southwest aspect on the slope of a hill—considerable moisture is needed during germination.

She skipped rapidly to the portions of the text that interested her most. The berries are full of dark, inky juice, and very sweet; in this lies their danger for children. There were several hair-raising little anecdotes of children stripping the attractive berries from plants in public parks with unpleasant results. On the other hand, a horse was known to have eaten eight pounds of the herb and an ass one pound of the berries without coming to any harm. Birds eat the seeds of the plant freely, but cats and dogs are very susceptible to its poisonous effects.

Deadly Nightshade is supposed to have been the plant that poisoned the troops of Marcus Aurelius during the Parthian Wars, she learned, and Buchanan's History of Scotland says that Macbeth's soldiers poisoned a whole army of invading Danes by liquor mixed with an infusion of dwale. The Middle English name (supposed to have been derived from Scandinavian "dool," sleep, or French "deuil," grief) probably led to the superstition that the devil himself guards the plant except on Walpurgis night. Its juice was used by Italian ladies of the Middle Ages to brighten their eyes, and in Italy the red berry is called Apple of Sodom.

The poisonous element of the plant is atropine, an alkaloid. The name comes from Atropos, who held the shears to cut the threads of human life. It was used as an anesthetic in the 16th century. *The leaves moistened in wine vinegar and placed on the head induce sleep.* For a moment Miss Pomeroy could not be certain that the words she so dreaded were not a hallucination. No, they stood clearly in unmistakable print. Immediately following them was the information that Juliet's sleeping potion was made of mandrake, a foreign species of the same plant.

Miss Pomeroy read on like a somnambulist through the directions for growing and harvesting the plant commercially. The alkaloid present in the root varies between .4 and .6 of 1%—but Mrs. Osgood must have used the sweet and sinister berries, the Apples of Sodom.

She had always liked Charles, Frank said, but to have been the instrument of so terrible a revenge still seemed almost incredible in a mother. But no, it was much more probable that she was another victim of Charles's scheme than a co-conspirator. Miss Pomeroy fitted the pieces together carefully. It must have been Mrs. Osgood who first found Charles's evidence against Frank. Had it been only the label on the case of Pernod, or was there more? In all probability something much more horrible, more unmistakable, to convince a mother that her only son had committed murder. Mrs. Osgood had been the first one upstairs on the first night. The chances were, then, that the evidence had been in her room. Miss Pomeroy shuddered at the thought of the old woman fighting alone against that knowledge.

The whole thing made better sense if the case of Pernod were left out altogether, and in the light of what she had just learned Miss Pomeroy could see how that was possible. The Spartan mother had made her discovery, and all alone had arrived at her decision. Or had it been something Kay told her, not something she had discovered for herself? There were now two women who believed that Frank Osgood had murdered his cousin, the two women dearest to him. Even though the fantastic revenge of the dead man's plot had miscarried it would have delighted its author. It was perhaps more apt that Frank's mother should constitute herself judge, jury, and executioner than that her son should stand public trial.

How she had administered the atropine Miss Pomeroy didn't know, but she was fairly sure that it had not been in the Pernod. She and Kay and Miss Pomeroy's own observation all testified that Frank didn't drink; the chance of poisoned liquor killing him was altogether too slight. No, Mrs. Osgood must have put the poison in something he ate at lunch—the milk or a solid food? Miss Pomeroy wasn't sure enough of the form atropine extracted by an amateur herbalist from the leaves or berries of the Deadly Nightshade would take to hazard a guess on that point. But it must have been something at lunch. And then she had withdrawn and waited for results without a hint of ' her inner turmoil—unless her irritability with Kay were a hint. But of course, Kay must have told her; that would account both for her bitterness toward the girl and for Kay's certainty that the poison was atropine. For that matter it would account also for Kay's horrified rejection of the proffered leaves soaked in wine vinegar.

Had the woman known in advance what she was going to do and come prepared to do it? No, unthinkable; action must have followed fast on the heels of discovery. And that would mean she must have distilled the atropine hastily from the leaves she had brought along as sedatives. And Frank, who certainly was familiar with his mother's passion for herbs, must have suspected the truth and lied to save her. The Pernod was nothing but a red herring he had drawn across the path.

Miss Pomeroy shut the book with a bang that drew a glance of annoyance from a tramp across the table on the verge of dozing off. She would have to go to New Jersey at once; there was not a moment to be lost. Not that she wanted to drag this story into the light of day, to brand Mrs. Osgood as a would-be filicide, to render Frank's loyal prevarication useless, but if the woman had made up her mind that her son must be killed and once brought herself to the point of attempting his murder she would not stop until she had achieved her end. Miss Pomeroy must get out there and somehow convince her that she was mistaken. And it would be no easy task; her experience with Kay made her realize that. Whatever Charles's manufactured evidence was, it was certainly convincing. It had convinced the two women who would most want to disbelieve it. And if Mrs. Osgood refused to admit that she thought her son a murderer and had taken his punishment into her own hands—well, in that case Miss Pomeroy would simply have to violate Frank's confidence and tell her the whole story.

What luck that the man had not spent the night under his mother's roof—or was it more than luck? Frank Osgood was not without a certain shrewdness of his own. If he knew that his mother had tried to poison him he must also know why, and he could reason as well as Miss Pomeroy to the conclusion that she would certainly try again. Perhaps he was deliberately avoiding her until he could prove to her that she was wrong. Still, the risk was too great to take; having worked the thing out Miss Pomeroy realized that she must go to the Osgoods' at once and secure all the missing pieces. Moreover she was curious as to the nature of the evidence so overwhelming that it had beaten down a mother's and a fiancée's unwillingness to believe. And finally, if she could ease the torment the old woman must be suffering in her terrible belief, she ought not to waste a moment in doing so.

She did take time, however, to call the office and report where she was going. Mr. Keene was complimentary.

"That was a good hunch of yours about the money," he said. "The guy had been cutting a swathe a mile wide all around town; every head waiter in the Fifties remembers it. It's a wonder it hadn't hit any of the gossip columns. I guess he wasn't quite prominent enough or quite rich enough. Anyway, you better wind this thing up in a hurry, and I'll send in our bill. They're not going to get one cent out of that estate except the house."

"All right," she said. "This call will finish it. I know who tried to poison Frank Osgood, and why, and I'll have to be sure it won't happen again."

"You'd better come in and finish your report," he said sharply. "It doesn't pay for an operative to run around on his own, and it's dangerous. We need to know exactly what you're doing."

"I'll put it all in the report as soon as I come back," Miss Pomeroy said, and hung up. It was a good thing she didn't care whether or not she kept this job. On the whole she rather thought she preferred to lose it if every case was going to prove as harrowing as this of the Osgoods.

She didn't mind the running about from place to place on suburban trains; in fact she rather liked the change and excitement, but the problem of the interview before her sobered her on this occasion. It was certainly the most difficult she had ever contemplated, and she would have shirked it if she dared.

"Mrs. Osgood, why are you trying to murder your son? I can assure you he is innocent."

Was there some way she could hint at it that would convey what she meant without having to crumple the defenses of the old woman's stubborn pride? She dared not leave anything doubtful or unclear, but there were things that could be said without words, and if she could somehow make Mrs. Osgood understand that she knew without having to say so she would ease things for them both. And then she would go back and finish typing the report which would say only that Charles Osgood had died of natural causes and that his money was gone.

It was a long journey by subway to Hoboken, by suburban train to Summit, and by taxicab out to the house Frank Osgood shared with his mother, but at the end of it Miss Pomeroy had not yet decided how she was to say what she had to say. It was a bright, warm day, the last of Indian summer, and as the taxi drew up at the house Miss Pomeroy had a glimpse of Mrs. Osgood in the back yard in a sweater and skirt. She paid off the taxi and walked around the house, glad that there was no excuse to postpone the painful interview. Mrs. Osgood was working in the herb garden, a piece of luck beyond what Miss Pomeroy had hoped for. She looked up as the visitor approached, and after a momentary surprise smiled a welcome as friendly and easy as might have been expected from any suburban old lady working in her garden.

"Why, Miss Pomeroy," she said, "what brings you out here?"

"I wanted to talk to you," Miss Pomeroy said, bravely plunging at once into what she wanted to say.

"You're not worried about Frank—he really is better, isn't he? He's in the house, but he hasn't gone to bed yet; Kay's in there, and I knew they'd want to talk, so I made myself scarce."

It was all so simple, so wholesome, so natural, that Miss Pomeroy could scarcely believe what she knew.

"They quarreled yesterday," Mrs. Osgood was going on, "and she gave him back his ring. I don't suppose she'd have come back for any reason but to make it up with him. Anyway, when I saw her on the porch I said to myself: 'Two's company, three's a crowd,' and I came out here in the garden. You haven't been in the house yet?"

"No," Miss Pomeroy said. "I saw you from around in front of the house, and I came straight out here."

"You know, Miss Pomeroy," the older woman went on, "it's just suddenly come to me what a terrible mistake I was making about Frank and that girl. I don't know what I could have been thinking of. There's nothing in the world I want as much as for Frank to be happy, and here I've been doing everything I could to spoil his happiness. Of course I'll be lonely when he marries, but if he didn't marry he'd be lonelier when I die. And I want to have grandchildren—and she's a good girl, she loves Frank, she's a fine girl in spite of everything. I'm ashamed of myself for the trouble I've made them."

"I think you're right," Miss Pomeroy said weakly. It was a sentiment that she would have seconded heartily a day or so earlier, but in comparison with the subject she had come to discuss, the question of Frank's mother's adjustment to his marriage paled into insignificance.

"I don't know now—Kay's acted so funny; she must have come to make up with him, don't you think? And yet she's so odd—pale and strained. It seems to me now if she'll just take back the ring and marry him that's all I'll ask of life."

It was getting more and more difficult to bring the subject around to atropine poisoning.

"This is the herb garden you were telling me about, isn't it?" Miss Pomeroy essayed, wrenching it abruptly.

Mrs. Osgood looked startled and a little offended.

"Yes, it is. Of course there's nothing to see now. I'd like to have you come and see it some time in summer. It's fascinating—so much more interesting than flower gardening—and so useful. I grow all my seasonings. You must let me give you some tansy and a bag of my lavender. Do you cook or board?"

"I cook," Miss Pomeroy said. "Don't you have any nightshade?"

"Frank pulled it all up late in the summer. Said it was dangerous with children running in and out of the yard the way they do. It was all along the fence there, and I do miss it; it's so pretty this time of year with the red berries and no foliage. I told Frank it was silly; children have been running through here for years, and no one's

ever been hurt with it. He gets notions like that sometimes."

"He pulled it all up when?"

"Some time in August. You can still see where it was."

"But those leaves you had with you in Connecticut?"

"Oh, I've preserved a lot; I wouldn't be without them.
I hope Frank will have forgotten another year. Anyway,
he's likely to have married Kay and moved out by spring,
and I shall plant it again if I choose."

"Did you know that atropine was the poisonous element of the plant?"

At this direct shot Mrs. Osgood remained singularly
calm. "The stuff that poisoned Frank? No, really? But how
funny! Do you mean you think he might have gotten it
somehow from my leaves?"

"It could have been procured from any part of the
plant—root, stem, leaves, berries."

"But the only leaves I had with me were those you saw,
and there weren't enough—besides, there weren't any missing. But isn't that queer, so soon after he took that notion
to pull up the plants—do you believe in presentiments?"

"No," said Miss Pomeroy.

"Come to think of it," Mrs. Osgood said, "he asked me
not to mention that he'd done that. I suppose he thought
it seemed old-maidish."

"I wonder," Miss Pomeroy said, and she turned and
looked at the house where Frank Osgood and Kay Waterhouse were deciding their future. She was breathless at
the narrowness of her escape from having said the wrong
thing to Mrs. Osgood. For now at last all the pieces fitted
properly.

Chapter 20

MISS POMEROY made no move to go directly into the house. She was not at all sure that she wanted to see her client or his fiancée just yet, not entirely sure, in fact, that she wanted to see them at all. Her confidence in her own judgment was considerably weakened by her earlier certainty that Mrs. Osgood had poisoned her son in a mistaken belief that he was a murderer. She did not want to hint at her new theory until she had an opportunity to put it to the test. But, although she was able to give only half her mind to an examination of it while she discussed herbs with Mrs. Osgood, the fatal simplicity with which every point jibed with every other was worse than ominous. It was so simple, so crystal clear, that she wondered how she could have failed to grasp it earlier. She wondered even more how the guilty person could have hoped to escape detection with so bungling and amateurish a scheme. It was its very crudity that had safeguarded it so far; Miss Pomeroy had been looking for something much more professional.

She realized that Mrs. Osgood had noted her wandering attention, and murmured an apology. The older woman laughed.

"I'm used to it," she said. "I know my hobby bores everybody, and I try to remember not to talk too much about it, but when I get started it's not easy to stop."

"But I am interested," Miss Pomeroy said, quite sincerely. "I was at the Public Library reading about herbs just before I came out here. I think it's a fascinating sub-

ject. You shouldn't apologize for your knowledge; you
ought to be proud of it."

"I guess I am secretly," Mrs. Osgood admitted. "I just
pretend to run it down so people will ask me more about
it. If you're interested in the literature you must let me
show you my books. I have some fascinating ones with
beautiful illustrations."

Miss Pomeroy permitted herself to be led around the
house and in through the front door. It was a mission
bungalow, the front rooms effectually darkened by a
roofed-over front porch. There was a dim little vestibule
with a gloomy library to its left, lighted only by narrow
strips of window high up on two sides of the wall. Underneath one of these, however, was a comfortable leather-
cushioned window seat, and when Mrs. Osgood had
switched on a light the dreary little room took on an unexpected air of comfort and of having been designed for
the pleasures of leisurely reading.

Mrs. Osgood lovingly drew half a dozen fat volumes
from the bookshelves and laid them on a table before her
guest. She hovered for a little while, pointing out engravings and reporting on plants that she had essayed without
success or that she had succeeded in growing when no one
had before. Miss Pomeroy could not make out the sound
of voices anywhere on the premises, although she strained
her ears.

"They must be in Frank's workroom down in the basement," Mrs. Osgood said. "I never interfere with anything there, so it's where he goes when he wants to be
sure of privacy. If you'll excuse me now I'll have to see
about supper. We don't keep a maid; I always say that an

able-bodied woman ought to be ashamed if she can't do her own work."

"Especially now," Miss Pomeroy agreed. "It's very patriotic of you."

"You must stay and take pot luck with us. Frank's friends think I'm a pretty good cook. Kay has asked for a lot of my recipes."

But at the risk of offending her hostess Miss Pomeroy shook her head decidedly over this proposal.

"I must get back to New York as soon as I've talked with your son," she said. "I left a report half finished, and Mr. Keene didn't want me to come away at all."

"I'd better call him then. I never do interrupt him when he's down there, but this once—"

"I'll be glad to rest a few minutes," Miss Pomeroy said. "If he's not up here of his own accord in another half hour I may have to ask you to call him, but I'd really rather you'd let him alone now."

"Would you rather look at the books, then, or will you come out to the kitchen and talk to me while I work?"

"I'll stay here if I may, thank you," Miss Pomeroy said. "This is all very interesting."

But when Mrs. Osgood was gone she turned back to the pages on the Deadly Nightshade and read it avidly all over again. On the following page was a description of Woody Nightshade, a harmless variety of the herb very similar in appearance to its cousin. Like Charles and Frank Osgood, she thought. What a shame the bungling criminal couldn't have got hold of the wrong kind and saved all this trouble.

Frank Osgood and Kay Waterhouse found her reading

when they came into the room, and the greeting died on
Kay's lips. Miss Pomeroy looked up and saw that the
diamond ring was back on the girl's finger. She felt old
and tired, but she did not shirk what she had to say.

"I have solved your mystery, Mr. Osgood." She spoke
formally, as agent to employer. "Your cousin's plot against
you was not of the sort we were looking for."

"I don't understand," he said. "His plot? I thought you
believed there was no plot—that he died a natural death."

She shook her head. "There was a plot—a diabolical plot
and a cowardly one. Haven't you realized what it was?"

His expression of dazed bewilderment gave every indication of being genuine.

"Your cousin discovered some months ago—probably
about a year ago," Miss Pomeroy said, "that he was suffering from a fatal disease. His life tenure was short, uncertain, and painful, and he found, I think to his surprise,
that he couldn't endure it. He had always considered himself a brave man; it must have been a difficult discovery."

She looked for the light of recognition in the two pairs
of eyes focused on her, but it was not evident in either.

"He must have considered suicide," she went on steadily,
"before he hit on the dreadful thing he decided to do.
You say he had always tormented you since your childhood." She looked at Frank. "He knew you hated him, and
it occurred to him at last that it would be amusing to fan
that hatred into flame, to goad you into murdering him."

"You think he meant—" Frank Osgood said, and all
the color drained away from his face. Miss Pomeroy
stopped, expecting him to faint, but he swayed for a moment unsteadily and then sat down. In another moment

his breath was coming more naturally, and there was a tinge of color in his cheeks.

"He wanted me to kill him?" he asked.

Miss Pomeroy nodded, and half consciously began to speak more rapidly. "He wanted you to put him out of his misery. He was afraid. He wanted death to come suddenly and unexpectedly and without pain."

"But he said—"

"He said what he thought was most likely to make you kill him. At first he thought of baiting the trap with money; that was where he got the idea of that large insurance policy. But of course he realized almost at once that he wouldn't be able to get it in his condition. He only mentioned it to make you a little more eager for his death. When he thought it over he understood that you couldn't be induced to kill for money. But he believed he could frighten you into killing him; he thought he knew your weakness that well."

"He was the devil," Kay said with quiet conviction. "He was the devil incarnate. I wish he was alive again so I could kill him myself."

"Hush!" Miss Pomeroy said sternly. "You have enough to regret."

"But afterwards?" Frank asked.

"Of course he had no idea how you might choose to kill him. But he knew enough of our police to know that the chances were very good you would be arrested and would suffer for your crime. And he thought he knew you well enough to know that if you weren't arrested you would commit suicide."

She spoke steadily, but faster and faster, warding off

interruption from either of the two.

"His knowledge of psychology was sound," she said, "but his experience of good people wasn't very wide. His scheme, you see, was to convince you that your choice lay between suffering for a murder you *hadn't* committed and committing a murder for which you would go scot free. He was cynical enough to believe that anyone confronted with such a choice would choose murder. Perhaps if he had lived long enough he would have relented; perhaps what he did to you eased his last months. I don't know. But before he had time to be convinced that he had failed his disease caught up with him. He died of a heart attack, and he left you fearing the results of a plot that had already worked itself out completely. It's finished; it's over. You have much to forgive your cousin but nothing to fear from him."

She was silent, but there was a breathless quality to the silence as if she were ready to go on talking at a moment's notice. The two young people stared at her wordlessly.

"That's my report," she said. "Your cousin died a natural death, Mr. Osgood. His money is all gone—deliberately squandered when he knew he couldn't live to enjoy it. You will inherit the house and the farm in Connecticut, nothing more."

"I've given those away," he said.

"Oh." Miss Pomeroy hesitated as if further comment might be expected of her; then she picked up her gloves and her coat and rose to her feet.

"Goodby," she said. "I'm sorry I haven't been able to do more for you. The office will send you a bill."

"But I killed him," Frank Osgood said thickly.

"You fool!" Kay whirled on him. "Don't you think she knows it? Haven't you heard her sitting here saying practically in so many words that she knows it and she doesn't intend to give you away? He deserved to be killed, didn't he, Miss Pomeroy? I knew you killed him and I thought it was right to keep quiet about it. And now she knows it and she'd keep quiet about it if you'd only let her. Why can't you let well enough alone?"

"How did you know he did it, Miss Waterhouse?"

"I saw him."

"You saw me?" He turned his dazed face toward her.

"Through the basement window. You were working down there in your room that afternoon when I got there. Your mother wouldn't disturb you, so I slipped around the house to call you through the window and surprise you. But I looked in first—"

"But how could you tell what I was doing?"

"I couldn't. It was your face that frightened me. You had that case of Pernod, and you were putting something into one of the bottles through a funnel. It—you looked dreadful. And then I saw the cup full of berries. I thought they were currants. I couldn't imagine what you were doing, but after I saw you I was afraid to try to find out. And I went around back and your mother said you had torn out all the Deadly Nightshade because you were afraid it might poison some children."

"I thought if there wasn't any growing out there I'd be less likely to be suspected. And you jumped to the correct conclusion that I was preparing a poison brew for my cousin. There's love and trust for you!"

"I didn't. I couldn't imagine what it was until he died,

and then suddenly I remembered and understood it all."

"But you didn't mind being engaged to a murderer?" Frank asked bitterly.

"Frank, be careful. Your mother."

"She'll have to know. What's the use of trying to protect her any longer?"

"Why need she know? I won't give you away. I'm glad you did it. And you won't give him away, will you, Miss Pomeroy? You've brought it off. It's like Miss Pomeroy said, it's finished. Nothing you can do now will bring him back to life, and I wouldn't let you do it if you could. I'm glad he's dead; I tell you I'm glad. All you can do by confessing now is bring misery on your mother and me."

"Kay, you should know by now we can't go on like this. I thought we could, I was going to marry you without telling you; even when I saw that you suspected I thought I could go on and marry you and we'd bury it. But I can't; I see that now. He based his last plot on my weakness, and he won. He's destroyed my life—no, that's not fair, evil as he was. He tempted me, and I destroyed my own life. But the thing that will bring pain to you and mother is already done; there's no use trying to cover up now."

"Miss Pomeroy, you've done so much for us, make him see he must be quiet now."

Frank shook his head.

"There was just one thing Charles couldn't foresee about me," he said. "He figured the strength of the temptation correctly; he knew I was a coward and that the long suspense would wear me down. He knew I'd kill him, and as you say, Miss Pomeroy, he thought I'd bungle it and be caught or else be overwhelmed by remorse and kill myself.

He was right all the way. I did it and then when nothing happened I hadn't the courage even to sit tight and enjoy the fruits of my crime. The waiting drove me nearly crazy —waiting and waiting and waiting, and nothing happening, while all the time I knew that bottle of poisoned Pernod had to be out there some place. That's why I came to Keene's, Miss Pomeroy. I wanted you to find that bottle and let me explain it. But he couldn't foresee that in the end I'd be man enough to come back to myself and confess. I have to, Kay; I have to, Miss Pomeroy. I must try to prove to mother that I have to; it's the only way I can show myself that he was wrong about me."

"No, no, no," Kay sobbed. "It's playing into his hands; it's giving him the final victory. Tell him he's wrong, Miss Pomeroy."

"Tell her I'm right, Miss Pomeroy."

"I see your point," Miss Pomeroy said wearily. She drew a long breath before she went on. "I shouldn't attempt to argue with you if you had all your facts straight, but you see you *didn't* kill him."

There was a momentary gleam of hope in his eye; then he shook his head. "I've tried reasoning that way," he said, "but it doesn't work. Chance took a hand, of course. I didn't know he had a fatal heart disease. And I'm a bum Borgia; it was just luck that made my dose strong enough. If he'd been a well man he'd have thrown it off as I did— even a not particularly robust man. But his heart was too weak to stand the strain. That's what you mean, isn't it?"

"Of course," Kay said. "It was his heart that gave way. The doctor said so. Your poison could never in the world have killed him."

"You didn't know about his heart?" Miss Pomeroy's own heart was lighter than it had been since she had made her discovery.

"Of course not. Why should I have killed him if nature was going to do it for me?"

"But then why ever did you choose such a poison?"

"I'm not a professional, Miss Pomeroy. I didn't know where to get poison nor how to keep it from tasting, and he sort of warned me himself against trying to read up too much on the subject. The only thing left was this stuff of mother's; the books were here and the poison was growing in the yard. It said that people sometimes recovered, but it was the best thing I could think of. The berries were sweet, and I was pretty sure the Pernod would disguise the taste."

"But how could you know he would drink it himself? Didn't you care about the risk to anyone else?"

"I knew darn well Charles wouldn't offer it to anyone else now. He was crazy about the stuff, and it's hard to get since the war. That's why I thought he wouldn't be surprised to get a case; he has a standing order with two or three dealers to send him a case whenever they can get it."

"But your handwriting on the label?"

"That was supposed to be a double finesse. I wrote it with my left hand; I thought it would look enough like my writing to make the police suspect me and yet be odd enough to make them think, when they examined it closely, that it was a forgery of my hand. I took it into an express office when they were busy and gambled on no one's remembering me. I'm not very conspicuous, and I was keyed up enough to keep from acting nervous. The return address was that of one of the dealers with whom he had an order." He laughed apologetically. "Even now when I go back over it, it seems to me the scheme was rather neat. I hope I'm not acting unduly conceited about it. You see it was all based on the theory he had manufactured some evidence against me. So instead of trying to avoid suspicion I was trying to make all the evidence against me look manufactured."

"But tearing up the vines?"

He smiled ruefully. "I'm afraid I counted a little too much on mother's discretion. I thought that if I asked her not to mention it she wouldn't. But really, need we hash this all over now? It will come out at the trial, won't it?"

"You didn't kill him," Miss Pomeroy said.

"Please, Miss Pomeroy, I've tried the Jesuitical line for all it's worth, and it's not good enough. I tried to kill him, and as a result of my attempt he died. If that's not murder let the jury acquit me for it."

"It was the wrong kind of nightshade," Miss Pomeroy said.

"What?"

"This that was growing out here was Woody Nightshade; it looks very much like the deadly kind but with the important difference that it's not poisonous."

"But, Miss Pomeroy, it poisoned Frank."

Miss Pomeroy shook her head.

"Mr. Osgood is a very suggestible young man, and he was in a highly emotional state at the time. He knew what the symptoms of atropine poisoning are; he expected them, and he had them."

"But the analysis?"

"We never had a report of any analysis that showed atropine. The doctor looked for it because we looked for it and because it would fit the symptoms, but he never actually found any."

"But wait now," Frank said. "Let me think. It can't be."

"Go ahead and think," Miss Pomeroy said harshly. "You sent him the poison and you expected him to die. Pretty soon he died, and you thought he must have drunk your poison. Do you know that he did? Were you there? Has anyone ever testified that he had a drink of Pernod shortly before his death?"

"And I," Kay said. "I thought so too. I never understood that scene in the basement until Charles died, and then I thought I did—that and the way Frank was acting."

"And then nothing happened," Frank said, "and waiting I grew more and more terrified until at last I couldn't wait any longer. I had to know about that bottle. And when I found it I was so tired of it all that it seemed drinking it was the only solution."

"You really wanted to kill yourself, then? You didn't think you'd recover?"

"I never dreamed of recovering."

"And I played up to him!" Kay said. "He expected the symptoms and so he had them, and I thought I recognized the symptoms because I knew what had gone before; that whole day was just a comedy."

"I didn't dare take chances," Miss Pomeroy said.

"I haven't killed him and I haven't killed myself," Frank repeated. "The only thing I have to blame myself for is the fire."

"The fire!" Miss Pomeroy literally jumped. "What do you know about the fire?"

"I was awake; I heard that fellow Perry tell you his story. And I made up my mind Charles wasn't going to do any more posthumous harm if I had to burn down the house to stop him. The first chance I had I slipped out of bed and started it."

"Mr. Osgood, you don't know how good that makes me feel," Miss Pomeroy said, "when all the time I've been blaming that poor Mr. Perry."

"It's hardly in it with how good you've made me feel," he said shakily.

"Well, keep still about it then, and don't let your mother know you ever thought of such a thing. Marry your girl, and for goodness' sake don't ever try to murder anyone again. You've got no gift for it."

Miss Pomeroy pulled on her gloves, feeling inordinately tired. Two of the fingers on her right hand were crossed so tightly that the glove wouldn't go on.

The lovers turned toward each other faces on which incredulity gave way to radiant relief. Miss Pomeroy slipped out quickly. She was ready with the arguments for her better self. She had told a lie, and a really colossal one. Without it three lives would have been ruined. Frank Osgood could never rise above his crime; even if he had been persuaded not to confess, it would have haunted him and his wife and mother. And Kay was not a woman who could be happy in the knowledge that the father of her children was a murderer. It would, of course, be impossible to fool Mrs. Osgood on what kind of nightshade had grown in her back yard, but Miss Pomeroy did not believe

Frank would ever mention the matter to his mother again.

Miss Pomeroy had the arguments all ready for her better self, but her better self remained strangely silent, if not openly approving. Although she lived alone Miss Pomeroy seldom talked aloud to herself. This, however, was a rather exceptional moment.

"For a first lie," she said judiciously, "that wasn't bad."

THE PERENNIAL LIBRARY MYSTERY SERIES

E. C. Bentley

TRENT'S LAST CASE
"One of the three best detective stories ever written."

—Agatha Christie

TRENT'S OWN CASE
"I won't waste time saying that the plot is sound and the detection satisfying. Trent has not altered a scrap and reappears with all his old humor and charm."

—Dorothy L. Sayers

Gavin Black

A DRAGON FOR CHRISTMAS
"Potent excitement!"

—*New York Herald Tribune*

THE EYES AROUND ME
"I stayed up until all hours last night reading *The Eyes Around Me*, which is something I do not do very often, but I was so intrigued by the ingeniousness of Mr. Black's plotting and the witty way in which he spins his mystery. I can only say that I enjoyed the book enormously."

—F. van Wyck Mason

YOU WANT TO DIE, JOHNNY?
"Gavin Black doesn't just develop a pressure plot in suspense, he adds uninfected wit, character, charm, and sharp knowledge of the Far East to make rereading as keen as the first race-through." —*Book Week*

Nicholas Blake

THE BEAST MUST DIE
"It remains one more proof that in the hands of a really first-class writer the detective novel can safely challenge comparison with any other variety of fiction."

—*The Manchester Guardian*

THE CORPSE IN THE SNOWMAN
"If there is a distinction between the novel and the detective story (which we do not admit), then this book deserves a high place in both categories."

—*The New York Times*

THE DREADFUL HOLLOW
"Pace unhurried, characters excellent, reasoning solid."

—*San Francisco Chronicle*

END OF CHAPTER
". . . admirably solid . . . an adroit formal detective puzzle backed up by firm characterization and a knowing picture of London publishing."
                                                    —*The New York Times*

HEAD OF A TRAVELER
"Another grade A detective story of the right old jigsaw persuasion."
                                    —*New York Herald Tribune Book Review*

MINUTE FOR MURDER
"An outstanding mystery novel. Mr. Blake's writing is a delight in itself."   —*The New York Times*

THE MORNING AFTER DEATH
"One of Blake's best."   —Rex Warner

A PENKNIFE IN MY HEART
"Style brilliant . . . and suspenseful."   —*San Francisco Chronicle*

THE PRIVATE WOUND
[Blake's] best novel in a dozen years . . . . An intensely penetrating study of sexual passion . . . . A powerful story of murder and its aftermath."
                                    —Anthony Boucher, *The New York Times*

A QUESTION OF PROOF
"The characters in this story are unusually well drawn, and the suspense is well sustained."   —*The New York Times*

THE SAD VARIETY
"It is a stunner. I read it instead of eating, instead of sleeping."
                                            —Dorothy Salisbury Davis

THE SMILER WITH THE KNIFE
"An extraordinarily well written and entertaining thriller."
                                    —*Saturday Review of Literature*

THOU SHELL OF DEATH
"It has all the virtues of culture, intelligence and sensibility that the most exacting connoisseur could ask of detective fiction."
                            —*The Times* [London] *Literary Supplement*

THE WHISPER IN THE GLOOM
"One of the most entertaining suspense-pursuit novels in many seasons."
                                            —*The New York Times*

Nicolas Blake (cont'd)

THE WIDOW'S CRUISE
"A stirring suspense. . . . The thrilling tale leaves nothing to be desired."
—*Springfield Republican*

THE WORM OF DEATH
"It [The Worm of Death] is one of Blake's very best—and his best is better than almost anyone's." —Louis Untermeyer

George Harmon Coxe

MURDER WITH PICTURES
"[Coxe] has hit the bull's-eye with his first shot."
—*The New York Times*

Edmund Crispin

BURIED FOR PLEASURE
"Absolute and unalloyed delight."
—Anthony Boucher, *The New York Times*

Kenneth Fearing

THE BIG CLOCK
"It will be some time before chill-hungry clients meet again so rare a compound of irony, satire, and icy-fingered narrative. *The Big Clock* is . . . a psychothriller you won't put down." —*Weekly Book Review*

Andrew Garve

THE ASHES OF LODA
"Garve . . . embellishes a fine fast adventure story with a more credible picture of the U.S.S.R. than is offered in most thrillers."
—*The New York Times Book Review*

THE CUCKOO LINE AFFAIR
". . . an agreeable and ingenious piece of work." —*The New Yorker*

A HERO FOR LEANDA
"One can trust Mr. Garve to put a fresh twist to any situation, and the ending is really a lovely surprise." —*The Manchester Guardian*

MURDER THROUGH THE LOOKING GLASS
". . . refreshingly out-of-the-way and enjoyable . . . highly recommended to all comers." —*Saturday Review*

Andrew Garve (cont'd)

NO TEARS FOR HILDA

"It starts fine and finishes finer. I got behind on breathing watching Max get not only his man but his woman, too."   —Rex Stout

THE RIDDLE OF SAMSON

"The story is an excellent one, the people are quite likable, and the writing is superior."   —*Springfield Republican*

Michael Gilbert

BLOOD AND JUDGMENT

"Gilbert readers need scarcely be told that the characters all come alive at first sight, and that his surpassing talent for narration enhances any plot. . . . Don't miss."   —*San Francisco Chronicle*

THE BODY OF A GIRL

"Does what a good mystery should do: open up into all kinds of ramifications, with untold menace behind the action. At the end, there is a bang-up climax, and it is a pleasure to see how skilfully Gilbert wraps everything up."   —*The New York Times Book Review*

THE DANGER WITHIN

"Michael Gilbert has nicely combined some elements of the straight detective story with plenty of action, suspense, and adventure, to produce a superior thriller."   —*Saturday Review*

DEATH HAS DEEP ROOTS

"Trial scenes superb; prowl along Loire vivid chase stuff; funny in right places; a fine performance throughout."   —*Saturday Review*

FEAR TO TREAD

"Merits serious consideration as a work of art."

—*The New York Times*

C. W. Grafton

BEYOND A REASONABLE DOUBT

"A very ingenious tale of murder . . . a brilliant and gripping narrative."
                —Jacques Barzun and Wendell Hertig Taylor

Edward Grierson

THE SECOND MAN

"One of the best trial-testimony books to have come along in quite a while."   —*The New Yorker*

Cyril Hare

AN ENGLISH MURDER
"By a long shot, the best crime story I have read for a long time. Everything is traditional, but originality does not suffer. The setting is perfect. Full marks to Mr. Hare."   —*Irish Press*

TRAGEDY AT LAW
"An extremely urbane and well-written detective story."
—*The New York Times*

UNTIMELY DEATH
"The English detective story at its quiet best, meticulously underplayed, rich in perceivings of the droll human animal and ready at the last with a neat surprise which has been there all the while had we but wits to see it."   —*New York Herald Tribune Book Review*

WHEN THE WIND BLOWS
"The best, unquestionably, of all the Hare stories, and a masterpiece by any standards."
—Jacques Barzun and Wendell Hertig Taylor, *A Catalogue of Crime*

WITH A BARE BODKIN
"One of the best detective stories published for a long time."
—*The Spectator*

Matthew Head

THE CABINDA AFFAIR (*available 6/81*)
"An absorbing whodunit and a distinguished novel of atmosphere."
—Anthony Boucher, *The New York Times*

MURDER AT THE FLEA CLUB (*available 6/81*)
"The true delight is in Head's style, its limpid ease combined with humor and an awesome precision of phrase."   —*San Francisco Chronicle*

M. V. Heberden

ENGAGED TO MURDER
"Smooth plotting."   —*The New York Times*

James Hilton

WAS IT MURDER?
"The story is well planned and well written."
—*The New York Times*

Elspeth Huxley

THE AFRICAN POISON MURDERS (*available 5/81*)
"Obscure venom, manical mutilations, deadly bush fire, thrilling climax compose major opus.... Top-flight."
—*Saturday Review of Literature*

Francis Iles

BEFORE THE FACT
"Not many 'serious' novelists have produced character studies to compare with Iles's internally terrifying portrait of the murderer in *Before the Fact,* his masterpiece and a work truly deserving the appellation of unique and beyond price." —Howard Haycraft

MALICE AFORETHOUGHT
"It is a long time since I have read anything so good as *Malice Aforethought,* with its cynical humour, acute criminology, plausible detail and rapid movement. It makes you hug yourself with pleasure."
—H. C. Harwood, *Saturday Review*

Lange Lewis

THE BIRTHDAY MURDER
"Almost perfect in its playlike purity and delightful prose."
—Jacques Barzun and Wendell Hertig Taylor

Arthur Maling

LUCKY DEVIL
"The plot unravels at a fast clip, the writing is breezy and Maling's approach is as fresh as today's stockmarket quotes."
—*Louisville Courier Journal*

RIPOFF
"A swiftly paced story of today's big business is larded with intrigue as a Ralph Nader-type investigates an insurance scandal and is soon on the run from a hired gun and his brother. . . . Engrossing and credible."
—*Booklist*

SCHROEDER'S GAME
"As the title indicates, this Schroeder is up to something, and the unravelling of his game is a diverting and sufficiently blood-soaked entertainment."
—*The New Yorker*

Thomas Sterling

THE EVIL OF THE DAY
"Prose as witty and subtle as it is sharp and clear. . .characters unconventionally conceived and richly bodied forth . . . . In short, a novel to be treasured." —Anthony Boucher, *The New York Times*

Julian Symons

THE BELTING INHERITANCE
"A superb whodunit in the best tradition of the detective story." —August Derleth, *Madison Capital Times*

BLAND BEGINNING
"Mr. Symons displays a deft storytelling skill, a quiet and literate wit, a nice feeling for character, and detectival ingenuity of a high order." —Anthony Boucher, *The New York Times*

BOGUE'S FORTUNE
"There's a touch of the old sardonic humour, and more than a touch of style." —*The Spectator*

THE BROKEN PENNY
"The most exciting, astonishing and believable spy story to appear in years. —Anthony Boucher, *The New York Times Book Review*

THE COLOR OF MURDER
"A singularly unostentatious and memorably brilliant detective story." —*New York Herald Tribune Book Review*

THE 31ST OF FEBRUARY
"Nobody has painted a more gruesome picture of the advertising business since Dorothy Sayers wrote 'Murder Must Advertise', and very few people have written a more entertaining or dramatic mystery story." —*The New Yorker*

Dorothy Stockbridge Tillet
(John Stephen Strange)

THE MAN WHO KILLED FORTESCUE
"Better than average." —*Saturday Review of Literature*

Henry Kitchell Webster

WHO IS THE NEXT? (*available 5/81*)
"A double murder, private-plane piloting, a neat impersonation, and a delicate courtship are adroitly combined by a writer who knows how to use the language." —Jacques Barzun and Wendell Hertig Taylor

Anna Mary Wells

MURDERER'S CHOICE
"Good writing, ample action, and excellent character work."
—Saturday Review of Literature

A TALENT FOR MURDER
"The discovery of the villain is a decided shock."   *—Books*

If you enjoyed this book you'll want to know about THE PERENNIAL LIBRARY MYSTERY SERIES

Nicholas Blake

☐	P 456	THE BEAST MUST DIE	$1.95
☐	P 427	THE CORPSE IN THE SNOWMAN	$1.95
☐	P 493	THE DREADFUL HOLLOW	$1.95
☐	P 397	END OF CHAPTER	$1.95
☐	P 419	MINUTE FOR MURDER	$1.95
☐	P 520	THE MORNING AFTER DEATH	$1.95
☐	P 521	A PENKNIFE IN MY HEART	$2.25
☐	P 531	THE PRIVATE WOUND	$2.25
☐	P 494	A QUESTION OF PROOF	$1.95
☐	P 495	THE SAD VARIETY	$2.25
☐	P 457	THE SMILER WITH THE KNIFE	$1.95
☐	P 428	THOU SHELL OF DEATH	$1.95
☐	P 418	THE WHISPER IN THE GLOOM	$1.95
☐	P 399	THE WIDOW'S CRUISE	$1.95
☐	P 400	THE WORM OF DEATH	$2.25

E. C. Bentley

☐	P 440	TRENT'S LAST CASE	$1.95
☐	P 516	TRENT'S OWN CASE	$2.25

Buy them at your local bookstore or use this coupon for ordering:

HARPER & ROW, Mail Order Dept. #PMS, 10 East 53rd St., New York, N.Y. 10022.

Please send me the books I have checked above. I am enclosing $ _____ which includes a postage and handling charge of $1.00 for the first book and 25¢ for each additional book. Send check or money order. No cash or C.O.D.'s please.

Name _____

Address _____

City _____ State _____ Zip _____

Please allow 4 weeks for delivery. USA and Canada only. This offer expires 1/1/82. Please add applicable sales tax.

Gavin Black

☐	P 473	A DRAGON FOR CHRISTMAS	$1.95
☐	P 485	THE EYES AROUND ME	$1.95
☐	P 472	YOU WANT TO DIE, JOHNNY?	$1.95

George Harmon Coxe

☐	P 527	MURDER WITH PICTURES	$2.25

Edmund Crispin

☐	P 506	BURIED FOR PLEASURE	$1.95

Kenneth Fearing

☐	P 500	THE BIG CLOCK	$1.95

Andrew Garve

☐	P 430	THE ASHES OF LODA	$1.50
☐	P 451	THE CUCKOO LINE AFFAIR	$1.95
☐	P 429	A HERO FOR LEANDA	$1.50
☐	P 449	MURDER THROUGH THE LOOKING GLASS	$1.95
☐	P 441	NO TEARS FOR HILDA	$1.95
☐	P 450	THE RIDDLE OF SAMSON	$1.95

Buy them at your local bookstore or use this coupon for ordering:

HARPER & ROW, Mail Order Dept. #PMS, 10 East 53rd St., New York, N.Y. 10022.

Please send me the books I have checked above. I am enclosing $ _____ which includes a postage and handling charge of $1.00 for the first book and 25¢ for each additional book. Send check or money order. No cash or C.O.D.'s please.

Name _____

Address _____

City _____ State _____ Zip _____

Please allow 4 weeks for delivery. USA and Canada only. This offer expires 1/1/82. Please add applicable sales tax.

Michael Gilbert

☐	P 446	BLOOD AND JUDGMENT	$1.95
☐	P 459	THE BODY OF A GIRL	$1.95
☐	P 448	THE DANGER WITHIN	$1.95
☐	P 447	DEATH HAS DEEP ROOTS	$1.95
☐	P 458	FEAR TO TREAD	$1.95

C. W. Grafton

☐	P 519	BEYOND A REASONABLE DOUBT	$1.95

Edward Grierson

☐	P 528	THE SECOND MAN	$2.25

Cyril Hare

☐	P 455	AN ENGLISH MURDER	$1.95
☐	P 522	TRAGEDY AT LAW	$2.25
☐	P 514	UNTIMELY DEATH	$1.95
☐	P 454	WHEN THE WIND BLOWS	$1.95
☐	P 523	WITH A BARE BODKIN	$2.25

Matthew Head

☐	P 541	THE CABINDA AFFAIR (available 6/81)	$2.25
☐	P 542	MURDER AT THE FLEA CLUB (available 6/81)	$2.25

Buy them at your local bookstore or use this coupon for ordering:

HARPER & ROW, Mail Order Dept. #PMS, 10 East 53rd St., New York, N.Y. 10022.
Please send me the books I have checked above. I am enclosing $ _____ which includes a postage and handling charge of $1.00 for the first book and 25¢ for each additional book. Send check or money order. No cash or C.O.D.'s please.

Name _____

Address _____

City _____ State _____ Zip _____

Please allow 4 weeks for delivery. USA and Canada only. This offer expires 1/1/82. Please add applicable sales tax.

M. V. Heberden

☐ P 533 ENGAGED TO MURDER $2.25

James Hilton

☐ P 501 WAS IT MURDER? $1.95

Elspeth Huxley

☐ P 540 THE AFRICAN POISON MURDERS
(available 5/81) $2.25

Frances Iles

☐ P 517 BEFORE THE FACT $1.95
☐ P 532 MALICE AFORETHOUGHT $1.95

Lange Lewis

☐ P 518 THE BIRTHDAY MURDER $1.95

Arthur Maling

☐ P 482 LUCKY DEVIL $1.95
☐ P 483 RIPOFF $1.95
☐ P 484 SCHROEDER'S GAME $1.95

Austin Ripley

☐ P 387 MINUTE MYSTERIES $1.95

Buy them at your local bookstore or use this coupon for ordering:

Thomas Sterling

Julian Symons

Dorothy Stockbridge Tillet
(John Stephen Strange)

Henry Kitchell Webster

Anna Mary Wells

Buy them at your local bookstore or use this coupon for ordering: